FAR ALASKA

FAR ALASKA

Mason Smith

GRAYBOOKS

LYME, NEW HAMPSHIRE

Title Page Image
Based on a photograph by marchello74 / 123RF Stock Photo.

ISBN-10: 1-935655-28-0
ISBN-13: 978-1-935655-28-2
Library of Congress Catalog Number: 2012943442

Published by
GrayBooks LLC
1 Main Street
Lyme, New Hampshire 03768
www.GraybooksPublishers.com

Softcover Edition

To Hallie

FAR
ALASKA

One

HE AWOKE WITH A PHYSICAL START, the sun suddenly bright in his half-open eyes. Over the tips of his toes poking up the thin covers (socks still on), it glared level and red through the light of the cabin door—made red and level, he reckoned, by glancing off the roof of the pickup outside. So it was even higher than it looked. Nine o'clock? When's the last time you woke in daylight, my boy?

Wouldn't call himself that no longer, the hot heap of female person right beside him, worn out and still snoring. Satisfied, to all appearances. Pretty good for a first try, more and better to come. Seemed only a moment ago he'd rolled over onto his back, for as good a night's sleep as he had ever had, over too soon. But lord he'd slept late as a gypsy.

Everything in close relation, bed, door, truck, the pine trees the sun had just cleared. In the other direction, behind his pillow, thin wall, six feet of gravel bank, a lake. Did he lay like this the whole night? Clarence did not generally sleep on his back, straight out like a corpse. If he was lined up as he guessed, north/south, it was worse: noon.

Or else further north than he thought they'd traveled yet. On the way to Alaska, but did not expect to be in the land of the midnight sun so quick.

Where might we be, cookie? Somewhere in a foreign land, Canada. Last other human being seen, your father, leaving out that door to drive three hundred miles to milk his leaking cows, and good riddance. Given up trying to make a honest man of him, or a honest woman of her, for the simple reason, getting to be too far from the barn.

She had taken off his watch. It never occurred to him to do so. Less fussy about his red-topped socks, which he slept in by habit, or else she never got the chance to roll them down, or him either. Looked like he would never shiver again, the heat she give off. Hester rolling her own brown stockings down, my gosh what a whiteness, them knees just like bread arising. This was a whole new category of things to astonish him and much yet to come, because he closed his eyes to save it, could only take so much and 'twas kind of embarrassing at seventy-two years of age. Some he had felt with his hands, some he imagined, but smart cookie, no hurry, leave something for dessert.

Always an imaginary critic to hear from. Sister, brother, brother-in-law, boss. Clarence what you doing in bed at this hour of the day? Well, what do you know about it? How much had he slept in the last ninety-six hours? How far had he walked, that wild night, the whole way around the lake and back to the home place. Then what he'd been through since, loaded up in a flash and made his getaway. Now, just the right season to be going to Alaska. Cold to start but getting warmer every day, all the way, lot of time to get there, couldn't have planned it no better. Truck, woman, and all the money in the world, and I know the direction, simple. North-west.

Sisters back there on the old sheep farm will be telling everybody Poor Clarence he don't know what he's doing, he don't know how to get along in a foreign country. Took everything he had ever earned out of the bank and stole a girl, now he will be the victim of thieves. Wilfred Gonyea may tell them where he last saw the outlaw, a cabin on a lake, outside of Sudbury, Ontario. Wilfred don't like losing his cook, wants her back and a captive hired-hand along with her. So, consequently, quite likely Royal Canadian Mounted Police may be on the case. For that reason, time to get up and be moving on.

But he was still an unfamiliar lounging boy, next to the warm heap of Hester. The pitch of the mattress slid him against her and held. Found he had no desire to fight it. Noon or after noon. It was a long virtuous wait to age let's call it sixty-nine, sounds better, to see what that was all about and now you might say he was on a honeymoon. Not married because not fit to marry, so much the better. Ask her why she come, without no wedding band. Two guesses and the second one don't count.

He was adapting fast but his new life had still taken him by surprise and in between his moments of levity and secret gladness he did experience the shock, not from the bullet that was not fired at him after all, but maybe something like it, enough to make a man stagger and stumble. The changes that had been thrust at him! Wave on wave of new things so late in life, after he had come to think there never would be any ballad sung about him, nothing to tell that he'd ever lived.

He was a ballad-singer himself, not a musician but at least he knew the words and tunes. All he ever asked for was to live on in one more song. Off to a good start, a boy in the lumber camps, taught a few old songs by his young stepmother, attracted to horses and given early responsibility for driving a team of Belgians, Center Camp to the Falls, Falls to Center Camp, every day, for Mr. Robert Purryer Senior. Loaded both ways. That was a lot of responsibility for a boy so young, twelve to fourteen years of age. But never so much responsibility the rest of his life so far. From those early years, downhill, because why, well, because the world changed fast and he was looking in the wrong direction. Liked what he saw behind better than ahead. Did not keep pace with the times. No good with machinery, not interested.

Worked at whatever he had to, lived anywhere but with his sisters if he could help it, kept a team of horses when he could, dogged in hunting season, gathered sap in sugaring but not the man to run the evaporator, no, never so much responsibility again as Robert Purryer Senior had given him at twelve years old.

Latterly couldn't afford to keep that team at all, not enough work for them to do. So, last few years, worked for Duke Arquit, the Town Supervisor, either at the town dump or on the skating rink or the campground on the river, part pay to live the winters in the log cabin he helped build, right there on the Project, rented to tourists in the summer. Sisters wanted him to live on the old sheep farm with them, listen to their belittlement day after day. But ha-ha, rather live in a hollow log, so in the summers he rented one poor place or another. Kept a truck to get around in. Saved up more money than anybody knew he had. And when all these recent events come upon him, help hunt for the killer, rescue the girl, knew ahead of time that he would have to leave his own country. Took out that money and bought his revolver and that outdoor cooker in the truck, finished the business and lit out. Used the revolver but once and then lost it, too bad. But all right, only other thing he needed was a cook, and Hester come when given the chance. He told her: Come or stay, but make it snappy, sister. She come and here she was, on fire deep inside her if you tell by the temperature of the surface.

One chuckle after another.

Said for the fortieth time, aloud: Fell a long way in a short while. That's Clarence Shampine.

"What's that, CW?" Hester said.

CW! Where'd she learn his middle name? Nothing to be ashamed of, as far as he knew.

"Did I say something?"

"Yes you did. Fell a long way, you said. You talking about me?
You think you fell a long way to get down to me?"

"You come up a long ways."

"I'm right where I was."

"No you ain't."

"I'm with you, and we done it. At last."

"Did you like it?"

"Couldn't you tell?"

"No you sounded like you had two feet in a bear-trap."

"Well it surprised me."

"I didn't have no more practice than you."

"That was obvious."

"I didn't no more know what was coming."

"Me neither."

"But we done it. We made a start. And look how we slept."

"It's tiring!"

"I don't see why."

"Nerves, I think. It gives your nerves a workout. Something."

"You make a lot of heat."

"You saying me?"

"No. We. Could do that in a igloo and be just as toasty."

"Maybe we will, where we're going."

"I tell you what."

"What?"

"We got something to look forward to, every day that goes by."

"Do it every night?"

"If the novelty don't wear off."

"It won't. It don't have to be novelty."

"No?"

"That was only just a glimpse, I believe. I was a little nervous. I just went ahead, but I was scared you wouldn't like me, and I didn't know if I would like you either."

"We had to do it, that was all."

"We got over the worst."

"If that's the worst, it'll be a picnic."

"That's what I mean. We won't be nervous no more. That's settled."

"Let's get up."

"Yes. I couldn't stand it to stay in bed and do it again. I would just feel awful guilty. Wouldn't you?"

"Well..."

"Let's not and say we did. I mean it. Slugabeds! Come on, let's get up and give some kind of a account of ourselfs!"

"All right."

"But CW. You promise. I'll be thinking about it something awful. Now you heat this little place up and I will get up some steak and eggs. We needs fortifying."

This was unlooked for, her companionableness. For all he knew when he stole her from her father she was a shrew and a harridan. Only took her because she was the only woman he could think of and knew her circumstances. Also that she had once clearly cocked her hat at him. That was when he was boarding his team at Gonyeas' and gathering sap with them in Wilfred's sugarbush. She made it obvious she thought he was a proper caballero and got him to take her out visiting. And to movies if there was a cowboy picture. But that led to a warning experience. They were going to visit Leo Weller, at the Weller camp at the Lake, and when he went to hand her out of the truck, coming around to her side like his stepmother had taught him, got her down out of the truck to the ground all right but then she slipped and hit the ice with all her mass, and he realized if he'd been underneath, he'd been flattened like a cookie.

That was how he made fun of her for years after. "If I'd a had holt of that, I'd been flattened like a cookie." So when he roared into the Gonyeas' driveway on his departure for the Injun territory, stormed inside and demanded she come or stay but don't waste his time deciding, he was black-heartedly taking her for no good and expecting none, expecting in fact to be afflicted with a harridan and shrew for the rest of his life, fair enough since he deserved no better; but with luck she would cook, and together they would do what people do in bed. If they'd be damned for it what difference did it make? For the rest he would shut his ears. As for liking, he did not aim to be likable himself. She started yakking at him just as he knew she would, a mile a minute, utterance like a waterfall that would drown a man, and he turned around and headed out as quick as he'd come. But then she'd shouted "Wait!" and clapped a hand over her mouth and rushed, as well as she could, so fat and wide, for the downstairs bedroom where she found the hope chest or trousseau she had been preparing all those years ago, when she thought she had him hooked, and came dragging it and half the scatter-rugs from the living room into the kitchen with it. He hauled it out the door and out through the woodshed and slewed it over the ice to the truck and heaved it into the bed, and next he put his shoulder to her buttock and hoisted her into the cab. No expectations of happiness at all, just meanness in his mind, meanness like Wilfred's, to serve the world right for the wickedness it had dealt him.

This morning's companionableness could not last. He remember Wilfred's last ploy before he left last night, hurry home to milk before the cows would tear apart their stanchions. "She does talk, gen'ly," he said. She had her hand over her mouth then too. Just so

15

afraid she'd spoil what was coming, send the only lover ever in her sights running again.

But goes to show you, if you are decent, other people will be decent to you. This didn't seem like the same woman. But so what, he wasn't the same man.

Two

THE CHINAMAN AT THE LITTLE HOUSE WHERE YOU PAID spoke in a way that Clarence could not understand, except for the word that wasn't so different from "dollars." He got that and he asked again and got the number, which he wasn't prepared for. Asked again and got the same, with short brown fingers flashed in his face that added up to the same. Well, he had the money but not in his wallet. He did not say "Waitee minee," as it came to him to do, nor put up a delaying hand. Just turned back to the truck. His breath turned white.

"Give me the loot," he said.

"What loot? You don't tell me where your money is."

"The big yellow envelope. Give me the plunder, sister."

When he went to the little brick cube that is the bank in Sabattis Falls and announced he wanted all his money, he didn't get it right away. The bank ladies wanted to know what for, Clarence, where was he going, did he need a companion, did his sisters know he was taking out all his money? Had to ask did he really mean all of it? None of their business. He said Yes and I put on my own pants in the morning too. Then the one who had touched her hair and invited herself on his trip to Florida went and asked the manager, another woman, and she frowned too but she said Well they had to give it to him, it was his. They put the money in a big manila envelope. It was still there, all but what he had paid for the Colt and the

17

cooker and what he had stuffed in his wallet, now apparently spent on room and board thus far. And that steak last night, red meat that gave him strength. Rather have it in a roll, and would, soon as he come across a rubber band.

She fished around, looked in the glove-box, felt beside her. Owing to her conformation she was no use at pulling anything up from the floor between or beside her legs.

"This truck ain't handy for traveling. We ought to have a sedan."

Huh. Sedan. Where would we carry the cooker then? Or the old silk wall tent he had never used, from the first World War, given him by Dr. Weller years ago. Threw that in at the last. Might be their home in the tall timber of Alaska someday. And the tamarack poles to it. They wouldn't fit in the trunk of a sedan.

The envelope was behind her, behind the seat. He went around and got it, pulled out some bills and put them in his wallet.

"How much is they, CW? I heard you had ten thousand dollars in that bank."

"None of your business and who told you that?"

He'd forgotten, account of money, what good terms they'd found themselves on when they woke up at noon for the first time in either of their lives. That was about pink knees and surprising fragrances and this was about cold cash. Clarence did not want that money to go out so fast. He did not know how long it would last and was not one to make the calculation. Worry yourself to death and what good was your money? Best thing to do, cling to every last penny.

The Chinaman accepted the cold cash and they were on the way again, go as far as we can today and every day. Whatever might befall them they'd do better than pioneers with a team of oxen on a dirt track like the Oregon Trail, so cheer up. Clarence looked across at his companion, not half as ugly as he'd always thought. Face of a bulldog, whiskers on the upper lip, one thick eyebrow like a ox yoke over both eyes. But now she looked right back at him with a twinkle in those eyes, or so he thought. Could hardly see her eyes behind them coke-bottle glasses but if that wasn't a smile he was a monkey's uncle. A face wasn't the whole story. A woman don't have to have a woman's hair-do. He blushed to think of the pile of pink under those drab clothes, gray fuzz and lip-whiskers. A gray-brown cardigan, worn to nothing at the fat elbows. You'd have to see it to believe it, which I have done.

They were thinking of the same thing, her sitting at her home kitchen drop-leaf table, cup in both hands, elbows wearing out that cardigan. Because she said, "We need a thermos bottle."

Cold cash again. Think of something to buy, quick as you smile at her. He scowled.

"Costs money, you think," she said. "But I think it would save money. We wouldn't have to stop for coffee. But you decide. I ain't bossing you."

There wa'n't no explaining this except what they did under cover of darkness. Is that all a woman needs, to learn to be quiet? This foreign land was nothing to write home about, supposing you wrote home. Middling small farms, the small houses too close to the road. That would be a unfamiliar project, writing home would. Clarence loved school, as a boy, though not good at school work. Had not used a pencil much since, no pretty young stepmother to bring it home to show, nobody to send a postcard to except his sisters.

Hester said, "We ought to buy some postcards and Canadian stamps, next place we stop."

He turned his head and looked at her, a long second.

19

Much more populous, this road, than he expected. Busier countryside than home, and this goes to show, you don't know what's going on, outside your own territory. Who would have thought there was this many Canadians. You'd expect the further north you went, the thinner the population. Pretty soon nothing but Indians, and after that, Eskimos. But he was driving right into a city. That was what it looked like.

Passed a garage or what looked like one with some kind of gas at a unheard of price. Imperial. Well ha-ha I come from the Empire State, right at home. Made him think of the truck, what he started to think when she said they ought to have a sedan. The truck, his truck, nothing wrong with it that Gene LaBounty couldn't keep watch on for him back home but here he was, headed west, left Gene LaBounty far behind. Skating on thin ice so far from that good mechanic. But what LaBounty had told him to do, he had done, all except pay extra for a automatic transmission. Changed oil at three thousand miles, except not lately. He had intended to stop to LaBounty's on his way out to Gonyea's to get the cook, but wasn't any sign of LaBounty there or across the road at the Restaurant. Nobody at the Restaurant at all. All the men in town gone somewhere except Arquit in his store, sold him the revolver, and what's-his-name at the gas company, sold him the cooker.

Automatic choke too. LaBounty said, "You'll forget to push it in, Clarence."

"No I won't."

"All right, don't. You'll thin your oil."

Now wasn't he pretty good, to think of that cooker, even before he got himself a cook. Clarence looked forward to the enjoyment of both, the cook in more ways than one. Never before had his own cook, sisters don't count. Boys! This was turning out good. Have to get himself a folding chair to sit in while she cooked. Take out his jack-knife and whittle. Take out a squeeze-box and play a tune. Never had one nor played it but wouldn't that make life complete? Keep my eyes open, that or a banjo. These old fingers would have to learn new tricks but other parts doing that already, ha-ha.

Good, yes, as long as he kept misfortune away from the truck. Not new. Six years old and a little banged up from hauling every sort of thing, a load of firewood left in it all winter, to hold the back end down. Bumpers, fenders dented, tail-gate bent. You couldn't keep a truck like new and do what 'twas meant for, or else he would have. But beauty is only skin-deep and this truck still run like a Singer sewing machine. Six cylinders. LaBounty says I ought not to have a standard shift, the way I wear out clutches, but I wouldn't know what to do with a automatic. Still had on winter tires, well, not winter now but good to have in mud. Close-ter to Alaska, dirt road all the way. He knew about that. Alaska Highway, who didn't? If you don't know where you are now, my boy, you will when you see the signs, Alaska Highway. Then, no turns, just go straight ahead. Keep a lookout but that won't be till next week or later.

What town this was he wondered.

Another gas station and how much we got, cookie? He looked between his gloved hands high on the rim of the wheel. Oh my goodness empty or so near it his throat closed in a painful contraction and he swerved in almost too late. Hester rolled against him crying out, "CW!" His mirth returned with the contact and he said, "Pit stop, sister. You got me dreaming so, I near run out of gas."

"You thinking of it, CW?"

"Yes I am, cookie."

"You know it's a sin. I been thinking about that."

"Sin when you're in the Garden of Eden. We have left."

"I feel funny when I think about it."

"I do too."

Here come a boy about twelve to pump the gas, wash the windshield, say Sir, and remind Clarence to check the oil, which was full and clean. Paid him cash and he saluted. If the wages of sin is respect I like it. On the road again, full tank and he checked to see if she was google-eyed or still thinking about matrimony. It would be a awful let-down to have that argument. Told her once that if she got on to that subject he'd be keeping his eyes open for every other good-looking woman along the way, Indian or white.

The city came and went and petered out along the north shore of a body of water that looked to Clarence like the ocean. There was no opposite side to it, so it could not be the St. Lawrence River, nor should it be, pretty sure he left that river behind when they crossed the International Bridge north of Watertown. Here, water went on forever, shining and blue, south, southwest and west. He knew the direction without thinking, because of the sun and the time of day. And the road wasn't going northwest at all but right west, close to the shore. This road had been worrying him for some time, for that reason. The water went on and on, and they went on and on beside it, westward. Looked like a ocean but couldn't be the Pacific Ocean. He was sure the Pacific Ocean was farther west than they had had time to go. Hester kept her hand over her mouth, not good for it meant she had a lot ready to say.

But then she took if off and said, "Why we goin' all the way to Alaska, CW? This is nice right here. This looks just as nice as Florida, even. Look, they's beaches."

"Why Alaska, why for the simple reason, beyond civilization. Haven't you heard, I killed a man?" Not telling you this but I done worst than that, all but done it, helped a young girl not-have her baby, kissed its head before it come out, buried it in a mud spring and handed a gun to the father to kill himself with. Do you think I

am fit to live among decent people anymore? I don't. Going to the
Injun territories and live outside the law.

I'll bid farewell to the canebreaks
In the state of Arkansaw-w-w -
Well, New York, but same principle.
If you ever see me back again
I'll extend to you my paw-w-w
But it'll be through a telescope
From hell to Ar-kan-saw-w-w.

Then aloud he added, lest she take him up about killing a man,
tell him he did not, "Also lumbering, sister. In Alaska, 'fyou didn't
know, they've got trees three times the size of ours, and they lumber
on the sides of mountains three times the height. If I was a cowboy,
I would gone to Wyoming. But I am a teamster in the logging
woods, and so we're going to Alaska. I hope you're ready to be a
lumber-camp cook, because that's where you're headed."

"I don't mind cooking, long's I sleep with the teamster," she
said. Good enough but then she added, "You sure they've got horses
there?"

He didn't want to say Does a bear do his business in the woods?
to a woman, so he stopped and started again. "Well don't you suppose? Horses is the best power there is in the lumber woods."
Though he remembered very clearly how the Linn tractor came to
replace the horses in his own time, in his own North Woods, already
a long time ago, a change that left him stranded. That was the story
of his life. Started good, thirteen years old, no more, entrusted with
a team of Belgians that weighed thirty hundred pounds. Then they
turned the tables on him. Them gas powered things come into the
woods and confounded his life, left him out on the end of a plank,
nowhere to go but learn some other work, anything that come along,
dock-building, roof-shoveling, caretaking; help some farmer gather

sap, sell Dr. Weller a hindquarter of venison, take a job here or there cutting pulp, work for Arquit on the town crew. What a relief to be a outlaw and shed of Duke Arquit forever. Been tied to that fellow's apron-strings too long, Arquit the town supervisor always wearing the cap and apron of a butcher in his store, chopping bones and giving orders all day long. "Clarence, what do you want to buy that revolver for? What'll your sisters think?" Hnn-nh.

With any luck, The Linn tractor had not yet come to Alaska, so hard to get to and such rough country. Further north and west you went, the later come change. What he heard, Alaska was a wilderness.

"Well," she said, with some care. "Anyways I'm goin' where you're goin'."

Yes, but. But what?

"You think my Daddy and me's just ignorant. But we had a TV, you know."

"Good for you."

"And we watched it."

Still didn't know what she was getting at. The lake went on and on beside them.

"This is the Great Lakes, is what this is," she said.

He knew what the Great Lakes was. He pictured them on the map of America. They are on the south side of Canada. He did wonder what were they doing here, when he had been going north-west. Except, he had to admit, the roads didn't go that way all the time, or even much of it. Sometimes they went west, and even south of west. A time or two, right south. That made the hair stand up on the back of his neck, driving south, right toward the noonday sun. But it's just like the woods, you can't always go the direction you want to. If you have to go west for a while, then what you do is go north for a while, and you come out north-west. This lake was good for one thing, keep him from getting any farther south.

Singing to himself to the even, quiet stitching of the Singer sewing machine:

Won't you gather round me children

A story I will tell

Bout Pretty Boy Floyd the Outlaw

Oklahoma knew him well.

Wrong state, but.

Now and again he'd hear something from over against the passenger door. Look out the corner of his eye, and she'd clap a hand to her mouth. If he'd turn his eyes from the two-lane blacktop right at her, she'd hold her hand there, smiling behind it.

After another verse or two, thought he would risk it, sang one aloud:

"Well the outlaw took to the country

To live a life of shame

And every crime in Oklahoma

Was added to his name."

Looked over at her. Smiling to herself. Thought of something to say to him but let it go, still smiling. Then all at once, "There goes that --!"

"What?" Always doing the driving, he missed things. She saw more than he did. Having a good time there, looking every which way.

"Haven't you seen that thing before?"

"What, somebody following us?"

"That what-is-it. Volks wagon. Like Patraw has, all around his place back home, works on. Most of them rusted to pieces. Like a little bus, and all painted up with flowers. I believe you can live in them things. Has a little sink in them, a little kitchen sink. We passed them before."

Passed them? Didn't think he passed anybody. Canadians fast drivers. That was because they measured the miles a different way, kilometers, not as long as a mile.

"They's stopped back there. Kid probably had to pee."

After a bit she said, "They must be going slow, too."

Something wrong with this speed? He stepped it up a little, but not much.

"That's a young girl, with children. I don't know how many kids, two ennaway. No man."

Very interesting when you are not worried if you are on the right road. If the sun goes under, no compass. Every road in Canada just like every other, none going in the exactly right direction. Good thing he was a lifelong woodsman or he might get lost.

"Probably a hippy," she said. "What was the license plate? Ocean State, it said."

Maybe we aren't the only parties heading for the Territories with a posse on our heels.

"Looking for a new life just like us, what'll you bet?"

Looked over at her. Big smile. Prettier mouth than he ever noticed, because for the simple reason, paid too much attention to the mustache.

Now, some reason, didn't notice the mustache so much anymore. Didn't mind it when he did.

Scrawny cows. Roofs turned up at the eaves. That didn't make good sense. Sometimes, a house painted a color that must have been on sale, no other good reason to use it. He associated that with French, but English was spoken everywhere they stopped.

They got back in the truck after gas and she said, "A boot?"

"What?"

"That's what she said, that policewoman. I asked her where is the next diner. 'A boot ten miles,' she said. I mean kilo meters. What is a kilo meter? How do you know how fast we's going?"

"Fifty miles a hour." Says right on the speedometer.

"That's what that says on there but here they has kilo meters."

Still seemed to Clarence they were going fifty. Felt the same. If they weren't, he didn't understand but he lived with many a mystery that he didn't lose sleep over.

"I don't want you speedin'," she said. Clapped a hand over her mouth, her smiling mouth. Then, "Other thing they say is withoot. A boot withoot. You hear that?"

"No I didn't."

"A boot withoot. I'm more observant than you are. That's because I'm here in person. You're here in a dream. I talks too much. I know it. I said it myself, to spare you the trouble. Give me something to eat, I'll be busy. She said aboot ten miles or kilo meters to the next diner, careful lest we misses it."

The diner didn't come in view very quickly. Or else they missed it. "Shoot. Aboot withoot," she said. "That's different. Otherwise it isn't hardly different enough to be a foreign country. Just neater. Every place is neat. Couldn't they drive on the other side of the road or something?" Then she turned halfway around, tried to. "Oh! I'd like to live there! Wouldn't you love to live there? Wasn't that a cute little farm? I wonder how much a cute little farm like that would cost. Goats! I always wanted to keep goats. Make cheese!"

Lord Almighty. But in the main she kept a lid on it. He came to wait for these eruptions, as long as they was small. Don't ask his opinion of these cute places. Canada nothing much so far, too flat for one thing and not his destination anyway.

Three

LONG TIME BETWEEN REAL CHANGES, then all to once they were on the moon.

What's this, the earth ripped up and piled high far as the eye could see and the sky full of soot. And the axles like to tear apart the truck. Slow down, son. Slow down more. Mercy, mercy, what if I broke a wheel off? Gene LaBounty far away when I need him. Clarence did you put in that automatic choke like I told you? N-n-n-no, LaBounty, er, n-n-n-no, afraid I did not, do you think my oil's too thin?" Even in the middle of the ribbed, pot-holed mine site, the truck jouncing like a boat on the waves, he chuckled to think what an incorrigible fellow he was, never to take that good fellow's advice, kindly meant. Now no help for it, drive on.

"How'd we get in the middle of a open pit mine?"

Just followed the road.

Thought it was a town.

Then, on through, farm country again. Hay, stacked outdoors from previous seasons, hnn. Hedgerows, houses like cottages and barns a little smaller than to-home and not many of them hip-roofed. One town with houses right next the road, another with houses set way back. Shade trees reaching right over the highway, some places, but no leaves yet, just buds barely opened. Clarence thought he ought to start paying attention but didn't see much of interest. Everything familiar but slightly off.

Hester likes things like windmills in the yards with a darky under a sombrero rowing a boat. Would turn her head around as far as would go, not tell him what she saw.

Noticed the roll of her stocking, a bulge just above her knee. Without thinking, he suspended his right hand over it. Once upon a time, rolled stockings baffled him. Now, different. Why don't she unroll it up no farther? Can't, that's why, far as it could unroll, can't stretch no more, ha ha.

Whereas, his knees, skin and bone, stringy muscle. Just as white as hers. Never cared for anybody to see his legs but now, whew! two pairs of knees and legs - it brought a blush to his face. Forgot I was steering. Hand still suspended there. He let it down on the roll and she looked right at him. Then she looked out the window again, with not a word and he took hold of the wheel with both hands. Second night coming, what time was it?

The country was not that different but something here inside the truck quite new to him. He drove on with a sense of proprietorship. He had not known what he was doing, bringing along this woman. Figured he didn't have to keep her if it didn't suit him. That was a different man.

Now, proud as he was of any team he had ever owned. Two teams only, come to count them. Not everybody would know his luck. Not everybody nowadays would know a good team of horses if they saw one, either. What other man wa'n't no judge of, why would he care what they thought?

Everything he owned, here in the moving Ford. Hester, her chest, some old firewood he'd had in there to hold down the back end last winter. Old Dr. Weller's silk wall-tent that he gave him, the tamarack poles he cut for it, the gas cooker, axe, shovel, fishing tackle behind the seat, manila envelope full of hard work at low pay, going north-west when the roads cooperated.

Himself? Same man, just given a break. That old town, Sabattis Falls? Place where everybody looks at a old-time woodsman like a creature from another planet. See that man there, Billy? With them high-laced boots and that beaver hat? Just stepped off a space-ship.

"What you so amused about, honey-pie?"

Honey pie!

Nice thing about being on the road in another country, you are free to reconstruct the recent past and the community you come from the way you want to without no contradiction. No belittlement, foolish hearsay and foolish opinion. Last thing he would ever get from home, credit where credit was due.

He had expected her to contradict him when he said 'killed a man.' But she didn't. Imagine if 'twas his sisters, or Arquit. Oh Clarence don't be silly! No doubt Hester was on the phone with them before he ever come to get her. Phones ringing all over town, somebody shot to Purryer Camp then another shot from the same gun at the mud spring, hnn. Didn't kill no one, what do you know? Is there somebody dead or isn't there and whose fingerprints on the gun?

But that would be too big a deal for Clarence to ever done it. Clarence Shampine? Clarence wouldn't hurt a flea. Clarence couldn't shoot that straight. Clarence would been hiding under the covers pretending he wasn't in bed.

Bump! Bump!

"Dear me suds!"

Everything in the back airborne a full second and came down hard against a truck bed going up, ka-bam!

End of paving, well-l-l. This can't be the best road to Alaska. Next thing, before you found a place to get off it, a curve they were still going too fast for, skidded way around to the other direction, stopped in a cloud of dust smelling of the driest stone, half off the shoulder, Lucky Teeter at the Fair.

No traffic, luckly. No one to see us but the trees.

Slowly they retraced the last few miles. The sun was hidden. They knew not which way they were headed.

"I got turned around."

"You's driving. Don't ask me."

Me I hate to go one mile out of the way to the furthest place from you know where.

He had been thinking too much, what the trouble was. Trying to reconstruct the past, to restore it to what it really was, all these years when he had been taken for less than he really was, and come to half believe it himself.

The action he had been involved in, the rescue of that poor girl, complicated as it was, as he might be the only person outside of Leo Weller to know, by her miscarrying her little baby in the very midst of her rescue, at his own family's home place—he hardly understood it himself, how the man he shot lived to tell the tale—not likely! But it had afforded him a chance to prove his worth. His knowledge of the woods and the ways of the creatures in it, human beings included. Stupid old Clarence, don't pay any attention to him. Well, h'nn. Who rescued the girl, all by his lonesome? Thanks to nobody. What he had done on his own set him free of that old version. So what if it cut him off from all that was proper and good. Set him loose, by God.

Here's where we went off, following the sun, shining brightly then, from the north-west. He got back onto the hard-top though it was headed too far south. Northern Canada, big land with nobody going there, no roads. Canadians all stayed in a bunch along the border, looked like, and if he wanted to go to Alaska he would have to go due west a long way first.

"Any map would of told us that," she said.

"Well, y-y-yes." Was I talking aloud?

When you know where you're going, you don't need a map. Some fellows need a map to get from Purryer Camp to Dexter Lake, why? because no road. He could get to Alaska without one, quite certainly. Ever heard of the Alaskan Highway? But maybe quicker with one. Less going down the wrong road, ha ha.

It was nice having her with him and worth making concessions. Nobody could know what it was like to be you. He had a feeling as old as his life who he was, long denied by everybody else. So you might better be on your own making it up as you go. Every mile of blacktop under that red hood bringing it closer, past as well as future. Maybe you can't share the past but the future you can.

"Which do you like best, CW? Maple Leafs or Canadians?"

"What?"

"Which? Maple Leafs or Canadians. Toronto or Montreal?"

"Never been to either."

"Hockey, Clarence! You get television at your sisters', don't you?"

Huh.

"You get it at the Senior Citizens."

Well, he did go in there sometimes, for a meal. Saved money. But didn't like the term, senior citizens, surprised to hear they'd let him in, not walking with a cane.

"Me and Daddy is fans. He likes Toronto I likes Montreal. Boom Boom Geoffrion! 'Course we could be Boston fans too, they's close and they's got Bobby Orr. You don't watch hockey on TV?"

"H'nn."

"Well, good. I'll give it up. Used to near give me a heart attack."

He didn't have any comment except how good-natured she was. If he was a new man maybe she was a new woman.

"Once I had a mini stroke, I ever tell you that? That wasn't nothing to do with hockey, though. Just come on me for no good reason. Slurred my speech. Couldn't say anything right at all for five-ten minutes. Had a glass of water and I was all right again. See them pills I takes? One of them's aspirin and something else, to thin my blood. Makes it thirty-seven percent less likely to happen again."

What was he supposed to do with this information? Take it easy on her tonight?

"Seize the day! I likes that expression. Seize the day. It become my middle name that day. Why I come with you. You'll see. I'll get a tattoo of it if I see a place to."

Tattoos!

"If I gets one tattoo, that'll break the ice. Get more later, maybe. Maybe I'll get Oot and Aboot!"

At other times that day they weren't so sure but what they were the same two people after all, he traveling with a fat and ugly fault-finding old maid that would soon show her colors, and she with a foolish boy of near or over seventy that never grew up or learnt sense. But that night they found out again that they'd been mistaken. They came to see, again, that they'd never known each other before, and just their good luck, come to find out, they were traveling with friends that had powerful pleasures to give and great appetite for their own. More than friends, each of them was traveling with a person whose smell, and glance, and look, were private excitement to him or her, a secret treasure under wraps by day but only by day and every day had a night.

Other words, as Clarence put it to himself, no disappointment the second time around. Contrary, there was new discovery, new basis for friendship. Embarrassment was night by night to fly out the door of the cabin (the next one just like the last) and pretty soon Clarence felt sure he would hear no more about sin, because it did not come across to her that way anymore, and if it did to him, so much the better. The point of the trip, to him, any sin he could do, make up for a life too cowed, too passive, far too good for his own good. Always a good boy, and what did it get him? They took the horses out of the lumber woods, that's what. If she ever brought up marriage again, down the road, probably it would be because they was really married, truth be told, and 'twould make little difference to say so with your hand on a Bible. However she wouldn't risk it now and not for a thousand miles, he could forget about it.

This time he had no need of pitch dark and neither did she. Well, she didn't the first night, she actually said "Why don't we have a candle?" because there was one on the lace doily on the little painted dresser, probably in case the power went out. Just as there was in this cabin here, which could have been the very same place, another lake six feet out the back and down a gravel bank, not four foot lower than the picnic table. It was Clarence that was bashful.

Turn north from the lake shore and you are in the wilderness again, quick as that. Low land and green timber, here and there a camp-ground or a set of cabins, canoes to rent no thanks and the season not open yet anyway, this lake still frozen because the fellow said it was a deep one. Deep winter or deep lake he didn't know which, same difference.

Clarence had bought another steak, in gallantry and to fortify them, and this time he'd brought the clerk out to tell him what kind of fuel he needed for the cooker, and he'd bought a bottle of gas, about a foot in diameter, foot and a half tall. The fellow said it would last him many a supper and it had better, for he had to go to the envelope again to pay for it. Again he tried to set up the cooker, in the light from the cabin door, but now he remembered it didn't have any legs or base. It was meant to be set in concrete, and what snow there was left from the winter wouldn't hold it up. So she seared the steak on a pan in the cabin again and with no Wilfred Gonyea to gnaw twice his share before going home to his cows for the last time, they had enough to set them up well for the job they had to do, see if it was as good as they thought the first time, see if practice makes perfect, ha-ha, as Clarence said. And to help with that, Clarence had his little flask of blackberry brandy, another one in his pack if that run out.

This time too he said no to the candle, though not so adamantly. And she seemed very visible in the dark, her overflowing whiteness glowing so, and hot to the touch as if alight. Again the surprising pleasantness to his nostrils, talcum-powder-like. He wouldn't have thought it, from the smell of the Gonyeas' kitchen as remembered. May be that come from the unwashed old farmer, certainly unshaved, and never took no care of his teeth, as his everlasting grin showed clearly. One thing to have her disrobe herself so willingly. Wouldn't have thought that, either, and didn't know where such freedom could come from, unless from so many years of waiting.

May be she did what he did, all his years of celibacy, known to no one but himself. May be she practiced in the imagination, ha-ha. Got the real chance and couldn't wait to get free of all coverings. It was just as well because he wouldn't know where the latches and catches all were, feared some little live creature might dart out at him. What held up the brown stockings he still didn't know and didn't want to, didn't want to watch them being rolled down either but when they were flipped away in the air with a gay kick, he liked what was left, the glow in the dark and heat to the touch when there weren't no more staying at a distance. Wouldn't have thought she could kick that high, either. Learn something every day. Thought that little kitten in between would scare him, but it didn't. Later found he could pat it fondly, stroke its head and scratch its ears.

Shoulders next. Already used to the routine, you see. It was as if she'd said, You just watch, CW. I like you looking. Here's the one. Round and white. Here's the other, the same. Then she said, "You take off my glasses, Clarence." Which was the biggest surprise.

Hers wasn't a face that he had ever sat still and looked at, for all the time they were going out, back there. Not so long a time in fact, just that she was the only one he ever did go out with, to come to any real danger of hooking up, and that just for the sake of the team. Why would you look at that, black-rimmed glasses thick as Coke bottles, behind which, eyes magnified until they looked like oysters. Under a brow like somebody's that didn't have good genes, close-ter to a orangutang than a pretty maiden. The only thing coming from the whiskered lips a rattle of Do this Do that and what is wrong with you considering your sisters is such nice people. Found himself actually coming to the defense of his sisters, one divorced and one widowed living together on that old sheep farm just as if they was in poverty, when everybody knew that Nellie had the first nickel she ever made and worked hard all her life, cook to lumber camps hotels and fraternity boys, and Bessie had the farm free and clear from Clark who never spent a nickel either, never even bought a sheep-dog. Trapped a wolf and trained it; what Clark insisted was a wolf. Oh, Hester didn't think that was right, the way those two old ladies lived, keeping a burlap sack over the Allis-Chalmers tractor, cranking it by hand, hauling their own firewood and cooking on a wood cook-stove too, electric one right beside it unused. What was the matter with them? yak yak yak.

Now he lifted off the black-rimmed glasses that looked like they were made out of old windows with the swirl of thick glass in them, poured molten hot and then cut off, and what come to his sight but as pretty a pair of eyes as he had ever seen, ordinary-sized, just sweet and smiling eyes with young wrinkles at the corners. Eyes the nicest mildest brown, with flecks of precious metal in them, and healthy liquid whites that glistened, eyes that looked right into his, left and right, trying to say something, ask something, find something back in the inside of his head, on some movie screen in there. His head was empty, except for this picture.

Not up this close was she ugly. Up this close even that single darkling eyebrow over both eyes thinned out to tender curving hairs in the middle, and the white skin behind the tender little hairs, seen through them, was the same flesh as of the knees and shoulders, peachy white and softly aglow. Putting the glasses on the bureau, next the candle, he touched those shoulders gently, both hands, still looking into her eyes, which now looked dreamy as if she couldn't see that well without the glasses, or as if the blackberry brandy had gone to her head. And her mouth? Did he want to look at that close up too? A smile does wonders for any mouth. She was smiling, he knew without looking, but didn't take the chance. Might not see the teeth for the tongue. What was to come after the shoulders and eyes was better, he knew. But he didn't see it, really, that time either. His head was empty but the contents of it had sunk down to his roots, he was too impetuous to prolong the answer. Learn that later, waited too long for this.

So the candle and more careful attention had to wait for the bear. Lying there in the dark like the dead, face to hips swamped in the pink cushions of her, top to bottom, left right and center, feeling her finger circle round and round the boyish cowlick on the top of his head, or the other one where his tail might have been, he heard the cooler dragged off the picnic table and down the bank to the shore of the lake. Heard the bear rummaging in it and seeing what jar-lids was screwed on too tight. Proof, in a minute, but he didn't hurry. Had no revolver to threaten it with anyway. Ought to be thinking what a bum deal that was, have the new Colt's revolver swiped out of his hands, whereas he needed it right now. Instead thinking, I have all of my hair, see? Pretty good for seventy-two. Sixty-nine. Only as old as you feel. He'd known what it was for five minutes while Hester got stiffer and stiffer until finally she broke the spell.

"What's that, CW?" Suddenly she wasn't a dreamboat but a bank officer. "Get up and see what that is."

He knew what that was. He had always been afraid of bears, and when he bought that revolver, it was not to do what he did do with it, it was to defend himself, most especially from bears, where he already knew he was going. Well, funny thing, sister. Not afraid of that bear today and, just the same, don't want to go speak to it without no firearm. Live and let live. But he pulled himself out of the cream-puffs and found his pants and pulled them on, went to the back door to look out. Moon light. Could not see down over the bank toward the steaming ice of the lake but the cooler that had been on the picnic table was missing. You're supposed to shut your food in a locked box, I know it. I thought those latches, metal ones, on the cooler was good enough, latched tight so no smell come out. But the fire and the tin plates stank of burnt meat and this was a bear that knew how to open coolers. He went out to the truck for his flashlight, fearless, then stepped carefully past the table and the fire ring to the bank, peered over. Where'd I get this courage, sister? It is just that I am a wanted man, ha-ha, and plan to throw the rest of my life away.

He did not need the light to see, and did not turn it on, but would shoot it like a pistol if charged, a beam of light in the eye. The bear looked up but then turned back to what it was doing. Had already pawed out the contents of the cooler, on its side with one hinge torn loose. A grapefruit floated away in the silver water out to the edge of the ice. Coffee grounds, he could smell. It was the peanut butter that kept the bear interested. She had twisted off the cap and with her long tongue was licking the last out of the bottom of the jar. When it was sparkling clean she looked up at him and put it down. She looked down again and looked over the rest of the food, arm's length. He said, "Go away, Bruin." Could watch just as well from indoors if she was through.

From the counter window he watched her head come swaying over the bank, then the whole creature slouch loose-shouldered past the table. She sniffed at the truck and he was afraid she would climb up in back and tear things apart but she strolled on down the campground road out of sight and Clarence went back for another snort of the blackberry brandy.

"Was that a bear?"

"A bear as ever was."

"You just told her to go away and she did?"

"That's right, sister."

"How do you know it was a she-bear?"

"Way she wiggled when she walked."

"I'm serious! How do you know she won't come back?"

"Peanut butter all gone."

"Come back to my arms, then, CW," she said.

This time he lit the candle. They were both wide awake and keen for experience. Excited by the close call with bloody death they went further into intimacy than either had expected. It had not seemed time for variation, but it was upon them forthwith. She did something new, touched him with her hand to see if he was back where he was before the first expiration. The breath went right out of him, and something like his breath out the top of his head, and he thought, Good thing I looked at picture-magazines. His sometime co-worker at the town dump papered the shack with those things, to keep the wind out. Some stolen pages, he now remembered, might still be hidden under the seat of the pickup. Thanks to which, not that surprised, and had ideas of his own. He wondered how his mustache felt. Might scratch anything so tender. Women, you know, born knowing all of it. Heaven help us if the redskins break in the door while we're in never-never land.

Four

WHERE WERE THEY? How were they coming? Well, road-signs tried to tell them to cross the Sault Sainte Marie, to get to where he was going, but what was on the other side? Michigan, which he knew perfectly well was a part of the United States, wrong country, no thanks. So up along the coast of Lake Superior, or, way they spelt it here, Supérieure, which sounded better to him. Lived among French Canadian people all my life and know how that sounds, foreign. That other lake, Huron, already put behind them. So you see we're in the Injun Territories before we've gone five hundred miles. I told you I would show you something different, cookie.

Clarence Shampine away from home is a different boy. Different to himself, having broken out of his old role of last old time logger, a curiosity to uninterested children, a joke to their parents. Different to onlookers, Canadians of one stripe or another who see a trim grey-haired (with all his hair) competent-looking man, mild-mannered but might be dangerous, packing an empty holster that makes you think his iron is near to hand. He wears an admirable black felt hat not unlike a Mountie's, brim flat all around, a high-domed top not indented, high-topped, laced boots well-greased, jodhpur-like hunting pants, thick grey wool with a couple of colored yarns woven through in a plaid. Made right in Malone but who'd ever know it? Multiple shirts, the outer ones open at the collar, his narrow waist cinched in by a wide leather belt with a big brass hippie sunburst of a buckle, silver cartridges glinting halfway around one side. The very things he was smiled at for back home make him a worthy serious traveler, passing through a Canadian hamlet in a respectable Ford truck now the color of mud, a truck that had been somewhere rough and touched a few immovable objects. Pausing to buy the thickest steak in the store, boxes of potato flakes, blackberry brandy if he can find it, unused to the liquor laws of Ontario and the other provinces to come.

He travels often on Ontario Route 17 but frequently turns off on some lesser road that appears to be heading more directly for Fairbanks, only to leave that one for another, and another, and that one for Ontario Route 17 again as it comes along having mended its way. He is not a map-reading individual, knowing the woods to-home in a way you couldn't put on paper, having traveled them in directions not marked on any compass.

These turnings do not cause him to pause or doubt his navigation and Hester keeps a hand over her mouth if tempted to question him. He is well used to the woods, and what are they in if not woods? Never saw more woods in three days than he has seen touring Canada. Woods and lakes is all it is and seldom anything you would dignify by the name of a hill. Did he turn and turn, left and right? Well, you don't go in a bee-line through woods. The woods is all connected up in ways that would surprise you. The shortest distance between two places wasn't always the first highway you hit. Even if the road goes straight for tens of miles on end with nothing but stick-timber, scrawny woods not worth logging and seldom a house or a farm on either side.

When he stops at a crossroads store and gas pump his attitude seems to command respect, or demands it. For he has little awe for what he sees about him and he puts on a humorous wily outlawish air. No one quizzes him or reads the essential shyness in his pale eyes, and if they look at the impassive rider occupying more than half the cab, they don't perceive an exceedingly homely if not ugly woman, or a woman at all, she seems a massive glowering presence suggesting important purpose and authority, chief of some far tundra tribe on none of anybody's business.

Somehow this subtle respect comes through to Clarence and confirms the sense of well-being that is swelling in his bony breast from the fulfillment of his bad intentions.

Shooting a man, saving that girl, cleaning out the bank, abducting Wilfred Gonyea's daughter, hitting for the territories, best things he ever done. He knows he has a long way to go but so far so good. With steak, potatoes, brandy in the cooler and his girl beside him, only needing a cabin with a big bed in it, ha ha, to stop for the night, he was full of good will when going due north just after full dark they passed an amazingly shabby, banged-up, rusted, broken-bumpered small Japanese pickup truck with a cap over the bed, and two figures by it, one down on his side on the road, half under it, the other standing at the rear corner like a statue with a rotating head, watching them pass. Briefly caught in their sweeping lights, this face neither male nor female except for the shining black hair wrapped around her neck like a scarf, this face something out of a book, a picture back in his cabin on the Project, the Last Indian looking at the Last Sunset; made Clarence think of a phrase out of nowhere, noble savage.

"That was a Indian if I ever saw one," Hester said.

He was slowing, but hesitantly. For all his new-found confidence he had to overcome the collective wisdom back home, well-ingrained by talk and confirmed by his natural timidity, that you don't stop for anybody anymore, not hitch-hiker, accident victim or dead body. If it didn't cost you your life, it might cost you everything else you had, because now-days they'll sue you for helping them out the car window when the door won't open.

"You en't stopping, are ye, CW?"

"What's it look like? Yes I'm stopping. This isn't New York State." He had no real conviction that Canada was any better, but here he was stopping because don't forget I'm a new man. At least he didn't know why else.

"Didn't you see that face? Like a tommyhawk."

"Well they are broke down. My step mother taught me the Golden Rule, if you never heard of it, Do unto others as ye would that they should do unto you."

Tomahawk, not so. In the rear-view it was a female Indian person with so rich a face that Clarence dared not look at it for fear of backing off the road. He was never a good backer to begin with. He stopped in front of the Datsun, leaving the road mostly open for passing traffic, if any, but they were far from anywhere and it was hugely silent outside the truck, the parking lights like a little campfire in the wilderness when he shut off the motor and stepped out. The woman facing him looked sturdy of body though not tall but seemed to grow large by her face and features and the sternness of her look. Also her color, a tone of brown to make any paleface feel humble. Hester stayed in the cab, but he knew she was turned around looking out the back window, a big oyster-eye behind each bottle-bottom lens.

Nothing external was operational on that truck. No way legal to be rolling. Clarence saw at once the bald tires, broken lenses, brown porous fenders and rocker panels. The person down on his side was looking for a place to fit a toy-sized hydraulic jack among the rusted underparts. The fellow seemed just as incompetent as Clarence knew he would have been to do the job, whatever it was.

Flat tire he supposed but no spare in sight. Not a word from the two.

"Well. . . ," Clarence said. "I'll give you a lift. Maybe you can come back in daylight."

The lady Indian said something he didn't catch, possibly dismissive. The white man—it was a white man, maybe younger than the woman—rolled on his back and stuck up a hand to be helped. Clarence wasn't quick enough and he rolled over and pushed himself to his feet. In a brush jacket, brown hair to his shoulders like a girl, he looked closely at Clarence. Looked him up and down. Took in his holster, boots, high quality hat and last his face with the pale eyes and small grey trimmed two-stroke mustache. Everybody always said Clarence had the look of a Indian, but for the eyes. He wondered if any of this pair would say so, just as soon they didn't.

Clarence gestured to his Ford, ahead of the smaller vehicle. The man looked that way as if he was checking the license plate, mud-spattered but brightly lit under the bumper. Back to Clarence now with a nod.

"I'll get you a bottle of whiskey. Your brand. Just up the road."

Clarence was about to say No I don't and No I couldn't but the white man and the Indian lady climbed in the bed of the truck with the cooker and the cooler and Hester's portmanteau and the firewood left over from weighting down the rear wheels last winter, so he just exhaled and got back in beside Hester.

"Arnold," the man said. The name came in the open window beside him.

Clarence said, "Well, all right." Up the road Arnold didn't have the cash for the bottle, needed a loan and it was Jack Daniel's not Clarence's favorite fruit-juice. Had the cash at the place, he said. "Well, hnnh." Clarence paid the shocking amount, never before given up for something that would knock you unconscious. Called for another visit to the envelope and they hated anybody to see their bank. Hester said nothing, seemed to be in a huff over there far as she could get. They trundled along north between walls of stick-timber, Clarence driving slow expecting the man to signal their turn. It got to be farther than Clarence was at all prepared to go, before the fellow pounded on the roof overhead and yelled and pointed in the rear window to the right, east, Clarence guessed, using inertial navigation. He didn't want to go east, precious miles wasted, but did. Then after about fifteen miles in the last direction Clarence wanted to travel, several more turns left and right on smaller roads that he would not remember when retracing them, no sun for a compass going or coming. Clarence had a feeling of going deep in a hole, a maze, nothing but black forest all around, no moon. Feeling of ought to know better. Golden Rule, hnnh.

Come into some kind of a clearing where everything was uphill from the end of the road, dim lights and shadowy buildings in all directions, perhaps a native village where they were going to be boiled in a iron pot if he didn't come up with something worthy of a folk song, ha-ha not so funny.

But it was a very different place they were pushed into, and Clarence stood impressed the moment he entered and even before his eyes adjusted to the amber tone of the light because it was all wood, or bark. Large inside, and high-ceilinged, a whole community under one roof, families in their own cubbyholes all around the out-side and in the middle, on the bare dirt, he knew right away what it was, a birch bark canoe, half built. Somewhere in his past, seen how they do that. Go out in the woods, search out the biggest straightest white birch tree you ever see, slit the bark twenty feet up from the ground and peel it off in one piece, done with a spud, tie it up in a roll and shoulder it back along the trail, leave the tree standing in the woods slaughtered, the way Clarence was taught never to do.

To take off the bark of a white birch, all the way around, even a little strip of it, kill that tree sure's you're born. Working for Robert Purryer Senior, as a boy, they was cutting hemlock trees just as big around, peeling off the bark for tanning, and leaving the good big logs to rot, same principle. Well, here's that bark, laid out on a soft bed of sand and needles, the sides of it bent up in the shape of a boat and staked to stay there, middle of it weighed down with stones. Two young braves that didn't look no more like Indians than Jehosaphat, except for black hair sticking out under their ball-caps, sitting near it on blocks of wood, carving with a horse-shoer's knife. They were clever to recognize what a good tool, for many a purpose, a horseshoer's knife made. People lifted their heads to see him and his lady, then put them down again, too polite to be curious. Didn't say hello to the other two either.

Smoky from different very small fires, nothing but coals, and warm. It had begun to be chilly outdoors. Hester kept a hand on his elbow, kept her mouth shut too. He could feel her nerves. But on through this big place like the inside of a whale and out the end and down a path to a white wall tent on a wooden platform, beside a running stream, where these two lived, it looked as if. Opened up a trap door in the floor which was the lid of their cooler, for some ice; and set to drinking the whiskey, right off, first things first. Looked like the white man, Arnold, was the chief drinker but the Noble Savage kept pace not far behind. She let her white man do the talking, which he was able to do quite well once he got his mouth open for the whiskey.

He didn't require any help and Clarence soon gave up trying to think what to reply to him. Wanted to tell them all about himself, how he came up this way to study the native crafts, especially the canoe-building, make a photographic record of how that was done, put it in a book. Then other books about other kinds of canoes, of other Indian tribes and regions, and also books that he just made up, stories, what he called novels, a word Clarence knew, somewhat, but that his people didn't use. A book was a book, and a book writer, well, that took a exceptional person, so much so that you doubted when anybody claimed to have done it. Or else, if they did, then you ought to show respect. When Arnold told them about the various books that he had written, The woman would put down her jelly-glass and scramble off their bed to find a copy and hold it in front of them. Sure enough: The Abenaki Birch Bark Canoe, Arnold Jepson. Dedicated to Evangeline McHugh, didn't sound no more Indian than the man. Seen that before with the Mohawks. Many a Indian not named Chingachgook. Put the book away before they could read more or look at many pictures though interesting.

They had so much to tell about that Clarence was confused, the North Woods Arts Center, was that what they just come through? Which Arnold started with Evangeline's help. Money from some rich man, owned the land. He took a sip about every time Arnold refilled his glass and Evangeline her smaller one. Hester had her bulldog face all shut and didn't put anything to her lips. Wanted him to get them out of there, which, going on their way, wasn't mentioned but for instance if they wasn't going, where was they all to sleep? Only the one bed.

Big one though, Clarence said to himself with an inner chuckle. Maybe that was the attraction. May be the whiskey was going to his head. He wasn't admitting this to anyone but himself, but he had seen pictures of more than just one couple naked all together, with various ways of hooking them all together, ring around the rosy like a snake eating its tail. Never had imagined such a thing in his own life but he had already fallen a long way in a short time. Maybe the way these two stern-faced ones pictured the night ahead, who knows? Could you do that without cracking a smile? Or else-t maybe they were to bed down up in the Big House where nobody said hello. That's friendly. Could always get in the truck again and roll on through the night, except, guess what, now Evangeline said they wanted them to take them back to their junkheap in the morning.

"Now here's my newest book," Arnold said. "Another novel. Show them, Evangeline." Blurry now, the title, and Clarence didn't read it but saw the name Jepson again and was duly impressed though it wasn't a very big book and looked like it had a lot of white to the page. But he said "Well I never. I could no more---. Good for you, Arnold. Anybody that could write a book." Clarence was honestly impressed with this man, his strong face and his deep voice and all that he knew and could say without pausing, supposing you could follow it. Clarence met a congressman once, McEwen, cousin of Leo Weller. This man could talk right alongside him any day. Could tell it was smart talk and he was flattered to be the object of any effort to impress. Wondered, What did Arnold think he was? Maybe this fellow was like Leo Weller, back home, saw something in him, liked to listen to him. Maybe Clarence appeared to be something he wasn't. Or was something he didn't know he was. Once you're out of your home country, you might not know yourself.

Hated to be under false pretenses. Tell a fellow you could teach school and come to find out can't write your own name. Leo Weller knew him very well. Other people, if they listen to you, it's to make fun of you; but not Leo Weller. That was one person he would miss visiting with.

Now Arnold was complaining that he couldn't get any money for his books. All he got went to the Art Center for the sake of keeping traditional arts alive and wasn't enough. Sounded like the whole world was against him even though he was a author. Cost money to print them books, well yes I suppose it does. So then you need to get them out in the stores, need some way to advertise them, get people to buy them. Yes, Clarence understood that. You apply for grants, that's all right for Native People, Evangeline and them others up in the Arts Center been living off grants for years but Arnold would never get out of the woods if he couldn't sell this book to a lot of people and neither would Evangeline. Clarence did not have any advice to give him, how to do that. Could see that that was a difficult thing to do. Glad he didn't have no such problem --

But Arnold said never mind, he had a plan. "I am going to rent the Concorde," he said.

That word brought Clarence right up short. Didn't know if he heard right. Clarence knew what the Concorde was, or thought he did, big airplane, went very fast, could take you if you want to believe such a thing. But what—?

Yes, the Concorde. Was going to rent the Concorde, he said. Everybody that paid a thousand dollars could go up in the Concorde, go faster than the speed of sound, get a look at the Earth from Outer Space for five minutes, then glide back down. Proceeds to go to the Salvation Army.

Now that was another surprise. The Salvation Army. Hnnh. "Did I hear you right?"

Yes, well, just checking. I pity anybody that wants to go that fast, but if you do, there's your buggy. First he ever heard of taking a hour-long ride in it, up into space and back, but that was exactly what Arnold Jepson seemed to be saying.

Hester spoke. "Why don't you keep the money?"

"I don't want the money. The whole purpose is to get the publicity for the book." How that worked Clarence didn't understand. He took another sip, a larger one. Might as well be hung for a sheep as a lamb. Arnold Jepson wants someone to drink this bottle dry with him, and I'm elected. Had a lot of bad habits in my earlier life and I'm breaking myself of them, teetotaling the first.

Begun to forget what he heard as fast as he heard it, and as far as you could tell by looking, Hester was already asleep. Clarence thought it might be better if one of them was vigilant. He could only stay awake by keeping up with Arnold, small sips, good likker. Arnold and he had a private understanding, now: no need to talk, we was drinking men. When he remembered to ask about sleeping arrangements, Arnold just said "Look around you, I'm sleeping here," and lay back with his glass on his chest. Evangeline said, "Come up on here, there's room." And she lay over against Arnold, the two of them taking up the middle. Hester was asleep in her chair. So Clarence fell on the left side of the bed, asleep before he hit.

Next thing he knows Hester is jerking him awake, still black night, the same old harridan she was before he'd sweetened her up. "Get up. We got to go." Them Gonyeas had a tendency to say "got to," which irritated Clarence as much as it used to irritate old Billy Wilson of Parishville, worked in Wilfred's sugarbush with him. Billy would answer, "Don't you say that to me, mister. The only thing I got to do is die." But Clarence didn't say that now. Loud in his ear though whispering, "I caught her red-handed, rifling the truck, going for the bankroll. Get up, Clarence! Clarence!"

What did she say? Evangeline rifled the—?

Evangeline was right there too, right behind Hester. "You people! Come in here and drink our whiskey, never offer anything for staying the night. You people!"

Hester didn't bother to answer her. She just pulled Clarence up off the bed with one heave backward of her massive body and a good grip on his multiple collars. He was dressed, if he could find his hat, which it occurred to him was the next thing they would try to steal. Was surprised to find it on the floor beside the chair he had sat in, and put it on. He found himself stiff and the vertical hard to maintain, but Hester was a squat pillar beside him. They started,

51

Clarence suddenly remembering the gauntlet of the Long House, full of Apaches.

But Evangeline stood in front of them. "You can't go. What's the matter with you people? We need a ride back to our car. You brought us here, you got a free place to stay, and now we need you to take us back. Jesus, what people!"

Clarence was easy to convince to lie down. He didn't want to go through the Big House. Beyond that lay a truck he would not remember how to drive. Hester must have agreed, he did not hear what she said. He crawled back onto the bed beside the snoring Arnold, just conscious enough to know he stank.

But Hester said, "No. This is not the way it is going to be. We are leaving. If you wants a ride back to your truck, you can come right now. CW, up! We ain't staying here the night. Not with these people."

"You people!"

"You people!"

"You people!"

"You people yourself! I never see the like! CW, come!"

Through the Art Center and on to the truck, Hester kept him awake with pokes in the ribs. Sure enough Evangeline was dragging Arnold after them, because he caught the argument over all riding inside. We'll freeze to death out there. Stay home then. He guessed they did climb into the bed, anyway Hester said "Go!" He made the engine roar and let out the clutch all at once, heard people rolling about cussing.

He caught a face in the back window, lit with what little light came from the dash and the illuminated boughs ahead. At the little store where Arnold had bought his bottle with Clarence's money, Arnold wanted to wake the people up and get breakfast, but Clarence, stiffened by another poke, refused to pull in. He was coming out of his half-slumber, in fact wide awake and feeling surprisingly good. "No, sir, I am taking you to your vehicle and leaving you there, no help, no breakfast. I will send you a thousand dollars next week, b'cause I do want to go into space and have a look around, ha-ha." No more words at parting, two seconds to jump off and if they don't let go, their problem. Looked back in the rear-view, saw nothing. Wished he had that Colt's 45.

"Good riddance to bad rubbish," Hester said.

"Good is right."

Except that about ten o'clock while they were returning by solar navigation to their original north-running road, order to get around Lac Supérieure, here come flashing lights and siren behind them. Clarence hunched over the wheel in a brown study as the RCMP officer came alongside. The Mountie rapped on his window which Clarence had not thought to open. Clarence cranked it staring straight ahead, completely fazed, deflated. He did not know what he had done wrong. Hester sputtered but spoke not.

"You know why I'm hauling you over, Mister?"

"No sir I do not."

"Because you left two people to drive themselves home that was not fit to drive. You plied them with your whiskey, hoping to steal from them when they were unconscious, but the woman kept an eye on you, so failing that, you took them back to their vehicle without sleep or breakfast. Don't you know you are responsible, when you have got somebody drunk? You can't put people out on the road in that condition. Give me your license. Do you have a passport?"

Guiltily, fishing for his wallet, Clarence asked, "My goodness, no. I didn't know I needed one. I never had a passport, never come to Canada before."

The Mountie handed the license back, ducked his head to look in at them, one after the other. "All right, now tell me. Did I get that story right?"

Hester burst out, "No you did not! Where is them people? They made us take them back. I near died for fear of crashing, the state him there…" nodding at Clarence "… he was in. Got them to their decrepit machine and yes, left them. Of course we left them. We're goin' to Alaska. They didn't have to go nowheres. That thing of theirs wouldn't go, anyway, and wouldn't be legal if it did. You know that your own self. They could set there till the cows come home for all of me, and sober up, and ask themselves what kind of people they is, to treat people that tried to help them the way they did. I never seen the like. All we wanted was to get away from them people. I hope they isn't in the back of your cruiser for I hope to never see them again." Which was one breath's worth and only the beginning. Clarence quit listening. That Mountie was getting a showerbath of her talk, couldn't get a word in edgewise. When she was done there wouldn't be no more to say. It would be just like the time somebody kilt Orrando P. Dexter, and several of the better people in the Falls and Risdonville was suspects, because they all had good reason to kill that fellow. Dexter fenced in their woodlots, wouldn't give them no time to get their timber out. That was his right by law but it was not the custom of the country. So, somebody drilled him. Bullet went through the seatback of his buggy, through him, and ended up in the backside of his horse. I felt sorry for the horse.

So Clarence was off on a parallel speech, internal, while Hester burnt the Mountie's ears until he sensed the best thing to do was let these people on their way, take the other two back to their wigwam, Clarence still on his inner anecdote about another famous talker, his father, if it ever got to that point.

Hester now sitting in the still truck beside him, hearing it:

"Well, all them men, good citizens, arraigned to the Court House in Malone, not one of them safe from reasonable suspicion. So, went to my father, because he was the famous talker, John they said, here's a jug of likker, come to Malone and do the talking. And when he was done talking to the judge, there wa'n't a case against a one of them. Nobody ever did get caught for that horrible crime, shooting anybody in the back, in earshot of his young wife just said good-bye to him, go to town and get the mail.

"Well, same principle here. A woman that can talk like that when she has to, not a bad partner to have along."

He took his right hand off the steering wheel to pat her big knee, right there beside him. Felt the rolled top of her stocking, that couldn't unroll no further up, they don't make a stocking that big. One of these times, roll that down himself, ha-ha. What's the next adventure?

"'You people!'" Hester said. "Can you believe them saying that to us? 'You people!' Makes me smile. I'll have to remember that."

Five

THEY FOUND THEMSELVES on Route 17 once more, going west again, skirting along the northern shore of that never-ending Lac Supérieure. Along came another road from the right, Route 11, a very familiar route to Clarence. He knew another part of it well, or so he thought, from Watertown to Rouses Point, the main road of the North Country, home. Happy to see it again, joining right in with Route 17, keeping it company to Thunder Bay.

That was a name he liked, Thunder Bay. Good names all along on this trip. Some of them were names he had heard of, many of them Indian names that called to him from boyhood, old days, old dreams, history books. They passed a couple of signs, could have turned off and gone north to Sioux Lookout. He would have liked to go there, stand on top and see what the Sioux saw, ha-ha. But it was out of the way. Wanted to keep Alaska straight ahead. This country so low, he didn't know what anybody could see from Sioux Lookout but flat land and a million pot-holes they call lakes. They were making good time towards another good name, Winnipeg.

Which, Indians, he never had no prejudice against. Just the opposite. When he said Robert Sochia could shoot like a Indian, it was a term of admiration, same as if he said he could shoot like a pirate. Likewise, those boys who could make a canoe with just a horse-shoer's crooked knife, give them a lot of credit. Evangeline, well, bad apples in any barrel. Handsome she was. Take away the bad act-ing, Evangeline was his idea of a redskin woman, maybe a little heavy-set but a face you could put on a nickel.

Winnipeg was a Indian name or he would eat his hat. Winnipeg, Manitoba. Almost finished with Ontario, that is a big territory, taken three days to cross. Let's see what Manitoba's got to offer. Truck running good, girl minding her manners. Money aplenty. Start of summer. What more could a outrider wish for?

"You know who talks a lot," Hester said.

"What?"

"I said you know who talks a lot, mister. You do."

Now he goes down the road wondering if in his long years living alone he has formed the habit of talking aloud to himself without knowing it. Might need to watch it. Not every thing he might think was meant for present company.

Did he still think he was alone? Hester was definitely there in the truck beside him. Weighed half again what he did, took up twice the space and ate like a lumberjack. Good thing there was plenty of money because it was running out the spigot like water. There she was, she wasn't nobody. But still did he think he was alone?

You know who talks a lot, when he hadn't been aware of talking at all. Hnnh.

Hoped she liked listening in. Probably having her setting there beside him provoked him to say things to himself that he didn't downright need to say, just to himself. Heard them before, many times.

That last remark of hers had to come from somewhere. Backtrack from that, what's she been thinking? Traveling alone too? Alone in her own mind just the same as he was in his, only not thinking out loud? Both of them used to it, lived alone so long, or, in Hester's case, as good as alone, living with that old skinflint. Meanest man Clarence ever knew, Wilfred. Just mean. Not nobody Clarence wanted to associate with, except he had a good farm, waste not want not. And a stall for each of Clarence's horses, that one sugaring season he needed a place to board them. And a daughter. That was the start of it.

Now he felt a touch of guilt for saying Wilfred wa'n't no company to Hester. Of course he was some company to her. They was company each to each, though not necessarily comfort. Maybe he ought to talk to her more. Be at least as good company to her as her father ever was. That wouldn't be no chore.

Back when he was visiting her, taking her to a show or to see Nellie and Bessie, or Leo Weller, she was a stream of talk from morning to see you later. He even thought of marrying her with the full expectation that he'd never have another minute's peace. Avoided that by the hair of his chin and thought himself lucky. But ever since you know what, hnnn. May be she never knew before what it was like to be content. Content to be still. It has made a nicer person of her, well worth the trouble. Picking her up for this ramble was the best thing I ever done but I sorely doubted it at the time, didn't know what come over me, just determined to do it. It was perverse, and I am not no pervert, normally.

Slush on the wiper blades. Whatever gave him the notion winter was over? Ever since that freezing overnight rain and sparkling morning when this trip began what with his ban on conversation he'd almost forgotten his favorite topic. Fair weather had speeded up the spring in his mind. Wanted high summer in Alaska, long time to prepare for taking over from Sam McGee. That fellow's measures to keep warm never far from his Alaska thoughts.

But winter wasn't over, really, here it was again, cold toes, feeble heater, all the hot air up on the windshield, had to look under the rim of the wheel between his hands to see ahead.

Pretty soon she would tell him if you can't see why don't we stop.

But when she just politely wiped herself a little window in the fog he relented and pulled off; and wouldn't you know the sun came out.

This place used to be a ice house or he missed his guess. Built on the side of a lake, ramp from the dock, signs of a rig just like the rail in her old man's barn that carried the honey-bucket down the walkway between the gutters and out to the manure pile, but this was for blocks of ice, held by tongs. Handy to a sawmill in the same family, so there's your insulation, sawdust. These windows put into it more recently and all the sawdust shoveled out, make it into a restaurant, or a store for people with their cabins on the lake. The slush was already melted, blond planks of a new deck drying. Sandwiches seemed cheap enough to him and she proposed sharing a bottle of Coke. Always something new.

But she said, "We'll have to cut this out."

"What?"

"Quit actin' like we're on a honeymoon or somethin'."

Don't say that word and don't even notice it.

"Get us lunch meat, cheese, fruit and bread and make our own lunches. This is living too high on the hog."

Well that's what we been doing. What the bear et.

First reference to his money. Not for her to know how much there is in that envelope though she had taken it under her wing and dished a few dollars out of it into her purse at times. Paid for their meals and lodgings in US dollars, which the Canadians took without comment, no surprise to him because the US was the greatest country on earth, well known fact. Gave change in their own kind of dollars to keep hold of all they could of ours. When you are travelling in a foreign land you do not argue over everything.

"Was you good at figures?" she asked. "As if I didn't know."

Well, not very, h'nn, never needed to be but who collected all that money, put 'tin the bank and let them keep track, not like some fools. Come to think, who knows what them bank ladies let out of the bag. Could hear his sisters asking, "My land, Doris, all of it?" How much was it, ennaway?" Doris would have said, "I'm not supposed to be telling you this but he's your brother, you look after him, you ought to know."

"You prob'ly was," he said. Good at figuring, he meant. "Anything like your old man." Who'd skin every penny he could out of anybody's wages.

Clarence had shoveled a lot of honey into that honey-bucket for not much.

"That was to feed your team, Clarence. Just when they couldn't earn their keep, only time he took anything out of your pay. Who do you think kept Daddy's accounts on that farm? Why'd you think he didn't go to the bank for everything and lose the farm like most everybody else except Silas Eakins?"

"Look, this is a old ice-house," he said. "Just like the Wellers at the lake, turned their old ice house into a cottage."

"Brr! I knew it. Still cold. Eat up, Lefty, let's we git agoin'. I likes progress. Give me electric refrigerators any day." Once he hefted her up into the truck she commenced to singing.

On the road to Mandalay-ay

Where the flying fishes play --

"You know different songs than I do."

"Didn't tell you I sang, did I?"

"Well, ha ha."

"When the dawn comes up like thunder

Out of China cross the bay."

60

The two routes separated and he took Route 11 north since he had been going west a good deal longer than he liked. His navigation was always hinting at him, north, north, north because 17 was always going west, west, west.

"I don't know about this," Hester said.

Sign said Lake Nipigon was up this way. Sounded good to him.

"I think we needs a map."

And a little later, "I thought we was going to Winnipeg."

He thought so too, why, because before that Y so many signs said Winnipeg, so and so many kilometers. Getting so used to kilometers he didn't know what he'd do with a mile. Map, hnn. "All right." Just to be polite and show her some respect. Get a map first chance they got. Meanwhile ask this fellow.

Now a T, with a turnout on the other side of the road. Clarence was already hesitantly slowing down. It was a bandanna'd hippie on a motorcycle, resting, feet or rather high black boots with D-rings on the ankles up on the handle-bars, leaning back against a high head-rest, or a back-rest for the missing girl-friend, sunning his blond hairy chest.

Hester didn't want to go near him but he was the only person they were likely to see before the Arctic Circle, and what Clarence knew of hippies—Robert Sochia was one—well, they weren't harmless in that one case, but Clarence had always found them interested to learn about the olden days, how to twist your axe-head just before it hit, for instance, when you're splitting wood. That way, see, it doesn't get stuck. Pries the two pieces apart and rings against the one, flies up ready for another stroke. Clarence was like this. Go right up to somebody he ought to be scared of, not thinking, get nervous too late, and here you were, pulled over and window down, ashamed to close the window and drive on, so saying hello across the road.

"Hey man," the fellow said, not moving his face much but slanting a look Clarence's way, lids mostly closed against the sun.

Clarence had a quick thought of Arnold and Evangeline, didn't want to be suspected of stopping to help. Not planning to stop and help anybody ever again. But the fellow said, voice like a college professor been out on a desert. "Can I help you?"

"Well, yes, you could if you know which is the better way for me to be turning on this road, with the aim of getting—"

"Don't tell him where we are goin'," Hester said.

"We are headed, sir, generally north-west," he said.

"Go right over that hill, then," the fellow said, with a silly giggle. He pointed, not in the direction of either road. "I just come from Hudson's Bay, myself." Patted the gas tank like you'd pat the neck of a horse and gestured backwards with his head. Clarence nodded, shut the window, and did a U-turn around the bike. Pretty soon, back on 17 again, and not a word from her.

Spoke too soon. "Before Winnipeg comes Kenora, and I need to stop," she said. "Besides, I want to see something besides the road. See the signs here, Forestry, Tourism, Mining. Twenty thousand people. Lake of the Woods. Bass. Muskellunge. History. Rat Portage, Hudson's Bay Company, Voyageurs. Slow down!"

He did, but it was too late, they were past the advertising.

"Clarence Shampine, you think you and your people are better than me and my people, but you want to cross the whole length of Canada and not learn anything. Now you stop in this city, right in the middle of it, and I'm goin' to get a tourist brochure." As if that was a little harsh, she went still for a minute. Clarence said nothing aloud, thinking just when you admit something, they hit you over the head with it.

But she didn't realize she'd already won. "I say we go in this town and get some Canadian money. I think you're being took, every time you buys anything."

"Well...." Hard enough for Clarence to make sure he got the right change as it was, from all them hundred dollar bills. Now if they were buying everything with Canadian dollars it would be like a foreign language only numbers.

"What'd you say?"

"Well, I said, all right."

There was a bypass route around Kenora to the Manitoba line but Clarence got steering lock when he saw it too late and went by, so into Kenora they did go, traffic getting heavier. The place was watery left and right and you wondered what you was on, island or peninsula, a big lake on the south side of the road and arms of it reaching up around every low hill, and then a couple of very long high arched bridges, he never saw the like, gave you the feeling of the roller coaster at the fair. Then they were plumb in the middle of it, city blocks one side of the street and the other a parking lot and a towering ferry-boat, for Heaven's sake. They could go to Minnesota, truck and all, if they wanted to. It was harder than he thought, to get away from America. He parked first place handy, desperate to halt this progress which was out of control. One good thing, it was a very nice day, nice air here, and sea gulls crying. Conversationally, he said, "Never used to see sea gulls to-home, until they built the Saint Lawrence Seaway. Then, they come with the ships over the ocean, and now there they are, even at Cook's Lake, normal as a loon."

"Clarence Shampine!"

"What?"

"You are here. This is now. There's the bank right there." She pulled out five hundred dollars from the big envelope and shoved them at him. "You go into the bank and change this into Canadian, and I'll get brochures at the ferry ticket place. Help me out of the truck, my legs is asleep from so much setting."

Clarence had just gone timidly through the door of the bank feeling like a conspicuous bank robber with his empty holster at his hip and the neckerchief on his shoulders that he could so easily turn around into a mask. He was standing in a short line, one person in front of him, good, gave him time to get ready. But before he re-membered which hand he had the bills in some loud words were spoken ahead. A fellow and the teller were talking, one loud, the other trying to keep it quiet, and other people were gathering behind the teller-lady in white shirts and bald heads, all looking worried or nervous. Clarence stopped, went sideways two steps, found the money in a pocket. He heard the fellow at the window say very slowly and not too loud and not too clearly, like he had something in his mouth, which is what he said he did, "You thee thith clothe-pin in dy douth? Now nodody touth be. Nobody touth be."

Clarence couldn't see the clothes-pin but something stuck part-way out of his mouth, with wires attached, a loop of colored wires dragging down to the floor. "Thith ith a dead man'th switch in my mouth." Clarence heard it clearly, "dead man's switch." Never heard of such. "Goeth to thith." Shows something under his arm, a box, those wires dragging on the floor behind him came back up to that box, or package. The man said, "Ish anydody toutheth me, I thpit out thith clothe-thin…" He took a breath and straightened up. "… the clothe-thin clotheth, and theeth lithle wireth touch togeddah, thee? And the bob goeth off. Killth uth aw. Jutht nobody do any-thing dumb, OK? Add had ovah all the cash."

There was a pause. The teller looked back at the angry nervous men behind her. Clarence had a mind to offer the man the five hun-dred dollars. He didn't want anybody to be blown up. "Here," he said, and held out his hand, but he didn't say it loud, or finish. "Had it ovah!" the bank robber said, louder. The locks of his long brown hair, the skirts of his thin brown coat were shivering. The bank men told the girl to give the man what was in the cash drawer. Which she did, fast as she could, and the man gathered it up and turned and went past Clarence very close, dragging his wires behind him, Clarence with his money still extended toward him just in case. He saw the clothes-pin in the man's mouth but still didn't see the man well, just that his lips were very pale and black rings around his eyes, and a John Deere cap with the long hair hanging.

He watched the man go out through the door and start to get into a black car that had appeared at the curb since Clarence stepped in. He just touched the door-handle, then a rifle shot, a sound familiar to Clarence, and the glass fell out of the bank door and a slug skidded across the marble to the base of the counter, tapped it sharply and set there spinning audibly, behind Clarence, who looked for it the second until the bomb went off. The blast knocked Clarence five steps further into the bank, kept upright only by hitting the counters where he stepped on the bullet and jumped again. That blast certainly killed the man with the John Deere hat. Killed him, surely, if the sniper's bullet didn't. Not a move, there on the pavement. Blew up under his arm, arm nowhere to be seen, let more blood out of him in an instant than Clarence knew a man had in him.

How about the fellow in the car? Nobody there. Anybody else? Clarence came tenderly forward to the vacant door-frame and looked right and left.

Where was the sniper?

Sniper was up on the ferry-boat, across the parking lot. Shot right over Hester's head. Clarence had that angle figured out in a flash, and the man that probably parked the car was standing over the body telling a sudden crowd that he was a policeman, not to worry, everything under control, stand back.

They didn't have to be told, they stood back as if there was a rope. Still, Clarence thought, that fellow was lucky to be alive, policeman or not. If he was in that car, the whole side of it blasted in and burnt. Well, of course, bank robbery every day. Clarence stepped through the frame, skipped around the puddle before the policeman could stop him. And here come Hester, as close to running as he would ever see. Saw the dead man before him and didn't know which was which, because at the blast she thought-

"Clarence!" she said, jerking his sleeve. "Is this you? Is you in one piece?"

"Well, I think so. That boy is gone forever. I perish to think, if you'd been coming to find me."

She had him by the arm, breathing hard and holding harder. They were in the middle of the street.

"I would have given him the money, if he needed it that bad. I had it right in my hand."

"Clarence!" Still could hardly speak, but broke away but for one arm, hauling him across to the truck. He stumbled pigeon-toed after her. Got to the truck, went to put his shoulder to her buttocks as usual, to help her up. He shook his head once, to clear the crook in his neck or else clear away the echo of that blast, walked around the front, away from the bank, got in. There loomed the bow of that ferryboat for America which seemed to have its clutches out for him. Glad to put his tailgate toward it. Come to find out they were still on 17. They drove away west. Soon put the tailgate toward Ontario too at last, headed for Winnipeg.

That would be one to tell and laugh about, for some people, he thought aloud. To me, it wasn't no joke. Just like a picture show except real as his hands on the wheel. For some reason, he felt as if he'd robbed the bank himself. The other fellow died in his place. Dead switch, you got that right. Hester was fanning herself. He looked at her. Very red in the face, fanning herself as fast as that brochure would go.

They were coming near to Winnipeg and the landscape changed tremendously before they were ready for anything new. They came off an escarpment and the land went dry and treeless and was flattening out to something, there way ahead, that Clarence could not bear to look at. Flat land, flat as far as the eye could see, colorless, and the city was no more inviting. Sprawling in front of it, biggest city he had ever seen, floating in a brown fog of its own making, you could see that with your bare eyes. Look north, look south, no brown haze, but over the city, soup so thick you could not see the tops of the tall buildings. Tall buildings in the center, straight ahead, but small buildings thick together forever in all directions. Hester reading, said "More than half the people in Manitoba lives right here. And Manitoba is big, CW, goes all the way up to the Arctic. They has polar bears in Manitoba."

Clarence said, "What I hoped they had was cows, and I don't mean dairy cows. Because where there is cows there is cowboys, and where there is cowboys there is cowgirls, and I am looking for a pretty cow-girl." There, mistake. He'd got to joking unintentionally, for he felt little mirth and didn't mean to insult her. What he'd meant to say was, "Where there is cowboys there is horses," but natural wittiness took over. He did long to see something he was an expert on. Anyway, made up his mind right then not to go through Winnipeg. Route 17 went through it, by the look of things, looking from where they come out on the brink of that vast westward flatness. Could see the road dropping down straight ahead, a bee line for them tall buildings. Well then, leave 17. Which way? You guessed it, northwest. Take the first road you see with a number on it.

This was a place to get away from, get past, hope for hills and trees and polar bears further ahead, anything's better than a desert, or any of these western cities where they have a bank robbery every day. Hester was hardly done fanning herself from the last scrape. Clarence had revised the story and now saw himself fearlessly moving toward the John Deere man saying, "See here, let me take hold of your clothes-pin and you take these hundred dollar bills, no reason to die." Happy ending once somebody disconnects those wires. Then mobbed as a hero by the teller-girls when all he'd done was hand out money, which, had more than he needed.

But he now was brought up short by the name of the river they crossed, or meant to. Got halfway across a bridge over it and up come a stop sign. Then the bridge turned sideways with the truck right on it, to let a barge go past down below. Barge went right under the truck. Made Clarence dizzy, as if he was on a ship at sea, had to open the window and put out his head, hold on to the door-handle.

"What river is this? I don't believe what I saw." What he saw was a sign saying Red River.

"Red River."

"Red River! This is the Red River?"

"The Red River goes right through Winnipeg."

From this valley they say you are leaving,

Do not hasten to bid me adieu

Clarence shook his head as if to drive the thought away. Red River shouldn't be nowheres near such a place. Seven hundred thousand people.

"Well," he said, "I always wanted to see the Red River Valley."
Holy words unthought for decade upon decade. When did he last
hum this tune?

Oh remember the Red River Valley
And the cowboy who loved you so true
Come and sit by my side if you—

He had sung past that word in the refrain without noticing it.
Didn't mean to utter it twice, so he clamped his mouth shut. Having
a nice trip with this woman so far, you don't want to spoil it. But
goodness gracious this was the Red River Valley. Sent a thrill
through him, just the name, and couldn't keep the song out of his
mind.

Once off the bridge they couldn't see the Red River anymore.
That was a disappointment, the Red River in a ditch where you
might as well chop it up and sell it by the foot. Never saw it again.

Couldn't escape Winnipeg either. Looks like they don't have
no north here, how would you tell, no roads that way. Couldn't go
bother the polar bears if you wanted. Pretty soon back on 17 and
going right through the middle of it, ready to cover their ears and
duck if these people started shooting. If they got too near a bank,
ha-ha.

Six

"OH MY LAND," she cried. "Brothels!"

CW wasn't sure what brothels were but he wasn't sure he wasn't sure. It might mean, hnn, whore-houses, a very distasteful word which he would not utter in mixed company. As they hummed along straight west with nothing in the world to look at except wheat fields and blistered earth, Hester was reading the tourist brochure for Kenora, which they had narrowly escaped with their lives. Clarence was still running over that bank robbery. If that was staged for tourists they done a good job. Also if that sniper's bullet hadn't shot the glass out of the bank window, the bomb would have blown it in his face.

She'd unfolded the brochure to the history page, straightaway, not interested in hockey or football, night clubs or shopping malls or heroic statues of the muskellunge. Brothels was the first form Kenora took, apparently, back in history, little shacks one after the others alongside the line of the railroad, while it was being built.

"They called it Rat Portage in the old days. I wonder why. Say, CW, we must of been coming northwest. Says here Rat Portage was the most north-wester-ly…" She slowed down on that word and dipped her head to the brochure. "…settlement of New France. Which is what they called Canada then. 1763. They was trading with the Indians. Doesn't say what for, for heaven's sake. Ojibway, Cree….It used to be part of Manitoba. The border ran right down the main street….Gold! They was mining gold here, twenty mines within twenty-four kilometers! We wouldn't ever of known that, see? If I hadn't of read this. The first ocean-to-ocean railroad train passed through here, 1886, the Canadian Pacific Railway."

Well it will surely be interesting traveling with you, sister, now that you found your hobby. You and the Great Plains here.

Boys it was a long way between places where you could get anything. Food, gas, or help. Suppose your truck broke down. Best hope you had was other travelers of which there was plenty, going both ways. She said this was the Trans-Canada Highway, maybe the only one, the one anybody going across this country would wind up on, same way they did. No choice. Well, that made for company. Once in a while, get passed by the same car or truck that passed you a hundred miles ago. A lot of people turning rubber tires into black dust. Where people used to walk alongside a ox and a iron-shod cart, axle-deep in the ruts. Sleep in a circle of wagons, all guns pointing outwards. Keep your hat on tight or lose your scalp.

Saw one of them little buses with little windows all up along the roof, to look at mountains out of, painted every color of the rainbow just like Robert Sochia's old Desoto before the rust flaked it all off. Or like the triangles sewed into the bottom of his dungarees. Had a big V and W on it, so same make as a Beetle and sounded like it couldn't go no faster, when it barely got past them. Saw it up ahead for a long way, the yellow back end of it.

"Say! That girl and two babies again! Rhode Island. You remember them?"

"No I do not."

"Yes you do."

"Funny you know that and I don't."

"Well we seen them way back yonder. Wonder where they's going. Hippies! You remember."

Clarence himself had a big sunburst belt-buckle like those people, hippies, liked to wear. If he saw something he liked, hippie or no, he wasn't too proud to wear it.

But traveling in this stream of traffic, over the plain, steady, noisy, just like a railroad train, felt wrong to Clarence. Might as well be all hitched together, save gas. Same thing in both directions. Some kind of two-directions migration going on that he wanted no part of. He was traveling on false pretenses in some way. Near got blown up, just a short ways back, and had a funny feeling he couldn't put his finger on, felt defenseless. Alive by luck, is all. What would become of Hester if he was blown to bits. Himself not worth saving. Done the worse a man could do and sent out from the tribe, that's why I'm traveling this route. Don't write home, nobody's looking for your letters. Well, what's all the rest of you people after?

As if she read his mind, Hester slapped the brochure down on her knees and exclaimed, "I should of got a postcard! I should of sent Daddy a postcard from Rat Portage! Tell him we was in the middle of a bank robbery! And you should write your sisters, CW. They must be worried awful about you. We been having so much fun, we didn't think of anybody but ourselfs."

Could see himself telling Nellie and Bessie about the John Deere fellow with the dead man's switch in his mouth and then his arm up in the sky and the whole side of him blown open. Take too many words. Arnold and Evangeline wouldn't fit on a postcard either.

He said, "You know what them two are saying."

"What?"

"Every day, look at each other, say, 'Don't you worry, Nellie, he's turned around by now."

"You think so?"

"'Don't you worry, Bessie, Clarence won't last long on the road to far Alaska.'"

"They didn't know we'd get along this good."

"That's right. They think you're wheedling at me, turn around, let's go home, Clarence."

"Don't know something we got, stay with you through thick and thin for that."

"Think I don't know how to navigate."

"Think I'd be homesick for my Daddy. Which I is, a little. But not to turn around for."

"What do you suppose Wilfred's thinking about us?"

"Well, about today he's given up, is what I think. He's begging Nellie come cook for him."

"Nellie! She won't do it."

"No, she won't. But he'll keep after her. He'll be sayin' your brother stole my cook, Nellie, have mercy. You got to come cook for me. He'll be over there at meal times, so they won't have no choice but feed him, till he gets it through his head."

"Then what?"

"Then somebody else. Oh dear, he has many a old sweetie, widows all around there. But don't make me talk about him, I'll get to feeling guilty."

Clarence didn't want that. Dangerous subject, home. Not to him, but to her, more a home person than he ever was or intended to become.

It came over him again how many people in how many carapaces of steel on rubber were shattering the air around the steadily grinding truck, the ones from behind passing almost as suddenly as the ones from ahead.

"What's all these people in such a hurry for?"

"Which people? They's goin' both ways. They's people, just like us."

"I'm a outcast."

"You're a figment of your own imagination."

"Whatever give it to you to say a thing like that?"

"I don't know, CW. It just come to me."

"I'll be a figment of yours."

"Oh I imagine you will, if you ain't already. Ennaways, I will just get us some postcards when next we stop," she said. "Get a road map too. I like seeing where we's at."

They departed from Route 17, or the Trans-Canada Highway, also called Route1, at a place called Brandon, which was another name from home. Town of Brandon, just south of the Falls, which was Town of Stark, if that made any sense to you. Brandon wasn't no town at all but just country. Woods. Here, this Brandon, flat land, wheat fields, scarce trees, nothing to see but they needed gas, and sure enough while the fellow was pumping their gas didn't she pick up a map of Manitoba and Saskatchewan. They sat at a booth to rest their ears. Splurged on coffee. And now according to his navigator if he wanted to get northwest they ought to go north here, pick up a road they should have taken long ago, not far from Winnipeg. Route 16. "Look here," she says. "Route 16, see, goes northwest, towards Saskatoon. Don't you want to go through Saskatoon?"

"Of course I do." Any place with a name like that, that I have heard before and like the sound of. Saskatoon, Saskatchewan, wouldn't miss it for the world. But first what's that in the counter there?

This place put him in mind of Arquit's Store, in SF. Same kind of a store, same size. Had meats, groceries, a little bit of hardware, work clothes, and guns. He wouldn't be surprised if a little fat man with glasses come at him from the meat-room with blood all over his apron, wiping his hands saying Long Time No See. And there under the glass counter lay the same kind of a pistol he had had swiped out of his hands at the mud spring by Mister Murder Man. Colt's Forty-five, holdster and all, shells fanned out beside it. Made the hair stand up on the back of his neck because he knew what he was about to do, and did not dare to do it.

One thing sure, he wasn't going to buy that pistol. Had plenty of money to buy it with but no, he was not going to buy it. For one thing, already bought it, same thing. For another, red tape, licensing, who knows what he would be getting into if he bought that pistol. Not a pistol, strictly speaking. Revolver, different thing. Bought the other one full price and got time to fire it exactly once before it was taken from him. Stolen. Clarence had waited for that revolver for many years, and Duke Arquit waited just as long for some'n to come along and buy it. Dust on it you could write your name in. Walked in there and said I want that iron, what's the price? Duke opened up the back door of that counter, picked it off the shelf, wiped the dust off it and read the price tag. He said, "Huh. Only a hundred and thirty-eight dollars. That's too low, Clarence. That price is years out of date. That'd be twice as much now. If you've got to have it. I don't think you do."

But Clarence did have to have it and didn't care what the price was, money aplenty burning a hole in his pocket, just been to the bank. Put a few bills down, let Arquit take what he wanted.

Not going to buy this one here but had to have it just the same. Or put it the other way around, had to have it, wa'n't going to pay. I was brought low long ago and it wouldn't bring me no lower if I stole it. Just like the bank robbery. That was staged for me just like this, and I done good. Did I run? No, stood right there and offered to save the fellow's life. Same principle. His mind was made up and he was deaf to any other voices in his head. How to steal it? Well, make up your mind and do it fast, he who hesitates is lost. But isn't that counter locked? Arquit's was, he had to go to his office to get the key.

Clarence could see himself getting the owner of this place, out there checking his oil, having him get his key and open it and bring out the pistol. The revolver. Then what. Get it in your hands and tell the fellow you got a dead man's switch in your mouth? Just let you get to the truck and everybody will survive. No, he did not see himself doing that. Come back at night and break that glass? Didn't like that deal either.

Well-well the case was locked but the key was hanging there in the lock. Clarence made without thought the assumption that he knew this place, laid out exactly like Arquit's, in fact was Arquit's, and Duke, if coming, would be coming toward him past the dairy aisle, wiping his hands on his bloody apron. But he was back in there cutting up a beef carcass, and the check-out counter was hidden. So was Hester, now among the greeting cards. He crouched behind the case, turned the key, slid the glass, had the revolver in his hand, and looked innocently about. No one, unless somebody was looking down on him from straight overhead, a thought which made him duck. He'd bought the revolver the first time square and square, no argument; paid double for all he knew. This was only taking back what was his. He stuffed it inside his many shirts, under his arm where that poor fellow had been carrying his bomb. Want the holster too? Shame to separate the two things. What about that? It wouldn't go in his shirts so good, but a separate price tag on it. Had no right to steal that, because he still had the first one. All right, he could pay for it.

The lady looked at him funny when he did. But shook her head and took his money. It was Hester who said, outside, "What you buy that for?" looking at his hip. He already had a holster there, put it on his belt when he bought the revolver the first time, been carrying it around empty hoping the bird would fly home, ha-ha. She didn't know what he had in his shirt.

Some people think you ought to put the holdster on the same side as your shooting hand but Clarence was of a different persuasion, had the holdster on his left side backwards so the butt of the revolver stuck forward. He had practiced in front of his shaving mirror in the log cabin on the Project, could bring his right hand around front and snatch that revolver out and up and around and have a bead on Mr. Grizzly Bear in one smooth spiral movement. Say good-bye, Bruin. The Colt has a long barrel, see, have to pull it a long ways up to get it free, that's why the cross-body draw is best, you don't get in the way of your arm. "Well good," said Hester. "Now you got two holsters and no gun."

"That's what you think, sister. Let's go."

Down the road five miles he pulled the revolver out of his armpit and laid it on the seat between them.

"Oh my land sakes," she said. "You bought a pistol. Why'd you put it in your shirt?"

"You don't know, do you?"

"Mean you didn't buy it?"

He didn't answer.

"You didn't buy it?"

Mum.

"What'd you do? Did you just steal it?"

Well, if I did what of it? Did you think you was on a holiday with a tap-dancer?

She turned her face straight ahead and was silent a long time. He began to wonder if this was all right. If she understood him at all or agreed with his premises. He didn't know, himself, if he had done right. Maybe he had been foolish. Could have got them in a peck of trouble. Just lately had gotten used to not having anybody looking over his shoulder so close. Wouldn't want to think he needed anybody's guidance, but... His sisters would certainly tell him he was a fool, for a lot less a foolishness than this. He had been confused in there. That place was so much like Arquit's store he expected to see Duke coming out of the butcher shop with his apron on, saying "What you want with that shooting iron, Clarence? You don't need that thing and you can't afford it. Put it back there and forget about it." Which he would have done. But he couldn't put it back, he'd already bought it once, and it was his, something he had wanted many and many a year, and had waited for, until he had to go after that criminal on his own, since he had figured out where he was and nobody else would listen to him. Purryer Camp was where he was, and Clarence had a long long ways to go to circle in on him there and rescue the girl he had took off, against her will. Bought that revolver for one purpose only, to say to that young man, got a bead on you, turn loose that girl, or else say your prayers, not asking twice.

"We'll be a long ways down the road fore they miss this weapon," he said.

She was silent another long time. Mad at him, so it appeared. Finally he said, "I told you I was gone to the bad. I don't expect to live among civilized people no more, so rules run off me like water off a duck's back."

It may be he was too willing to go bad. Folks might well say that against him. But if so it was because he had been innocent for too long. Nobody ever thought him dangerous his whole life. Took him for granted. Way back to his young stepmother, that knew she could count on him to be good, as she could not count on his older brother. For some reason, it don't do you no good to be good. People take vantage of you. Make fun of you. But who saved the girl from Robert Sochia? Clarence Shampine saved her, all alone, no thanks to the posse, and from that day on, different man. Sabattis Falls couldn't keep this man no more.

Now heading into the Canadian West, look how the bullets fly. You seen it yourself, cookie, whizzing right over your head. He needed that gun and he didn't need to say May I and I am a American citizen here's my driver license and maybe not get it, maybe get hauled back to Kenora to explain that bank robbery, or back to Timmins to explain why he left them two people to get their Datsun home staggering drunk, or worse, the fingerprints on that other one in the other dead man's hands. Now Hester was moving, smoothing her skirts over her knees and putting her hands together in her lap, about to speak. He was humble, ready to hear.

"I did not really believe you, Clarence," she said. "I guess you said so, but I confess I did not know I was running away with a real outlaw. I didn't never suspect no such a thing."

Well, that was mild, so far. He did not know if he was a real outlaw yet, so's to say it right out loud. More coming.

"But I am a long ways from home and I haven't got nobody else. I am with you, Clarence. I'm right here beside you. I been happy on this trip and look forward to more of it. Something new every day, just as you always say. I will take the bad with the good. I got a feeling that I just went over a waterfall but so be it."

They'd always found little small wooden cabins, in woods, by a lake, where Hester could cook up some chili and they could sleep in a bed apiece if they weren't getting along, ha-ha. But this was not a land of lakes. Nothing but wheat farms and Hester said, "Well, if we don't find no cabins that is quite your style, Clarence, we could always stay at a motel, like other people do."

"That isn't my style."

"To tell you the truth it isn't mine either," she huffed. "I never meant to even say the word mo-tel. When I was a lass there wasn't no such a word."

"There wasn't no such a thing when I was a boy."

"That's what I just said, didn't you hear me?"

"I was a boy before you were a girl." Her a lass was hard to imagine. "You said word, I said thing."

"What's the difference? We's talking nonsense. We needs to get a few things if we's not staying in mo-tels."

"Same as words?"

"Things. Articles."

"You said what's the difference. I'll tell you one article, don't plan on buying a lot of stuff to clutter up my truck."

"What brings that up? I haven't been buyin' ennathin'."

"You're thinking of it, I can tell. Money don't grow on trees and there aren't so many trees anymore."

Miles of wheat-fields, large fields, elevators large and small and the sun now smack in front of them so low that Clarence had to turn down the visor to see ahead without eye-pain.

Trouble with them both was they could see they had to start sleeping in different circumstances. Had a wall tent back there, pretty as you ever seen, oiled silk, and folding cots. Quite a lot of trouble to put it up every night and take it down. Plus, folding cot wasn't made that would hold her, let alone the two of them.

A car with a little teardrop camping trailer went past them and Hester exclaimed "Oh that's so cute! That's what we needs, one of them!"

Cute, hnnh. Dr. Fred Weller had been a brand-new doctor at the end of that war. First World War. Clarence had seen the officer's cap and the hard-leather puttees the doctor had worn, and this was the tent he had used. Well, one day, Clarence had been building

80

a dock for his cottage at the lake, helped by his nephew Leo Weller, brought him half a hind-quarter of mountain lamb too, and Doctor asks, "Clarence would you ever have any use for a tent?" Quite a old man by that time. Bald, like all the Wellers that age.

Clarence living on the sheep farm at the time, thought right away, he could set up that tent out behind the barn, wouldn't have to listen to his sisters. Just go in the house to eat. Otherwise, live in peace. The folding cots come with it.

Just his luck that little tear-drop trailer happened by. And now here come another pickup truck much like this one, Clarence seeing the house on it in the rear-view mirror before it very slowly overtook them. All but a house-trailer built onto that truck, sticking forward over the cab and out over the sides. She said, "Lookee there, CW! Room in there for a kitchen, sofa, TV, bathroom and you know what, a queen size bed! Wouldn't you and me have a good time on that!"

Or a little Airstream trailer, next thing she'd see. You would see them now and again, shiny aluminum, slip through the air like a fish through water. Clarence wouldn't mind having one of them either but only one problem, and not telling Hester what that was. Something about how many things you can tow all to once.

Besides the problem that if you bought everything you thought you might like, pretty soon you got a lot of stuff and no more money. I didn't waste money twice on the same pistol, did I? No I did not, and that's the plan for this trip.

"Wasn't that cute, CW? That camper on top of the pickup."

But something else on his mind. Something else they would see, more and more often the further west they got into this prairie, this wheat country which it seemed to Clarence, flat as it was, and straight as the road, was rising, rising a little bit all the time, so that he felt higher, ever higher since the Red River. The air felt different and that seemed to go with the increasing numbers of trailers carrying a horse or two, tails fluttering out over the gate behind. Fellow driving with his brown arm out the window. Boys! That was a life he would have loved. Cut out for that life, he was, more than the life he'd led. Take a horse with you everywhere you go, never be seen on foot.

Well, a logical man. If you ever want to be towing a horse-trailer with this truck, which somebody might, you can't have no camper-top on the bed, can you. Nor you can't have no cute trailer behind. So get certain things out of your mind, cookie.

After a bit of silence, Hester said, "That'll be nice, that tent. I look forward to it."

After another, she said, "We got candles?"

"No."

"We'll get us a Coleman lantern. If we's going to be camping now they's several things to buy, next place we come to."

Is that all? he wondered. Don't she care about you know what?

Glanced over and saw her smiling sweetly at him with her glasses off and her eyes closed. Could feel his ears turn red. He ducked his head a bit and concentrated on the road. A homely woman could be a surprise at every turn.

Seven

IN SASKATCHEWAN BEFORE HE KNEW IT, which might be the West, he wasn't sure but getting closer certainly. Now that he had the pistol on his hip he felt different, more the way he intended to feel on this trip, a dangerous hombre. He wore it around camp, setting up the tent, building a fire for the cook. Wore it in the tent right up 'til undressing for bed. On the road he wrapped the revolver in a towel and kept it behind the seat, and as he passed through towns he peered at men going into or coming out of taverns, diners, feed-stores, above all banks, to see if they were wearing guns. He hadn't seen any side-arms so far, guessed he wasn't far enough west and so continued to leave his holster empty when they stopped. As soon as it appeared to be the normal way to do, he would wear the revolver. Might wear both holsters, the second one, on his right side, might come in handy. If he ever came upon another weapon, who knows, buy it and fill both. Many a gunman carried two pistols, it was nothing to make fun of.

They seemed more and more to be in a stream of travelers. Clarence did not drive fast, the contrary, believed in steady progress, the turtle gets there as quick as the hare and surer, and so the stream flowed around them all day long. One time he heard a deafening, battering roar all of a sudden, at his side, and veered to the right almost off the road and slowed in bewilderment at first and then amazement as fifteen or twenty motorcycles went by, each one like a string of fireworks next to his ear.

Sometimes they'd see the same vehicle again and again, maybe from an earlier day, further east, somebody going faster than they did but getting up later in the morning. They'd see somebody at a diner they'd seen before, a young mother and two small children once at a truck-stop, and nod to each other, and Hester would stop and chat with her. Clarence kept to himself, wasn't looking to make any new acquaintances, nobody needed to know who he was.

Now they'd pulled the rig into a little park just off the road, a patch of trees with one of these pot-holes of water in front of it, between it and the road, otherwise just desert. It was work putting up that wall tent but second time, team work, not so bad and he enjoyed the smell of that oiled silk and the way the light came through it.

She'd been doing something with the frying pan, no fire tonight, something else that cost money, now set beside him to watch the sun go down.

"Well? I knows what you think of buying anythin' but aren't you glad we got these folding chairs? And the Coleman stove. And Clarence I got to do a wash some day."

"So you want to buy a washing machine?"

"No, I'm just saying." He hadn't turned a sweat since he left home, why wash? Had quit wearing his long johns before they started walking around without him. They'd had showers in the cabins, or at least wash basins. Now, tenting, it would be different, have to find campgrounds with showers, if they had such things. So far hadn't noticed.

"You know where I would like to stay one night. That Delta Bessborough Chateau in Saskatoon. The last Canadian National Railway Hotel. It looks like a castle, CW!"

Been reading the billboards. He'd seen that too, what was it doing out here in the West, ten stories high, made of stone, looked like he didn't know what.

"That's my style!" she said.

"Hnnh. You got a sense of humor."

"I don't suppose you'd ever let us do that, just for a treat."

"No I don't suppose I would. How long would my money last if we paid a hundred dollars a night for a place to lay our heads."

"I been a cheap date up to now."

He was trying ideas for a clever response when another truck passed, over on the highway. Reminded him why he was worried about more junk in the back of the truck. His secret plan. When you see a horse riding in a box on a pickup like that, ears pricked to the wind, tail flying out the back, you see somebody living the good life. A dream denied to him, already no room for a bronco in Clarence's rig.

Couldn't be helped. One of them cots was flinders in no time, first night camping. A person could of been pinched in the wreckage, less said about why the better. Then, no floor to the tent, and the ground made of cinders.

A lot of these grain farmers in their trucks, type of people that don't wear side-arms. A lot of dusty ordinary cars, I mean dusty. A bus now and then. And then every so often what he saw just now, a pickup truck with the next best thing to a wooden horse-stall built into it, or slid in onto the bed and hooked. And a cayuse standing in it looking ahead over the cab, just as happy as a dog, mane and fore-lock blowing back. Sometimes you'd look into the back end of it after it went by and the horse was wearing a saddle. All you'd have to do is hop on and go for a ride.

Not a rider himself but only because he never learnt, worked with draft-horses in the lumber woods. He guessed that the cowboy must back the truck up to a bank, if you could find one, or maybe use the back door to the rig for a ramp, but it would be awful short ramp, consequently steep. Had to be a smart, well-trained willing horse, handy with its feet. That is just what a cowboy had, a smart horse willing to do what you asked.

Good question could I learn to ride.

And now here goes by a whole stream of pickups with a one- or two-horse open trailer behind every one. Another and another. Then what looked like a four-horse trailer all enclosed. All going the same way, west. What's the attraction, I wonder.

Then here was chili con carne, tin plate on his lap, cooked up as easy as kiss your hand, while they both was sitting on the verandah, how'd she do that?

"I see they has these folding tables too. Coleman's does." Mouth too full to answer.

She changed the subject herself. "This air in Saskatchewan, the clear skies and low humidity, my goodness it feels good. I likes it, don't you?"

Yes I do. Chili good out here too.

As soon as the sun neared the earth it turned red and the air went cold. She put on a cardigan and heated water, did the pots and plates. While the sun fattened on the rim of the world she stood behind him twirling his cowlick with a finger. He tipped up his little bottle to his mustache. She said, "Now CW, we got one cot that is up on its legs and one that isn't but they is more ways than one to skin a cat. I likes the skin contact. We can have it if you don't try to climb all over me."

"How will I resist?"

"I'll make sure you do. I don't want to lie in a pile of splinters again."

Wondered what tricks she had for skinning a cat. When he found out, taken by surprise. "Well, I don't know," he said, too late. There she was, looked like the moon.

"Oh they do it all the time, CW. Variety's the spice of life." She led him by the hand.

Didn't like it quite so well but Hester seemed to like it plenty. Sounded as if she was wounded and calling for the doctor but that was just a woman's way of giving pleasure, make you think you're too much for them. Sensing tremendous movement, put his hands around under the front, almost more than he could reach, and found the large globes of her chest separated from her by a lot of loose skin, and swinging a mile front and back. Thought they needed to be saved, and pulled them back up to her as well as he could without collapsing on her rolled neck but they spilled all over his hands. All tender flesh to him, pink and smooth and warm and soft. Heard of this way of doing it and seen pictures but always looked away. Didn't think God would have planned it that way for humans, though for dogs, of course. And horses. And now, well, all right, now you know how a stallion feels, and it was certainly easier on the cot, just her forearms and her head on its side, almost catching his eye. The rest of his life was a sacrifice anyway. If anybody was reading about me doing this in a book, I would put a piece of paper over the page with the one word on it, "Private."

The way they found the rodeo next morning was simple. Follow behind one of the rigs with horses on it or in it. If you get separated, can't go fast enough, let it go and follow behind the next one. Because surely these rigs were going somewhere, the same place, had to be a rodeo.

"You're the one in charge, I guess," Hester says.

"You don't want to go to a rodeo?"

"Sure I do. It would be entertainment. Which I don't need thanks to you but which I could enjoy without needing it. Some things you both need and enjoy, so you don't know whether you even do need them and it doesn't matter, huh! I don't know what I'm saying but you know what I mean. Sure. I'll go to a rodeo with you, CW. I was just pointing out that you didn't ask before you decided. What we was doing. Where I thought we was on a trip together. I am not trying to start a fight, I am just finding my tongue. You had me tongue-tied with your pecker up to last night! All I needed was to do it with you doggie-fashion, not looking at you, to find my tongue again. Now really, Clarence, I don't know what's come over me, I's flustered this morning, and I will stop. It is not going to be like this, don't you worry. Whew! Mum!" She put her hand over her mouth.

Took it off in a minute to say, "Just a temporary flare-up, that was."

And then went to giggling to herself, sputtering all around that hand to where it must be as wet as a dog's tongue.

But she did come under control. Or he hoped it wasn't under control, because if it was, it wouldn't last. Flare up, you better hope. He had to laugh himself, running around the world with a silly girl can't stop giggling. What you get for robbing the cradle.

Hester was silent, still smiling to herself, when they had followed a line of horse-trailers into a town with grain elevators like connected silos everywhere you looked and off on a secondary street of low houses to the rodeo grounds. This was on in the afternoon, way past Saskatoon, near to the other side of Saskatchewan, as he knew because by now (without deciding together) she had bought them a Hammond's Road Atlas and kept it open on her knees with a finger inching along the route. Manitoba was nowhere near so

wide as Ontario and neither was Saskatchewan. The Provinces of
Canada were falling under the wheels like dominos.

"I don't see no cows in this country yet but looks like they got
cow-girls." A dust-coated pickup cut sharply in front of them, with
a bunch of them in the back with a few bales of straw to sit on; cut
back in line so sudden it half threw them over the side, to their great
hilarity. Clarence kept well back in case one of them fell out under
his wheels. They held onto one another laughing. He knew they
were cow-girls by the bright colored satin shirts and the white ten
gallon hats. They waved to him and Hester coming along behind
them. One of them brought out a small brown flask and tipped it up
and the others cheered and reached for it. One was standing, playing
with a lariat, serious. That was a girl that could stand on a sap-sled
thumping along the ways of a sugarbush without grabbing onto the
spout.

Signs to a Agricultural Fair, Dairy, Heavy Horse, Light Horse
but this was not the fair, just the fair buildings and signs, wrong time
of year. It was what they called a CCA rodeo. Canadian Cowboys
Association. They followed the cowgirls right through a wooden
gate into the grounds where the other vehicles ahead were looking
around and finding themselves places on the grass to stop and unload
their animals. Nobody stopped Clarence and Hester or asked what
they were doing there, their truck looked pretty good too, muddy
as any but only two wheel drive, and so, lower than most. Clarence
felt conspicuous for that but not for his girl, she wasn't the only large
size woman on parade. They parked and got out to look around,
Clarence's heart beating to see the horses backing out surefooted
from those trailers. Nobody here had a horse standing up in the bed
of a truck. He wanted to see one of them unload.

Heavy Horse, he wondered, did that mean draft-horses? Did
they still use work-horses, growing wheat? He remembered photo-

graphs in the old draft-horse magazines, hundreds of horses in the wheat-fields, staggered rows of them pulling plows and sowing and cultivating and harvesting machines over smooth-topped rolling hills all the way to the treeless horizon. Even drawing steam-powered combines. He thought by now there would not be a real working work-horse on the prairie, no more than there was in the lumber woods and farms back home. But you could still have a few, kept by old-timers, like back home, compete with them in the Malone Fair, pulling a stone-boat, imitation work. And they would bring the Budweiser horses, fancy horses to Clarence, Clydesdales, light barrels but feet like frying pans. He would like to be here at Fair time and see these Heavy Horse competitions, that was his kind of horsemanship. If anybody's short a driver, volunteer. Still, interested in these cow horses too.

Used to be a girl back home, married one of the Weller family. She rode Western and used to win the barrel races with her Morgan mare, Babe. That was a very good horse. Died of a twisted intestine, having a foal. Foal come out weak, the mother had the same thing as Bang's disease in a cow. With a twisted intestine the horse just starves to death, that's what kills her. No sooner the mare dead, the foal just learnt to stand, with Clarence's help, learnt to drink from a Coke bottle with the thumb of a rubber glove put onto it for a nipple, coming along good and standing up but the third day, he slipped the other way and died too. A sad event that was. Double-sad for that poor girl.

These people were in a hurry to get their horses rigged up and get somewhere and they could hear the announcer the minute they came in the grounds, rodeo was already going. These people he come in with were late but they were the last. The gate swung shut.

They were in the grounds but not with the audience and couldn't see the bleachers. The sky was turning steel gray, the sun so low above the flat prairie that it was hidden behind anything as tall as a man or a vehicle and throwing shadows clear to the other horizon. It lit up dust that rose behind everybody's boots. In the general hurry they drifted towards a wooden tower very much like the fire tower on Blue Mountain where Charley Plumley used to live, watch for smoke and talk to the hikers that came up. Very much like that but here it was the announcer's booth and at the bottom of it a bow-legged half-crippled cowboy was pulling roll of bills out of his hip pocket and peeling off his entry fees to give the lady writing down his name. You give your name and event and leave ten dollars. The lady said, "Ain't you got nothing but hundreds?" The cowboy said, "I don't never carry nothing but hundreds. When I get change I give it away to little children."

"Well," the lady said, "at this rate I'm gonna run out of small denominations. Are you the last?" She looked at Clarence. "No, you're not a bull-rider, I don't think!" Took a quick look at Hester too.

"Well ha-ha maybe I am."

Hester said, "And I's a barrel-racer for all you know," and slapped a hand over her mouth, giggling. All it takes is imagination. The question was, which way to the stands. Next beyond the Entries table was the chutes where, other side of wooden boards that didn't look any too heavy, the huge bulls were being run in. They had to wait to go around as these rough customers, Injuns by the look of them, big dark round-faced men, pounded and whacked the animals to get them off a trailer and into the gate. One of the bulls was in there beating his head against the gate and the cowboy way up there beside him tenderly stretched a leg over and somebody give him a rope to hold on to. "My goodness," Clarence said, "that is a brave young man, not much more than a boy." The cowboy was small, at least. After he nearly set down on the back of that animal three times and changed his mind, he did set down on him and went out under the lights with his boots up in front of him where Clarence couldn't see what become of him, but knew he'd hit the dirt quick when the crowd let out a soft sigh. Crowd said oh-oh-oh a couple times more, probably that bull come after him before they shagged it away and he limped off. See something of him hitching himself out of the way, through all the rails and posts and heard the announcer joking about it all. Hester got him by the arm. She was excited, tugging at him, said, "I want to get around where I can see what's happening."

The lights were high up on poles all around, lit the arena like day even after the sun went behind the barns. Everything stood out against the brown dirt clear as if it was outlined around the edges. They never saw such evil monsters as the bulls, such crazy horses as the broncos, such bursts of speed as when the steers and horses came out side by side and the cowboy dropped off his pony beside the animal, behind the horns, and put his heels out front of him, try to dig in and slow that animal down, wrench his neck around until he falls on his side, feet swinging up. Clarence kept saying, "I never saw such a—" Or what they called dally-ropers, he had never heard of that event, slower but not always, of the most intense interest to Clarence for the mystery of it. Two horses come out, one steer between them, both riders swinging ropes, one for the head, that didn't look impossible but the second one did, come riding around behind that steer once the head was caught, slap that loop at the back feet and come up with the hind legs, quicker than the eye can see what happened. "Well I never—" Once, got only one foot, and the two horses both backed up fast, opposite directions, riders wrapping the rope around their saddle-horn, calf stretched out on three legs, head one way, one back leg the other, like a figure-skater. Then fell on its side as the timer's arm went down with the flag. Not quick enough, them other two boys did it in less than ten seconds. "If I ever see that again—" Turns out one fellow got his fingers wrapped under the rope. Announcer said, "Broke any of 'em, Merle? That'll learn you. Merle's a newcomer to rodeoin', folks, only been ropin' since he was six."

"Gee," said Hester, still like to smile. "You don't get much sympathy, do ye?" Clarence's breath was short, his heart pounding.

Suddenly a bronc rider was in the dirt, his chaps twisted around, one boot-toe upside down, white bone sticking out of his thigh. Clarence shielded his eyes. Announcer said, "Folks, this is the fellow that delivers your bottle gas, here in North Battleford. Looks like he won't be around for a couple of days. Let's give the pore boy a hand. Stay on longer next time, Darrell."

Kind of quiet for a few minutes while they let the ambulance in. The announcer said, "Now get set for a prettier sight. Come on in, Melody, and say hi to your fans while they set the course up. Soon as old Darrell gets out of the arena. Give that boy another hand for good luck. He'll be back next Friday riding the Braymas or else we'll send him East with the other dudes. Here comes the World Champion Barrel Racer, I kid you not, Miss Melody Rodriguez, and her Appaloosa, Dorothy."

Applause from all around Clarence and Hester, and the serious girl with the lariat from the back of that pickup come riding around waving right at them. Announcer saying, "Melody, honey, can't you rename that horse? Buckshot, or something? Dorothy just don't sound quarter horse, to me. But ladies and gentlemen that horse can turn in its own length going sixty miles an hour. That leaves Melody still going sixty miles an hour all by herself, o' course."

Clarence wished the announcer would just do his job, like Melody Rodriguez and her horse did theirs. It was a science, to him, a beautiful execution of a hard task without no waste motion, didn't look like anything because it was perfect, you had to know what you was looking at. No show and no whipping. The clock told the whole story, and that fellow ought to shut his mouth. He slapped his hands on his knees when it was done.

Must have been thinking out loud because Hester said, "How you know so much about barrel-racin'?"

"You watch these other girls close, you'll see the difference."

"Is that so." Almost giggling, not over last night yet.

Going back around the chutes to find their truck outside the lighted area they saw the bowlegged cowboy with the bankroll standing in a circle with three other men, in a space between trucks and trailers. One of the men said, "Old Winchester here used to be a pretty fair roper. That was before he lost his eye-sight." Winchester was pulling the cap off a bottle of Jack Daniel's. He threw the cap away in the dark and said to them, "Now you're stuck."

Jack Daniel's again. Where'd I last help polish off a bottle of that? Good going, fellows. Clarence thought he would have to get some his own, carry it in the cab, sip it by the camp fire. Someday, might have one of these fellows, or the likes of them, stop by for a visit. Blackberry brandy might not be everybody's cup of tea.

Eight

C LARENCE WAS GETTING CLOSE WITH HIS MONEY. He noticed it himself but in case he didn't, Hester mentioned it. She hadn't yet taken total charge of the envelope, something he was watching for. She still asked him every time she came to the bottom of her purse and couldn't make another purchase of the things they carried, things they liked to have with them in the truck to eat or drink. Sun lotion for his arm, when it got warm enough that he took off some of his shirts, put his bare elbow out the window. "Hadn't we ought to change some more money?"

"Well," he'd say, "there isn't any more where that came from."

This time she said, "No, but we can't work for money and still keep going to Alaska. We got to get there. Don't you have money enough?"

How much did she think he had? And now that she mentioned it why'd she come on this trip anyway if it wasn't for that money? He wasn't born yesterday. Doubt if she would have run to get her trousseau and never looked back if it wasn't for that bundle of bills. Word of that probably got all around the countryside by kitchen telegraph before he'd driven up the street to buy the Colt's, let alone driven further up to the gas company to get that cooker.

Yes, dawned on him now that Hester would have been on the phone to his sisters, or they to her, before he was out of the bank with that envelope in his hands. Knew all about it and more than he did about the fellow he was supposed to have shot at Purryer Camp, Hubbard there that his mother run the hotel. What do you make of that?

She said, "You think that's going to run out before we gets to Alaska?"

No answer. Why you pretending you don't know? Stepping on sore toes, sister.

"What're we goin' to do when that roll runs out?"

No answer to that, either.

Stop to pee and get gas. He never used to say pee but she said it which shows people are not all brought up the same. Way he was brought up, anything that you didn't want to picture in your mind's eye, you didn't say. That was what was unpleasant about her saying pee. Didn't want to see no picture of her doing it. But say anything often enough, it don't bring up the picture anymore. So he would say it himself now. Don't forget you are a lost cause anyway.

Laughing little Indian man pumped the gas while she got the key and squeezed through the door of the rest room on the side of the gas station. The Indian appreciated her with a big smile until she was shut in there and turned to Clarence with his hands apart to represent her beam but Clarence pretended he didn't know her.

"She a hitch-hiker, is she?"

"Found her along the road."

"Leave her here. I like 'em like a mountain."

"No?"

"Where you going with her?"

"I'm going, sir, to Alaska."

"Alaska?" He whistled. "Looking for work on the pipeline?"

Clarence didn't know about any pipeline but apparently he should.

"Next year, prob'ly," the fellow said. "That's what they say." Clarence not answering, the slow pump still running, the fellow made a comment every few gallons. "Next year."

"Your Congress, you know."

"They got to get used to the idea."

"But they will, eventually."

"Trans-Alaska pipeline. Oh that'll make a lot of work. A lot of work."

Then when he was waiting for Clarence to hand him some bills. "What kind of work do you do?"

"I can do most anything and she's a cook but by preference I am a team-es-ter." That is the way Clarence said the word, three syllables.

"Teamster. That's a truck driver, ain't it?"

"No, I drive horses."

"Well, say. They still use horses in the woods where I come from, Manitowoc. But in Alaska, I seen on TV, you know what they skid logs with? Helicopters! You're outta date, man!"

Hester squeezed back out the rest room door. The laughing Indian shook his head with pleasure. "Here she comes, man. Leave her. I'll take care of her."

"Not that easy when anybody's sweet on you."

"She sweet on you? Well then you're all set! Alaska here we come!"

Back in the truck motoring up the road, Clarence was in a brown study about that laughter. Was that fellow teasing him about his woman? Too much of her, you think, boy? His defense of her was feeble. More the better, may be. Would I like a slimmer girl, may be, but where would that leave all the large ones, to waste is where. Somebody's got to look after them. Laughter.

Nothing new under the sun. Clarence had always been made fun of, victimized, teased for his willingness to be nice. Never built up no defenses around him. Stepmother taught him the Golden Rule and he never veered from it but the thanks he got was little. Not every other person kept the rule. If you was the only one using it, you just laid yourself open, you got your shirt taken off your back.

"That's right, CW."

She was friendly but he was in a black mood, ready to pick a fight. "Your mother teach you the Golden Rule? Your father don't know nothing about it."

"Don't you put down my Daddy."

"Why not, the meanest man I ever met."

"Is not."

"I'll take you home to him, if you want."

"What! After comin' all this way. We's having a good trip!"

"I'll turn right around and take you home to him."

"Foo! I'm not leaving you to go to him. No way. I like you better."

"You do."

"Yes, I'll admit, I do, strange to say! But after this honeymoon we're on, we could go home. Together. That would be all right with me."

"This ain't no honeymoon."

"Well. Speaking artificially."

"No. One thing, we ain't married and won't be because I like sinning more'n I expected. Second thing never coming back. Going to the Land of the Midnight Sun and die in the woodstove like old Sam Magee. Stick with me, you'll never see that wicked man again."

Not sure she wasn't softly crying to herself the next few miles or else trying to get his sympathy. But she was just holding back. She cackled suddenly, "You call that the Golden Rule?"

But clamped herself down again or else he did it, shut her up: he said, "I'll unload you right here. I'll take you back to Arnold and Evangeline. Want somebody to go back to the farm with you? They'll go back to the farm with you, they'll take it right off you and your Daddy's hands. Them two would. If your father's farm is what you want."

"I wouldn't never give you up, CW."

"Well then be content with the way I am, not by my own choice, unfit to live among decent peoples. My stepmother wouldn't recognize me, desperate character."

"I don't know why you're talking like this, Clarence. Something bothering you?"

No answer.

"You worried?"

No answer.

"Worried about somethin', baby?"

This was unfamiliar to Clarence, all of it was. The sympathy of the woman most of all but he skipped over it ("baby!") quickly to the greater mystery of his heart. A private, phlegmatic man without many words, though proud to have his own way of looking at things, and saying things, he did not know when he had last had unfamiliar emotions. He had emotions, he had pleasures and angers, more angers than otherwise in his later years and for good reason, so few of the things that other people enjoy having come his way. He had no woman until lately. That was a long time lacking, and he could not forget the long time womanless. Years on years of solitude, living in a hollow log. He had no close friends unless you count Leo Weller. No children to teach what he knew to. He did not know that he would have wished to have children, but other people did have them and that was a part of a person's birthright that he never experienced. His brother was dead, his sisters still treated him like a child. No property, the family land, lumbered-over woodland, inconvenient but a lot of it, all left to one sister because no one thought him capable of handling such things as deeds and taxes. All he had was the clothes on his back, you might say. In hunting season, when he dogged for the guests at his sister's and brother-in-law's little hotel at the lake, Morley (the brother-in-law) called him stupid to his face, paid no attention to his suggestions about the drives. That rankled worse than anything else, that disrespect of his woodsmanship. They all, all his kin and in-laws, made fun of him and his horses.

All the same he had never complained, he had kept his dignity, worn good new work-clothes on Sundays, made shift to have some kind of a place of his own, whatever he could rent, or lived alone at the Home Place, with Bessie's permission, oh yes, had to ask her if he wanted to hole up there, cut his own firewood. He could have made himself a good living off that land, and kept a team in good condition with the work and fed them well, but no, couldn't have her permission to log a part of that land, she thought it was ridiculous for anybody to think of logging on such a small scale, but he knew better. Simple arithmetic. Not complicated. Other people was always substituting something complicated for something simple. Something expensive for something cheap. Nowadays, computers. Don't know anything about computers, only that computers are expensive. Heads are cheap.

Just like a dairy-farmer, they all thought they had to go to the bank and borrow money for new barns, blue silos and bigger machines, else couldn't make no money making milk. Well, he didn't believe that. Used to be, every farmer raised enough grain for his cows, oats mostly, enough corn for silage, and enough hay for the winter, and from the oats he had all the bedding he needed, as nice a thing as you could see, all down the barn, the cows bedded deep in bright clean yellow straw. Plenty straw left over for your horses. Nowadays, oh no, you can't raise your grain, better buy it; can't dry your hay and bale it, oh no, got to chop it and lay it in a trench silo, run over and over it with tractors all day to pack it down, cover it with old tires. Wasn't that a pretty sight along the road. Don't make no hay at all and what do they bed their cattle with, nothing. Or sawdust. Look at them animals! Stand all day knee deep in their own—. Makes you hate to drink milk. Well, if you have to pay everything you make to the bank, where did you get ahead buying that machinery? He wasn't as stupid as people thought. Who was stupid?

Well, now what was bothering him, because yes, that woman wasn't imagining things, but it wasn't how stupid other people was, because he wasn't a farmer and didn't care if they went broke. They just had a nice day at the rodeo. What was bothering him? Her not telling him she'd heard it all from Nellie and Bessie. No. Just possible she didn't.

Could tell her, Responsibility, sister.

Could say, Point of no return. Ever heard of that, sister? Say you're flying over the ocean, like Charles Lindbergh. So much gas in your tank, so far to go. Comes a point, maybe just a little past half-way, you don't have enough gas to get home, if you was to turn around. May be that's what I am thinking of. Maybe that's why I talk about giving you back to your old man. Now or never.

Maybe there's more to it than that. I have always had a lot of time to think but I have not always had this much to think about, or anybody listening.

Want to know something I did at that rodeo, that you didn't notice? You was so excited to get back around the fences and corrals to the truck. I surprised my own self, and I am afraid you would begin to wonder about me. Probably you didn't even see that farrier's trailer setting there, nobody in attendance, but I did. And I see something, just like I see that Colt's revolver, that I had an idea I could use on this trip. Crooked knife. Farrier's knife, for trimming hoofs. Picked that up off of a block of wood there, next to his foot-stand, a nice hoof-rest made out of a tree just like I used to see at home when I was a boy, very nice for the front feet, when you're fil-ing them down to the shoe with your rasp. George McAfee, out to Brushton, had one, older than he was. Well, on that block of wood, some horseshoe-nails, his nippers, and, guess what, a crooked knife. Everything the fellow needs except the new shoes, which is on a rack on the door of the trailer. Hammer and anvil on the bed of it, at a good height.

Well, that crooked knife, cookie, is in my pant-leg pocket.

Well, why? Why because could be some day we have to get across a lake or a river. I might need to make us a canoe, on the spot, ha-ha. I am more than halfway to Alaska and I have got to think ahead.

The slope of the land was upward but only so slightly, still looked flat, still wheatfield after wheatfield, ten wheatfields to a small house and a few outbuildings mostly sheds for machinery. Animals was scarce. You just felt that the engine was working a tiny bit harder than it would on the level. Speaking of which when was this truck going to break down. Since when you go this far and nothing go wrong? When was the last time you looked at the tires?

Trans-Alaska Pipeline, what they going to do with such a thing as that?

Well, there I changed the subject again. Hester over there might be crying for all he knew. Too quiet. Maybe same reason I am mad. His job to comfort her but when you are the cause of it what help can you be? There wasn't never any point of no return, because there was never no chance of me turning around. I always knew that, but she didn't. Maybe she just come to know it. If she don't trust me to take care of her, good for her, she's smarter'n I thought.

I'll show her how far from trustworthy a man I am.

He reached down his right pant-leg and fingered out the crooked knife, brought it up and left it on the red vinyl seat between his skinny thigh and her bulging fat one.

She followed his hand, saw the crooked knife there.

Now she could either go to crying all the worst, or get a charge out of her baby, he thought.

She just turned to him seriously. "You see that movie, Bonnie and Clyde?"

No I did not.

"They had a good time too, stealing and breaking the law, Bonnie and Clyde did. They was good to each other, is all, but that's the only Golden Rule they knew. They was sweeties like us."

So what?

"Well Clarence I see you convinced yourself you gone bad. That's what I got to bear. I won't tell you how they ended up, in a hail of bullets but I liked that movie. I imagined I was Bonnie and I thought if that was the way I had to die, so be it."

I didn't say nothing about dying.

"Otherwise they would lived the rest of their life in jail."

"What's that you're looking at?"

He hadn't meant to be so obvious, looking in the mirror. Mirrors, all three of them. Didn't want to worry her. Also, she might scoff at his worries, didn't want to risk it.

The action he'd been through, violent deeds at Purryer Camp and the home place and the mud spring, h'nn. Broke him free, yes, and welcome. But certain animals do not forget. Wilfred Gonyea followed them for two days trying to get his cook back 'til it was just too far back and forth to milk his cows. The law was something else again. No cows. Could follow you to the end of time.

"What is it, CW?" Twisting her head around to look back but it don't twist that far, too many chins.

"Well, I see that vehicle before."

They had passed the girl with the Hippymobile again, seen her twice now, but it was not the Hippymobile behind them.

"What vehicle you talking about?"

"Never mind."

Not sure, anyway. Many similar vehicles on the road. Police not always in Fords painted blue and yellow.

"Tell me what it is, I'll watch for it too."

No, too many chiefs spoils the pow-wow. It was just what you would sneak up on a fellow with, last thing anybody would suspect. "You said Patraw. Well this is another kind of Volks wagon."

"That beetle? That's a white-haired lady in that and the thing's piled to the roof. She's going a long way too and the license plate… I see the license plate, not Ontario, how many states has them on the front. New York. That woman looks just like Stella Knight, if it was her own sister!"

"Stella Knight. Never spoke a kind word to me boy or man."

"Shoot! Stella Knight never spoke a kind word to anybody. Thinks she's so strict but I tell you what, Clarence: she married her own cousin! She did. Mark Knight's her own first cousin. Was, I should say."

That was another matter. Mark taught me to file a hand-saw, so that a sewing needle would slide right down the blade in the notches between the teeth. You want a saw that will cut! Smooth! And a dead shot with a rifle. Mark Knight did not go without venison. In the saw mills, who do you get to set your teeth and file your saw? Mark Knight, that's who.

"He drinks. Drank, I should say. Well so that's Stella's sister. Where's she going? Somebody must have let the family secrets out of the bag."

The Beetle slowed down and stopped on the side of the road and they went by it. The woman was studying a map opened across her steering wheel.

"She don't look that much like Stella," Clarence said.

"No, she don't. And you know, CW, I don't want to be seein' the same cars and people day after day. You know it? This is our trip. I wants to be the onliest peoples on it."

Well we'll be off the main road looking for something pretty soon, ha ha.

"Stella Knight! What on earth could bring that cross old gal to mind? Cripes but she brings a lot of memories with her. But we gots to shake them loose. I don't want to think about that old set of hills and dales, them old people. Had enough of them. Sisters, and the like. Ain't we?"

They came to a fork in the road where the arrows said left to Vancouver, right to Edmonton. "Where is that? Vancouver. Edmonton. Heard of Vancouver. Way out on the West Coast of Canada, I think." She looked, turning pages of the atlas forward and back. "Off this map, ennaways."

"We go right," Clarence said. Solar navigation.

The beetle behind them curved away to the left with the silver-haired lady and all her stuff piled to the roof.

"Good riddance," he said.

"That's the last I's going to worry about anybody following us! Seeing anybody from back home. Foo! You too?"

Stop at a place where you see plenty cars and pickups pulled up, that's where the food'll be good. This one was crowded and the only thing not like home, the people skinnier, they fit on the stools along the counter, wheat farmers come to share their troubles. Alone, Clarence would never take a booth but lately had to. Had to pay tips too which he never understood or believed in. Something they do in New York City. If you hire somebody to wait on the booths, pay her. Don't ask her to go begging of the people that eat. They already paid for the food.

Hester ordered a steak and gave him a wink. What is it, suppertime? He hated to be tight all by himself, that was just self-punishment.

He was still eating when she went up to pay and when he followed, happened to see a drawing on the next table but one toward the door, a drawing being made by a little brown arm with a crayon in the fist, the paper turned just right for him to see it, a man with a wide-brimmed black with a high round crown. Under that, neckerchief just like his. Under that, big belt buckle and holdster and pistol with the butt sticking forward. On the wrong side.

Of the little boy, all he could see was a spray of golden hair and some dirt in the bare scalp at the center of it. Not to criticize, might be some dirt in his own cowlick by now. The picture was clear as day, almost stopped him, made him stumble against the next table. Hope he did not disturb—. Yellow crayon for the belt buckle. Bowed legs and cowboy boots. Cowboy boots was something Clarence had been thinking about.

Embarrassed, he kept going, brushed behind Hester at the cash register, fingering out a toothpick, on out to the truck. Boy was too young to draw that good. He wanted to tell the little boy that the side-arm was on the wrong side, but maybe that's the way he looked from in front.

The hat was what had caught his eye. That hat was right on his head. Took it off only to eat, and put it back on when he stood up.

There was twenty clouds sailing across the sky if there was one, twenty shadows sailing over the prairie.

"There was that mini-bus again" Hester said when she got her breath from getting in herself and they were down the road a way. "There in the parking lot. What you so amused at?"

He could not have told her if he tried. How many times in your life would that happen? You tell me how it would feel, catch a little boy's imagination like that.

"You feel better, ennaways. That's good."

She let quite a bit of time pass and then said, there a "Back there a ways I thought you was worried about something. I thought, what could be bothering my man? I thought, could be we's half way to nowhere. This is a awful big continent we took it upon ourselves to cross, and nobody even knows where we are. Just like bein' in the middle of the ocean. I would want to be a comfort to you in that case."

Now that would be something new. Somebody trying to be a comfort to him, and him ever thinking he needed it. He was a idol to a little boy that just saw him in a restaurant. That boy knew at a glance what he wanted to be when he grows up. Clarence's confidence about the continent not in question. Instead, question in Clarence's mind about whether he believed in unselfishness. When did anybody ever say such a thing to him, or when did he ever say such a thing. Couldn't remember his pretty young stepmother. She was a comfort to his boyhood, certainly. Otherwise, grew up in a comfortless world and got used to it. He would be pretending, if he said he wanted Hester's comforting. Didn't want it, didn't need it.

But wished he could pretend, like a normal man. Pretend he wanted comforting and let her give to him, if that was what she wanted. That picture was not of no normal man needed comforting.

She picked up the crooked knife.

She was turning the knife over and over in one hand, rolling it by its angled wooden handle, between their legs there, not looking at it. "Why do you think I ever liked you, Clarence?"

"Why because I wear pants."

"That's a insult. No such a thing. I liked you because I thought you was a good man. You was good to your horses and you worked hard and didn't waste your money. You was a gentleman to me, opened the door and helped me into your truck. All 'til you quit coming around, which, that was not nice. Then you come and asked me to come to Alaska with you and I came, but you don't know why. You don't know much about me and I got to wonder why you come for me."

"Obvious, because you got the right places under your clothes. I was a lost soul anyway. That's all you need to know."

"You're missing the point. You always do. You run right straight away from it."

"If that's your last word, you got it."

"No, it isn't. This is important, Clarence. You're just mad, for some reason."

Mad? I was happy a minute ago.

"I think you's worried. No, I know you is. We come a long way and we get along better than we might of thought we would. It's two of us, Clarence. You got me to hold you. I will. I know what you's thinking."

You do? I don't.

"I know what's got you worried deep down. Lord love you, Clarence, before you do something like steal a horse let's talk it over."

"Is that what I been thinking?"

"Well, you tell me. Isn't it?"

Nine

ALBERTA, NOW (gosh that was quick), and ahead, a work crew, look to be half a regular road gang and half a bunch of boys in striped suits, convicts out of some penitentiary. They weren't substituting something complicated for something simple here, these fellows had short-handled shovels and picks and grub-hooks in their hands and were swinging them hard. Clarence slowed abruptly too late, the tires of his pickup dropped off the end of the pavement with a bang, and the truck rattled and bounced over rough gravel and stones, the crews pausing and straightening their backs each side of it, very close. Clarence was driving with a smile of wickedness on his face, imagining these prisoners and the road crew looking at the mud-covered pickup truck as it passes slowly between them with the horse-trailer behind, New York, USA plates on the truck and a Alberta one on the trailer.

There goes a nice outfit, they're thinking. Boys I would like to be traveling like that.

Man with a woman and a truck and a horse trailer. You can't tell there's no horse in it until it goes by, no tail flying out the back.

Last night in the tent with the additional hardware parked close-by, it was something different, hard to say how. What he felt it was, somehow, tragic, just as if he was the dying hero. Never felt so much sadness, the two of them, sad right in the middle of it, deep in each other's arms and legs, deep in being two animals in one, maybe the deepest yet. Something about it, every time was different, as if you couldn't go no farther, and then next time you did, and at the end you said, "Well that's a new record, certainly. We ain't going to beat that." And next night they would beat it again. But last night it was tragic. It was deeper because it was sadder. He did not know any other way to put it. They did not talk about it, after. What they talked about was what to do. Right there all bare naked and wrapped together, just enough space in all that flesh to breathe.

She knew there weren't no stopping him. He had to get a horse. They was going to go to Alaska with a horse, or even a team of horses, because he was set on it. Alaska meant something to him, and he was not going to present himself to it as just a two legged thing with no horse. Only way he could picture it, horseman.

Well, all right, a horse, if not a team of horses. May be you could buy them, if you knew the country. But the money would run out quick enough in Alaska, without buying a horse. But seemed like Clarence's spending spree was over before they left home. Buying a horse, nnn. That way you would be getting a horse from a horse-dealer. Bad enough that they had to buy a trailer first.

There wasn't any other way to transport the horse when you got it. You could not have one of those deals where the horse rode on the pickup, in the bed of it with the sides raised and a gate behind him which swung down and made a ramp. That was a saddle-horse kind of a rig anyway. Impossible because they had her hope-chest and the tent and cooler and the cooker and his things too, in the back of the truck, under a tarp, not to mention the firewood to weight the back end down last winter, still there, and now a couple of bed-rolls that you opened a valve and they sucked in air and un-rolled themselves, much better than bare ground and warmer. Should have got three, look for another Sporting Goods.

Long ere yesterday she'd been pleading for a metal roof over all that back there, what they call a cap. But if he'd wanted a cap on his truck he'd have had one long ago. Tarp was good enough and if they got a cap, she'd see, someday that truck cap would just be trouble, be in the way, you'd wish you never got it, in a fit of anger someday he'd throw it off and leave it 'side the road.

But all right, they both come to see, had to pay cash for the trailer. They reasoned that out, the two of them, aloud, her as much as him. Maybe this is why it was tragic, in among the cots last night. Hester become a fallen woman, bad as he was. Had to buy it, cash outlay, and license it. She said it herself. You couldn't be going down the road through provinces and territories of Canada and through customs at the border with a stolen, unregistered vehicle. What's a trailer cost? They didn't know. But it wouldn't break the bank if you didn't go and buy the horse or horses too. This is where she come to be the banker. "Isn't that right, CW?" Well, yes, good woman, had good sense.

First time he ever see Wilfred in her. Crafty and sly once she decided to be crooked. That's who he was with last night, a outlaw's floozy. The two of them past saving, not just himself.

The trailer had cost them $800 Canadian dollars, in the middle of Alberta. Still rodeo country, cow-ponies everywhere, mostly for the children. Experience showed that until you look for something, you don't know it's there. Soon as they watched for a trailer for sale, found one first thing. This one, in front of a yellow ranch house on the main drag of a small town, used to be green, four wheels, heavy-built, two horse. Had a cow-brand painted on it, Minus Plus.

Clarence was not one to hesitate. See what you want, take it. Sign said, Blow Horn, and at that everyday come out of the house, the man, wife, kids, kids's friends and a hired hand, if that was what he was, or a brother, shifty looking fellow with no part in the transaction, but explained that how you say the brand was Bar Cross.

So, come to hand the man his money and get the bill of sale, well, she had to bring out the envelope and fish in it. Clarence didn't like anybody seeing that envelope but this was a nice family, with the exception of the brother. No smiles from him.

Of course, first thing they had to do, the brother led them downtown to the Motor Vehicle, get a new license on the trailer. Which is where Clarence first realized he didn't carry enough tools to do with. Knew enough to put on the license plate but didn't have a wrench and screwdriver. But the shifty brother had a little thing in his breast pocket, miniature vise-grips screwdriver wrench hammer all in one. Had a lock of hair over his face like a horse's, kept shaking it out of his eyes, helped them get the plate on. After that, led them someplace to go get a ball to bolt onto the bumper, and someone to put on the wires for the trailer's lights. And then, all set to go, now he tells them, says "You ought to have a bigger truck, to pull this trailer."

Well mind your business, mister. This 6-cylinder is a hundred forty horse-power, you boys is spoiled if you don't think that's enough. Pioneers had two oxen to pull far more than this, without no road. "Just my opinion," the fellow said. Hnnh. He drove a little green Pinto, good one to talk about power. Chip on his shoulder about something and he'd seen that envelope from the bank. Clarence watched the rear-view mirror. If he ever saw the Pinto or any vehicle following for too long, take evasive action. One of these little towns, turn off and go around the block. If he's still following you then, it isn't by accident.

Now, next morning, soon as they start looking for a horse to steal, wouldn't you know first thing you see is a bunch of convicts playing the banjo.

"You know what I mean by banjo," he said.

"No. What?"

"Short-handled shovel."

They didn't put you on the chain gang for stealing a horse. They shot you on the spot, or if they wasn't in a hurry, sent somebody for a noose. That'd be a nice picture for a postcard home, him and her dangling from a live oak tree.

Responsibility. Did I ask for this? Be better if she was fighting him every inch of the way.

Heavy Horse, or a team of same. A Belgian or Percheron or a Shire that somebody had put out to pasture and didn't use no more. He had seen a few of them, not many, on this trip. Now, get off the main roads, start looking. How to do this, they didn't know yet. But they didn't know how to do the other thing either, when they started. If they hadn't learnt, been like driving across the continent with a trailer you never filled.

They kept forgetting to look for horses, there wasn't any to look for and different things pouring in. How different the farms were out here. The houses and sheds smaller, farther apart, the fields larger. Even though they were further and further north, the soil looked richer, the fields were greener, not just wheat everywhere. Peas, beans, potatoes he would recognize. These crops, they didn't know what they were. In the towns, the people they saw, Chinese, Japanese, Indian, Eskimo. Couldn't tell what they was. She was reading the brochures, said Chinese, Japanese come to build the railroads and highways, work in the mines up around Great Slave Lake

He was waiting for the mountains. Seemed as if the roads were always rising, climbing very slightly. The air felt good and the truck run good but labored more with the heavy trailer and the gas went through it faster. Sometimes he thought he saw the mountains far ahead or off to the left but they would turn out to be only clouds, very good imitations. He wished for a gear half way in between second and high. That would been just right. Remembered Gene LaBounty warning him keep his foot off the clutch, but he had to shift a lot. It jerked the truck to change gears, and the hitch banged when he did it. If he had a team of Belgians in that rig, another thirty hundred pounds... He whistled at the thought.

They avoided Edmonton, another set of skyscrapers surrounded by a low spread-out city they had no desire to see. Hester told him where to turn, to get around it, good navigator. All the horses they saw was Light Horse category, children's playthings. She navigated them to pass to the north of the city and they liked traveling the smaller roads, so the navigator tried to keep them parallel to 16 and they kept on, west or a little north of west, sloping up.

With the atlas open on her knees, she traced their route ahead. She said they were going to go through Dawson City and Whitehorse, and he felt that legend was upon him, look out. She said those two places were in the Yukon Territory and he ducked his head between his shoulders in awe. The gold rush! It was as if something was driving his head down to his lap. He could hardly believe these legendary places they were approaching, the burden, the responsibility of it. More reason they had to steal a horse but he feared, he feared to do it.

But that was just the suddenness of it. In a moment he was chuckling. "Maybe we will pan for gold. Stake us a claim."

"Better get a donkey instead of a horse. Didn't those old miners always have a burro, or a donkey, or somethin'?"

He didn't know anything about it really. Dawson City! Whitehorse!

"Yellowknife!" she exclaimed. "Turn north! We're goin' by it! Too late!"

They had to pull over and read the atlas together. But Yellowknife was far, far to the north, the other side of Great Slave Lake, and that was far the other side of Lake Athabasca, not on the way to Alaska at all. You can't hit every famous town on one trip. Already seen the Red River Valley. He didn't like the sound of Yellowknife anyway, sounded like bar-room murder. Far as that goes, up in the Yukon Territory people kill you quick for a bag of nuggets and who do you report your demise to?

Here, very surprising, they were still passing through prosperous settled farm country, very green, very rich soil, very many small farms where people seemed to be doing fine. Doing much better than the farmers to-home. He wouldn't have thought a place like this existed, this close to the Yukon. Thought it would be poor empty land here, badlands, tundra maybe, nothing but stunted trees and fur trappers. Instead of that, long long vistas from the high places and mountains to the southwest but come down from the ridges and all the land was settled, ordinary, everything that wasn't woods or gulches plowed and sowed to unfamiliar crops, and the roads full of farmers' trucks going to and fro.

Various signs about oil and gas, and something called oil sands. Potash, what was that again? Lots of new little houses. People was coming into this country right here, for some reason. Maybe it was the oil sands, whatever they were. He didn't see any oil wells. Too civilized here but now, never mind the towns, those were not clouds, near to the west and southwest. Those were solid ground, those were too dark and the wrong color, those were mountains, snow on top, getting higher all of a sudden.

Plenty of horses here, like any good prosperous farm country. Girls ride them, mostly. It was like that old game you used to play when you were a child, on a road trip in the family truck, counting the horses you saw before the other people in the truck saw them. If you were the first to see any horse, you counted it. See who got the most before you got to Malone. Soon's you saw a cemetery, holler "Cemetery cemetery bury all your horses." If you was the first to see the cemetery, other players lost their count, back to zero. So you was always looking for cemeteries and horses. Just looking for horses now, but for some reason couldn't help noticing the cemeteries too.

Said, "You look on your side, I'll look on mine."

"You look at the road or we'll be in the ditch!"

He got a wheel in the gravel and swerved back on the blacktop.

Checked on her, and she was smiling behind them coke-bottles.

"Well, I see horse after horse."

"We don't want one that's kept right up near the house."

"No and it's just too settled here, for horse-stealin', don't you think? I does."

It would be just like that very good Colt's revolver wrapped in a towel behind him, behind the seat. Very glad he had that. Glad he never stopped to pay for it. That might of led to a license, what're you doing in Canada, what you need a gun for, got to register that with the Royal Mounted Police. No thanks. Well, this horse, same principle. You wonder why I am a outlaw, well, reasons like that. You make it inconvenient for me to play by the rules at my stage of life. Cemetery just around the corner. Many a man don't live to be seventy but I am just entering my second childhood, ha-ha, thanks to the fact that I have quit trying to please.

There was no hurry finding the right horse in a land of plenty. "Look for Heavy Horse," he told her. "See one of them, I will slow down and think. Where there is this many horses kept just for riding and rodeoing as there is around here, there will be a draft horse once in a while. Then we'll have a closer look."

Back there at the rodeo while they were in behind the chutes and among the horse-trailers one fellow had called him Pardner and asked him to punch his knee into the belly of a horse he was trying to cinch up, get the horse to let out his breath. He didn't know how you saddled a western pony but his hat and his neckerchief had got him recognized. He saw the fellow wonder at his boots and the green work-pants he was wearing. Now he thinks he maybe ought to swap these pants for straight-leg jeans and cowboy boots. Tried them long ago when a boy and could hardly walk. Question was, was he too old a dog for new tricks?

Thoughts of that rodeo brought back the smell of manure and the look of springy fetlocks and muscled rumps, not to mention the pretty cowgirls. One point in the middle of that rodeo, four girls on blonde ponies with fancy surcingles and breastplates, holding up four gold-fringed flags, galloped side by side all the way around the arena while the Canadian anthem played on the loudspeakers up high on the light-poles. That brought tears to his eyes and he wasn't even a Canadian. It embarrassed him, he didn't have any control over it. That was a puzzle, how that happened. Didn't make any sense.

Unless it was just to see pretty girls riding good horses. Or the flags. Or just the horses. Just the horses. That was one thing. That was the main thing. Horses. No such thing as a new life without a horse. Not for this boy.

One of his favorite images of his father came before him now so strongly that he pulled off the road for fear it would make him forget his business. Outside the window of the old log house, he saw his father plowing in the hillside field behind. At the same time he heard the sound of old Mrs. Bryant's Cadillac on the road, going up along the row of shady maples on the other side of the house. It was spring thaw, and the road was turned to mud. In the field, the two horses, a grey Percheron and a chestnut Belgian, stopped, while his father watched the car try the hill. He knew without waiting to hear the roar, wheels spinning. He unhitched the whiffle-tree from the plows and drove the team out the gate onto the road letting it drag on the ground. Clarence ran after him to see the team swing in front of the Cadillac and come back to his father's chirping, until he could hitch onto the front bumper. Then he saw the giant buttocks drop and twitch, the muscles crease them, the gaskins tremble, and the Cadillac follow them up and over the crest of the hill, around the curve, toward the Lake where Mrs. Bryant, and Mr. Royal Weller also, brother and sister, each had a camp. His father come back down the road behind the team with a dollar in his blue shirt pocket, all he would take.

Later, when he was ten, Mr. Robert Purryer Senior entrusted Clarence with just as heavy and just as good a team and a good wagon, every day, start before day light, on bare road or ice road depending on the time of year, drive from Center Camp the other side of Miner's Hill, all the way to town, for potatoes and eggs, hay and grain to feed all the men and horses in the lumber camp, there and back again more than twenty miles. Just a boy, with all that kindly and patient power, those brave and intelligent beasts without malevolence. Whatever you asked them to do, they would do. Do it without hurting them was all Mr. Purryer asked. That's what sealed his fate. Use them so as not to hurt themselves. Made a teamster of him and stranded him among the Gasoline People for the rest of his life, up to now.

What kind of a man had he been, before this trip? Well, not a success. Had to live inside his own world, always at the mercy of a boss, and make himself somebody else to fit necessity. One good friend of his own age, that he could be himself with, Millard Shampine, the last farmer around home that kept a team. Who would Millard get to help him sugar, well you can guess, who else? And that was a good team, but lazy! Come time to break roads in March they hadn't done no work in ten months. But Clarence would go over to Millard and Grace's about the end of February, of a Sunday, set in the parlor with his hat on his knee, clean new wool clothes, have a glass of milk and fresh doughnuts. She was always baking, Grace was. Her old father there in the rocker by the Estate Heatrola, other part of the room, never said a word. And we would finally say, Well, it's about time to break roads, en't it? One of us, Millard or I.

So next week end, down in his stable there, half underground, harnesses hanging right there by the sliding door, we would hitch them up, then drive them outside and hitch them to the double-bunk sled and see if we could get through the snow, make a loop through the sugarbush with them. If all went well, make another loop. Long as they could do it without breathing too hard. Next weekend, again. That way, by the time we had to scatter buckets and tap the trees, roads was ready, and horses was ready. Knew their business and was in shape.

Well, when we get a nag here, may be the same situation: a horse that ain't done a lick in a long while. Who knows what they ever taught them. Maybe just a toy to them.

One kind of people Clarence always respected was a successful farmer, which they was here, one after the other. If I come into a restaurant full of these farmers, I will take my hat off.

"There's a cemetery. Bury all your horses."

Little patch with a picket fence around it and tablets of stone everywhichway but the grass was mowed and there were pots of red flowers.

"I ain't been counting."

"Well I am counting," she said.

"I ain't see one heavy horse. Not one."

"Me either. But there is bound to be some. Why we've got to look close, go slow."

"I think we looks suspicious." He stepped on the gas.

"You know Clarence, I like you, but you really is a awful person."

"I know it."

"No you don't. You think you are a desperate character, an outlaw, which you ain't, hardly, even if you did steal that crooked knife. You had a better excuse to take that pistol but I don't think the Golden Rule would have any part of that, you's just making excuses. I do not believe that O'Neil was after you, back home, unless just to testify. But I don't think there was goin' to be any trial, after Robert Sochia killed himself. The girl went home, wherever that was. I never heard of no baby, except from you. That was the end of it. You could have stayed right to home."

"Said you was with me and wasn't going to give me the benefit of your thoughts."

"What? When did I ever say that?"

"I can't remember."

"Well I might give up on that promise which I don't remember either. Start paying attention to where we are and what we are doing, not the olden times back home. This horse is going to be trouble. Just having it, let alone stealing it. You thought about how to feed it, up in Alaska?

"Same as other people do."

"You going to have the onlyest horse in Alaska."

"Well won't we be something."

Hay, grass, grain, bark, pine needles. I'll feed it something. There's moose in Alaska. Much like a horse. Animals in Alaska eat something.

"What they are doing up there now, is getting ready to build the Trans-Alaska Pipeline. You probably don't know what that is. I don't either, exactly, but that is where they's jobs in Alaska. They been arguing about it for three years and now they are starting to build it, a pipe-line for oil all across Alaska. That oil, it's right next to the Arctic Ocean I believe. Looks like there would be a better way to get it, or else leave it where it is. But they's going to make a pipe and put the oil through it, all down across Alaska to this place here, Skagway."

Couldn't drive and also see what she was talking about and didn't care. The mountains had risen up in front of them, or aslant off to their left, and Clarence had dumbly, unconsciously, turned the truck and trailer toward them, or Hester had, navigating the smaller roads suggesting the turns, both of them amazed, amazed. High gray sharp-toothed layered mountains such as he had never seen except on implausible calendars, the highest peaks bare, the highest saddles brilliant white under glaciers, here they were, nearer and nearer, setting the long low hills and vistas of the prairie with their glowing wheat and greening crops in another context, making Alberta now the glory they hadn't dreamed of. It lifted both of their spirits, drove their self-doubt out of their minds, confirmed their trip and drew them onward closer and closer. And as they came closer, moved slantingly to converge with the Rocky Mountain ranging northwesterly at the edge of the prairie they were moving more and more into cattle country. Red Angus, Charolais, Hereford and Siementhal cattle grazed on the less-divided land sloping ever more upward toward the foothills, the regular grid of towns and sections and homesteaders' quarter-sections gave way to larger and larger ownings and they began to see, without knowing what it was, the Crown lands where cattle grazed in the summer on allotments, recently driven there and to be brought back in the fall by cattle drives like those of the storied

West south of the border, in Montana and states further south, only smaller, the ranches here in the thousands of acres not the tens of thousands, the herds in the hundreds and not thousands.

It was here that they found a town called Cora, and Clarence bought himself a perforated white straw hat, cooler than his black felt one and with the creases already formed for his thumb and two fingers to put it on with. Didn't fit the shape of his head but he hoped to torture it until it gave in. Hester saw him come out of the store and said, "It was just a matter of time. I knew it." He'd buy Levis and a shirt with pearl snaps on the pocket flaps next and not long after, pointy-toed boots. "Well," he said, "I don't want to stand out too much, for a good reason. Might be posters everywhere with my picture on it. When in Rome do as the Romans do." Also since Cora Clarence affected a long very thin cigar that kept the smoke away from his eyes which watered otherwise. Inhaling was out of the question but the cigarillo looked good in the mirror. All in all he was working towards a disguise.

"Who do we know named Cora?" Hester said. "That's just the dearest name."

From Cora they rolled out along the highway parallel to the foothills, so not to get so close you couldn't see the glaciers, or have to zig-zag around the long promontories between dry drainages. Up above the grasslands, what looked like poplars in light green foliage and above the poplars, very dark stands of straight crowded sticks, spruce, not worth cutting but he did see logging operations, followed a log truck full to the top of its stakes with the little poles. The old log homesteads with tarpaper roofs were down in the valleys near the creeks, with outbuildings sided with board and batten and roofed with slabwood, and there were corrals and chutes made of poles. At the road there would be a cattle guard and a gate attached to an overhead frame wired back along the fence to carry the weight of the gate, and on the frame a placard or shield or sign with the brand, he supposed it was, of their cattle, same as the name of the ranch. His ranch, now and when he really got one when he got one, was the Minus Plus, already painted on the trailer. He'd thought that by this northern route in the general direction of Alaska he would miss the real cowboy West, just see make-believe West as at the North Battleford rodeo back in Saskatchewan. Real enough when you get your thigh-bone broke. But here was a little corner of the cowboy west slicing up along the front of the mountains. Glad to see it and especially so when they came on this band of cayuses hanging their heads over the fence just waiting for them.

Deep in solo conversation at the time, wondering how Hester knew so much about the Trans-Alaska Pipeline. Buys a newspaper or a magazine, says she can't sleep if I don't wear her out but Clarence had come to feel sore. It begun to hurt to have fun. She wasn't in agreement with him on resting for a day or two but that only made him to smile. Better than the other way around which was the story of his life. Wishing and not having. Used to have thoughts he should not have and knew it, young girls too, at his age, for shame. It was a secret but he had no shame in his thoughts. Just thoughts, no harm done. She was right if she didn't think he was such a good man as she used to. She's learnt something useful.

But you see. Quick as I stop servicing her, which is what you would say if it was horses, she starts to talk. That's good. I can regulate it. I can regulate the one thing with the other, ha ha.

Some ways, a man that lived alone and didn't have any part in the way other people lived, the news, the thing they talk about so much now they called the Economy, which he didn't really know what it was, a man that was outside of all that might know something, or see something, that people that is in the middle of it can't see. Now that he was out here on the road in the Canadian west he had time to think and be prepared if anybody should ask him where we go from here. It would not be enough to say, as he would like to, Backwards. I used to like it the way it was, better than I do now. When I was a child, I thought you had a right to grow up in the same world you was learning about. You wanted to be a adult. Then they change the world, and you are a child in this new world even if you are old enough to be a adult. A lot of people pretend they are adults in this new world but they have never had time to watch adults in it, to know how to behave. So they are just as much children in this new world as he is. That's why change happens so fast. No grown-ups! Things that was unthinkable a little while ago, common now. If you are old fashioned like me you might get left behind on purpose.

"Why don't you speak up," she asked. "'Always muttering." Then she saw the band of horses, same time as he did, on the north side of the road, twenty of them if they was one, all on a tear. They broke over a low ridge covered with trees in a bunch and poured down right toward them to where there was a willow-bordered stream, across a space in the willows which must have been a ford, a faint trace of a road where they came down, and they crossed in a great splashing of water and dashed up the near slope clear to a split-rail fence beside the stopping pickup and trailer, front ones looked like they was thinking of shoving it over just out of high spirits.

There they piled up against one another's rumps and tails and now just as quick they turned and raced farting and bucking along the fence, to turn again at a corner and tear back down the slope at an angle for the ford, where some of them splashed across and stopped a little way up the other side and others held up, looked at the mess they had made of the crick, all muddy, shook their heads. One of them delicately stepped upstream and put his head down. That was the one Clarence took note of, a tall light-barreled bay.

Counted, twenty-one of them. Their feet were all grown out, curved up like slippers, nobody looking after them very close. One of them looked every bit a thoroughbred to Clarence, that tall dark red bay, much too good for the company. That was a riding horse and to his eye a good one, therefore nothing he would generally want. Some of the others were draftier, perhaps not workhorses but not saddle-horses, either, or at least not to show at the fair. Pack-horses? It was a motley crew but it was a good deal of horseflesh running loose and un-cared-for and no house near. A wonder they could run at all with feet grown out and broken like some of them. Thought he caught a glimpse of a wall-eye. Bet he knew how the horse got that eye. This place, with the clumps of shade trees and most of it open, would be a good place for a horse to go stand under a tree in a storm, get hit by lightning.

They lived on their own, these horses. Nobody breaking bales for them this time of year. Wintertime neither, he suspected. They pawed in the snow. Their coats had grown out shaggy and not all shed yet. The only one that looked at all smooth was the thorough-bred. Maybe not thoroughbred but got thoroughbred in him or Clarence was a monkey's uncle. What you would need was a pocket full of horse-bisquits and that thoroughbred, at least, would come right up to you. You put a rope over his neck, and he would be your animal until he found out you didn't know what you were doing.

The rest of them would come too but he would come first, that gelding. He'd come sniffing at your pocket even if you didn't have your hand in it. Shove you right backwards with his nose. He's been around people.

"You ain't going to find a situation like this again," he said.

"Who you talking to?"

"You."

125

"Well, you could probably buy one of them cheap. They's so many."

"That is not what's meant to be."

"I don't know why it shouldn't be. It would be safer, Clarence."

"Good has come to me since I quit trying to play it safe."

"You don't know what caused what. If you're talking about me, I would just as soon—"

"No you wouldn't."

"What was I goin' to say?"

"Be married."

"Is that any way to propose? Clarence Shampine what has come over you?"

"Opened my eyes. This western landscape's what done it to me."

"Well that is exactly what I was going to say. Only to mean, you didn't have to drag me off like a cave-man. It would be just as good. Anyways I don't think stealing is how people gets horses out here. Else these here would have been stolen already."

"Maybe they was stolen already. I don't care if they was or wasn't but buying one is too complicated, too much trouble, and would slow us down. Anygate, there isn't anybody here to buy them from. You prepared to drive all night?"

"If you are stealing one of these horses I want to get as far away as possible before morning. Steal the horse, if you're goin' to. I'm a accomplice, I guess. Which one?"

"Which two?"

"No, Clarence, no!"

"If pack-horses is what they are, why not? It's a two-horse trailer. I bet that up in them buildings there, beyond that old corral, in the trees, I'll bet there is a tack cabin, and saddles and pack saddles, bridles, nosebags, ropes, panniers. You know what this is, cookie? This is a dude ranch. Used to be. Or still is and this is the off season. I have heard of the likes of these. I used to read Western Horseman. This here is a remuda, they call it. This is a pack-string, plus a few of the sorriest saddle-horses and one that somebody can't handle, too hot. I would like to take the whole outfit."

"Maybe you could get a job working on the dude ranch."

"Not lookin' for a job. Is that how you are thinking?"

"You got to, or I should say we got to, get a job, somewhere, in the end."

"You are just like your old man."

"I am not."

"Are so. You listen to yourself."

"What did I say, like him?"

"Said 'Got to.' Twice't."

She clapped her hand over her mouth. Took it off to say, "I like living without them words much as you do." Left it off and went on volubly, "You think maybe we don't have to get jobs?"

"If we don't spend too much money on the way we'll invest in the Trans-Alaska Pipeline and sit back and live on the rent."

"Knowing you you'd bore a hole in it and steal oil." They were putting off stealing the horses and knew it. "Come on, let's do it if we's doin' it. I ever tell you I rode horses?"

The way up to those buildings was not obvious. Some gate ahead, or one back a ways that they had passed, and a driveway across that brook. Didn't want to go in by the main gate anyhow. What they needed to do was get in there by some other road, a ranch road that went along the north side of the place, say, where they went out a gate to go up into the mountains. See where they could get the rig to, first, then come back after dark with horse-biscuits and get that bay to lead the other animals into the corral. Pick the two he wanted and skedaddle. That is, after finding some panniers, halters, nose-bags and a bag of grain for starters. Be way up in British Columbia before morning. Nobody would miss these skins for weeks, but don't count on it. They were still leaning on the fence, watching the horses, scheming. Then he said, "You what?"

"Me what what?"

"You used to."

"Oh. Ride horseback. Yes. Little you know about the girl I was. I rode horseback a lot. Back at that rodeo I had a hard time not telling you that. You telling me all the finer points of barrel-racing."

"Why didn't you?"

"You liked that Melody Rodriguez so much. I could no more... Come on!"

It was like taking candy from a baby except that he couldn't get rid of the big bay. No padlock on the gate up the side road, drove the rig right in as if they owned the spread. Horses raced up in a bunch to see who they were. Everything worked. Lights in the tack-shed went on when switched. Moonlight to see by outdoors. If anybody should come they looked good, like they were in their rights, behaving naturally, need two of these horses that's all. There was a gate from the pasture into the corral, gate the other side of the corral for the selected animals to step right into the caboose. They opened the back gate of the trailer and that animal walked into it before Hester could shoo it away, which she wasn't ready to do with him towering over her. Made Clarence realize her proportions, wider than she was tall. She got out of the way and the bay went bang bang bang bang up the ramp with a nicker, as if he thought he would find his favorite kitten in the manger. Clarence had put grain in the feed bin at the front and water beside it and of course he was determined to stay to dinner and many another to come. Seemed to say "Let's go!" instead of where are you taking me. Next come his side-kick, a buckskin, as good as any, so they let him aboard. So Clarence had to throw a old cavalry saddle and a bridle into the pickup along with the pack-animal equipment. There was a nice tooled old western saddle with silver conchos on it but he could not take it. He tried and Hester tried to make him but he could not. Just didn't deserve it. Didn't want to make the owner mad, add insult to injury. Did take a Navaho saddle-blanket. The bridle with a spade bit come from a hook that was labeled Merlin and fit the beast so that was his name. Halter the same, Merlin's halter, and one for the pack-horse too.

Water, buckets, brushes, a rasp. Hammer and clenching iron, some No. 4 shoes. Any nippers? These would be barefoot horses for some time, maybe never get shoes again but be prepared. Clarence hoped the thoroughbred wouldn't lean too heavily on him when he was trimming his feet, or thrash or kick. That horse was too big and Clarence never set up for a farrier. He could trim a hoof but set a shoe or drive horseshoe nails without piercing the quick, have the points come out on a line, that was an art. And make the horse run true, not swing the foot inwards or outwards. George McAfee where are you when I need you? Yes there was a nice pair of nippers that Clarence dearly wanted but it seemed criminal to take them since he could make do with a rasp and the farrier's knife, and the other fellow still had nineteen sets of feet to do.

Sent the rest of the beasts back through the corral without their chief and shut all gates and drove away with the headlights off, which was a decision, who could say whether good or bad, but had to be made. No traffic on the highway that time of night; and on to the north, lights on. Hester chuckled at one time and he looked across at her. "You people!" she said.

They went back and forth. "You people!"

"You people!"

They decided not to drive all night after all since if you were not on the run why would you? Come on the outskirts of Grand Prairie not much after ten and took a cabin, a place with its own corral where Merlin and his little buckskin sidekick could have a good roll on their backs under the streetlights after a feed. In the morning they would remember where that came from. Clarence, still sore, would try to keep discipline even in the presence of beds but if a hero was required so be it. Drank enough brandy to calm a certain jumpiness like the feeling when a owl just flew over your head close enough to pluck hair from it.

Ten

CUTTING OVER TOWARD THE MOUNTAINS to find the horses, they had left the farm country and driven through a large boreal forest with every species of evergreen tree that Clarence ever heard of and some he didn't recognize. Tamarack, lodge-pole pine, jack pine, black spruce and some kinds of fir tree, he suspected pulp cutting was the business here, not logging, and they did see many truckloads of sticks on the road. Sticks to him, much smaller timber than to-home but at least they were in the midst of a kind of work he knew.

Now when they returned to the highway in the morning it looked as if they were on the edge of another huge prairie extending to the north and east far as the eye could see, and even west again, where they were headed. The altitude of Grande Prairie, said on the welcome sign, was only 2,172 feet, not that much higher than home, amazing to Clarence. Come all this way, two thousand miles and more, and haven't climbed but a thousand feet. Cook's lake, to-home, was 1,200 feet above sea level, or such a matter.

And this was still farming country! It amazed him that they could still be in farming country. This far north! This close to the Yukon Territory! Hester was reading to him out of a brochure she picked up at the cabins. "This here is the Peace River country. They calls it just The Peace."

"The Peace." That was a nice name.

"The Peace. Yeah, man." She waved her vee'd fingers in front of him. Then back to her atlas.

"The Peace. And do you know what? Lookee here! The Peace River runs east and northeast all the way over to Lake Athabasca, and from there up to Great Slave Lake, and turns into the Mackenzie River and flows north up into the Arctic Ocean!"

Clarence was trying to comprehend the continent they were wandering on, where after driving for two weeks northwest and climbing higher and higher toward the Rocky Mountains they could come to a place that was so low and flat, still home to the unromantic agricultural classes and the rivers flowed toward the north which therefore must be lower and flatter still, contrary to common sense.

Also that for all the farther you thought you were getting away from cities and shopping centers and overhead wires and big buildings here was a huge construction project, acres of steel frames and towers going up, clouds of dust and moving Caterpillars and big signs to read as they drove by. Paper mill. A Kraft mill, it said. Proctor and Gamble. That company that made soap, they didn't know that company made paper. Maybe to wrap up the soap in. She asked him, "You know what a Kraft mill is?"

"So happens I do, some. They do it same way at Cornwall, also at Deferriet, where our pulp goes, to-home. Very clever, all chemistry. Use the same chemicals over and over, burn off the results to make all the electricity, like a perpetual motion machine." Clarence chuckled to think of the cleverness of the paper company chemists, himself for remembering so much. He did not expect to find a paper mill up here but one good thing about it, they was building good roads too.

"Well," she said. "There's going to be plenty of work in the woods around Grande Prairie."

"I will pretend I did not hear that."

"I didn't mean ennathing. Just a observation which it says here. Also says the climate is nice. Dry, so you don't feel the heat or the cold. Sunny. Very sunny."

"I think you are scared of Alaska. Ascared of anything but a farm."

"Not long as I have my comforting."

"Well we ain't looking for jobs just yet."

"Is they any brand on them nags? You call them nags, I calls them horses. Is they? I didn't take note."

"Not the same as on the trailer. Not the same as each other, neither. They been adopted before. We got a family to take care of now and we better get far from this country, fast as we can."

"A farm is a comfort to the mind," she said. "The Peace."

It had felt very easy for the Ford to pull the trailer with the new cargo in it from the foothills to Grande Prairie. Now he knew why. Slightly down-hill. Here northwest of GP the grade was the other way, had to use second again, every little steeper section. You could hardly tell when you came to them but the engine told him, it lugged and labored until he clutched it carefully and shifted down. If they get so steep he would need first gear, he would have to double-clutch and wasn't too sure he could do it. Been told how but daren't try. If the RCMP come after them he couldn't outrun them, have to think of something else, ha-ha.

"They's discovering oil and gas too. This place is going to grow."

"What you getting at?"

"Nothin'. I'm just reading information to you."

"Well, keep reading. I like information."

"You're a changing man, CW. Always something new."

Well that was a surprising thing to hear. He guessed it was true, who would know better? May he had been feeling it himself. If it was true, that's because it was necessary. He was not in his own country. If you go away from home, you find out who you are. Nobody telling you who you are every day, same as yesterday and the day before. Might just be that I am my father's son. Nobody ever thought of that, back home. John Shampine, well known for having his own mind. Could have been a rich man but rather not.

A prophet is not without honor, save in his own country. Remembered that from school. Once he got it figured out, it stayed in his mind. Means, the last people to tell you what good you are is your sisters.

"Before we get too far away from the city, let's get a newspaper," Clarence said. "See what's going on in the world. Tourist brochures only tell you so much."

She looked at him a minute. Then she said what she had been going to say. "Dawson Creek British Columbia is Mile Zero of the Alaska Highway."

The only story Clarence was in the habit of telling about his father was that one about the suspects in the Orrando Dexter murder case coming to him with a bottle, to get him to talk to the judge. John Shampine was a suspect in that murder himself, on account of the fact that between where he lived, on the Cook's Lake Road, and Dexter Lake, at the foot of Catamount Hill, where Dexter was killed, was no more than five miles of woods that John Shampine could navigate blindfolded. According to the story, the Judge looked at John Shampine very sharp, asked him just how long it would have taken him to walk from the Home Place over to Dexter's and do the dirty deed himself. His father said, "That, sir, would depend on how fast you walked." How much was story and how much was truth Clarence did not know. Judge might not of thought that was a answer.

134

He did not know much about his father, come right down to it. Called himself a farmer but why would anybody attempt to farm where he did, up in the rocky hills. First wife died middle aged after having children late, Clarence's mother, so he didn't know much about her either. What he knew was that his father was a enjoyable talker and liked his younger second wife to sing, which she did. Some people enjoyed Clarence's talk also, Leo Weller and his father Loyal to name two. Encouraged it. Clarence had got in the habit of telling the same stories over and over again, about the good old days. One way he had changed was, he had some new stories to tell. Arnold and Evangeline for example. Bank robbery. Somehow, didn't think he would tell the old ones any more. Like the one about the time he was supposed to set the brake on that railroad car of Mr. Purryer's, filled with hemlock bark, and didn't get it set in time, and the car started to roll, and down the bottom of the hill the switches jumped straight and on he went, and so on until he would tell how when he got back up where he started, Mr. Purryer said, "Well, Clarence, I said to myself when you went down that hill, if you came back just as fast as you went, you wouldn't be gone long." In my new life I won't tell that one anymore. "That was the fastest anybody ever went on a railroad without no locomotive." No, I won't tell that one anymore.

"What you chuckling about now?" Hester asked.

"Got a thoroughbred-quarterhorse cross and a pack animal in back and here we are heading for the Land of the Midnight Sun."

"The days is getting longer. I did notice that. But it was chilly out last night. Thirteen degrees. We would of froze in the tent."

All the Wellers liked his family for being honest workers, decent people, firm in their speech and morals. It didn't matter if we was poor and uneducated. What was so good about being uneducated he did not know. But his father, smart man that he was and a

135

hard worker too, never made money. Never went far. He must have chosen the life he had but Clarence didn't choose it, didn't have no choice. Neither did his stepmother, or maybe she did, since she chose John Shampine. But that meant having dandelion wine and spruce tonic to drink and no refrigerator. Clarence would have been glad to go to school more than he did. Get a education. Instead, went to school to Mr. Robert Purryer Senior in the lumber woods. No regrets about that. Loved every minute of it, don't tell nobody.

Well now I take that back. That is what I used to say, have said it a thousand times if I have said it once. I'll quit saying that too. Try a little harder to remember. If you said you loved every minute of being a errand boy for a lumber camp cook you are not remembering good. If you said that was your education, you didn't get one. I don't need to make things up no more.

Now it was coming to Clarence that there might be something to life besides the past. That was change right there, because he had for so long wished the past had never gone by. Woe for the day they took the horses out of the lumber woods. Time to get over that. Maybe when they come to Alaska these skins in the trailer will be useless. Wouldn't that be a fine cup of tea?

"I'll give you a penny for your thoughts," she said.

Why I don't just fill the truck with my palaver? It isn't fit to listen to. But he made an effort. He lied. "Thinking about that bay, way the red lights of his coat shimmered in the sun, after you brushed him this morning. You just look at him and the word thoroughbred comes to you. Well, what they did out west to make a good cow horse that had speed and endurance was, cross a quarter horse, which was a ratty little animal from Texas that had a lot of cow-sense, with a Arabian. That's how Merlin came to pass."

"Per Hinman had a quarter horse," she said. "Big hindquarters higher than the withers. You think—?"

"What?"

"Never mind."

They were both shaken by the landscape, thrilled by it. She'd say, "Oh my land!" The mountains still far away to the west and southwest and they going northwest but the mountains coming again and again into view around long wooded escarpments with sparkling rivers running northward, crossing their way far below, under bridges, flowing into this surprising northerly agricultural land north and east. The Peace. Headed for the Arctic Ocean.

Now he had such a jumble of thoughts that he couldn't speak aloud but he had the resolution made. If I talk aloud without knowing it, well, let it happen. Where was I?

"Remember how your father played his ace, cookie?"

"Don't know what you mean."

"When he was persuading us to come home, that one last night, near Sudbury Ontario. 'Mountains out there like you never seen,' he said. 'See them mountains once,' your father said, 'you'll never come back.'"

"Yes I do remember that," she said. "That's exactly what he said."

"Well, we see them now."

"I wish you hadn't reminded me of him," she said.

Dawson Creek, not interesting. Flat, dry, and grain elevators. She read from her papers. "Capital of the Peace." Capital of nothing, to Clarence. "Mile Zero City." Zero is right. There was a tall black silhouette telling them where to turn left for Alaska, and in the middle of the main street, on the double yellow line, a little post with flags on it, the start of the Alaska Highway. "Five hundred refugees from the Sudetenland in 1939, I am afraid I don't know the meaning of that." Must of had noplace else to go. Clarence carefully drew the rig around the Mile 0 post, watching the left wheel of the trailer in the rear-view, and they started off for mile one, two, and three.

"Says big business here is tourism. People going to Alaska. RV convoys get together here, says. Huh. Must be they make the trip like a wagon train. I guess we's ahead of them, they don't go this early."

"I don't want to see tourists in Alaska."

"Why not? We's tourists."

"We are not."

"I said to myself when I woke up, I will not argue with him whatever he says. Eleven thousand people. Few visible minorities." Dawson Creek could have been Potsdam, New York but more grain elevators. Still could not believe growing wheat this near Alaska. The main street went straight for the horizon, a distant wooded ridge. She said, "Lowest educational levels in the province. Highest crime, but not heroin-related and not murder."

"Not murder?"

"Disappointed? High in cannabis-related."

"What's that?"

"Marijuana, I think."

"Which is dope."

"Some say so but it's a nicer name. A real nice name. High crime rate in shoplifting, breaking and entry, theft from cars, and assault, non-sexual."

"That's more like it. Bar brawls. I want to see men going into bars with their guns on hip."

"So you can do likewise at last."

Going on through the small unthriving city Clarence took particular notice of taverns like the Dew Drop Inn, which reminded him of the Grand Union Hotel in Tupper Lake where he had once boarded, working for the Oval Wood Dish. Nobody going in or out.

Streets mainly empty so he parked and Hester changed some money in the Bank of Canada with him standing by empty-holstered, no shots fired. Found a farm store and bought rope, had a little, got plenty more and when he thought of cutting it added a carborundum stone. They drove out of that disappointing town. What you needed for western excitement he guessed was cows and here was mostly wheat. Still wheat! Will wheat never die? Though there was also mines. Different kinds of mines all along this trip. Back in Ontario a huge open mine that the ore was smelted for copper. Copper, you heard right. Then in Saskatchewan potash, whatever that was. Around here, asbestos, also oil and gas, a propane plant. Always wondered what made Canada tick and now he knew, digging it up and selling it. The wheatfields that continued to surround the highway to his surprise were beautiful though and he had to be grateful that the road builders were able to stay low and run the highway in the long slopes of the alluvial plain sloping very gradually east and northeast, same reason it was good farming. The grades were easy for the Ford only it took more gas pulling the heavy trailer, let alone the inhabitants which never seemed to have enough to eat. Had to stop frequently and he was glad he hadn't spent money unnecessarily on the revolver and legitimate ownership of these expensive characters in back. He regretted shelling out for the trailer. That kind of thing was getting to be against his religion.

"Something different about you today."

"Something different about you too."

They were sitting in their folding lawn chairs, the rig parked along a side road, letting the horses graze. Something out of a calendar, cobblestone stream, green grassy slope, aspens above that, firs above that, end of the valley granite going heap after ridge up to snow country and sawtooth peaks shaded against the dark blue sky and the sun which slanted all the way back down to the riffles and bounced into their eyes. Merlin and the buckskin cropped the plants along the shore a bit and then dragged their ropes uphill to the end of their tethers and eased back to where they could feed without jerking the tethers. They didn't pull against their stakes too hard and it was a good thing and Clarence said so, under his new resolution, don't just think, say.

"I'll probably have to try to hobble them some, other places. If I can remember how to tie up a hobble. I think Merlin will come to the dinner bell, that's the good news. Buckskin will follow close, by the looks of them. But Merlin, once he gets away the first time, he'll be trouble forevermore."

A word to the wise, he thought but did not say.

"My clothes are falling off me," she said.

He had not noticed that. They come off quick enough in the tent, ha-ha.

"They is getting loose. Look."

Not sure how he was supposed to see this looseness.

"I see some of the Indian women, or Inuit or whatever they is here, in Grande Prairie there was lots of Indians, ten percent they say, well, I see some of them that looks a bit like me. I mean they are built like me and in a kind of way they have faces like me, and do you know, I like the looks of them. I needs new glasses. I am going to get a hat or else you let me wear your old one, now that you've got a cowboy hat. Let me use that old black felt thing with the high crown. I seen some of these Indian woman on the street with a hat kind of like that one of yours. Did you know that some of these Indians here are Iroquois, that come all the way out here in the nineteenth century? Do you know what that means? Iroquois are New York State Indians. That means that we took all their land and they took off and kept looking for some land they could have and they come all the way to the Peace River Valley of Canada to get away from us, talk about refugees. I am going to get some clothes that fit and I don't care if they is Indian dresses. I would just as soon go around like one of them Iroquois women."

When he could get a word in edgewise he said, "I'll get razzed for being a squaw man."

"I think you would be flattered by that, knowing you."

"That's right, I will. Do they wear glasses, them Indian women?"

"Some do. Nicer ones than these."

"You can't help it if they have to be thick."

"I want some contact lenses. Or else prettier frames, at least. Colored ones, something that goes with my new hat. You said my eyes is pretty."

"I don't remember nothing of the kind and I don't know about giving you my hat. With any luck it wouldn't fit." That was backsliding, saying he didn't remember anything of the kind. But if he changed too quick she wouldn't recognize him.

"Let's see. Go back to the truck and get it."

"Did I hear right?"

"Sure. I asked you nicely and I said please."

"Well it won't fit, I've got a narrow head, have to get a special oval model. Cooler weather I'll need it. Don't think no more about stealin' my hat."

"I need pants, too. I need some jeans and boots."

"You start thinking about your wardrobe when we just left civilization, sister."

"You are so right. I wish't I'd went shopping in Grande Prairie, that was quite a city. Where you got your hat was a department store, if I'd of known we was shoppin'. Nobody tells me ennathing. But up ahead they's Farmington. Then Whitehorse the capital of the Yukon Territory. Take me there at once, I's getting impatient."

"At once, ha-ha. Opposite of that, we are slowing down, stopping like this to feed the animals." Animals do that for you, regulate you to a reasonable pace. But it was a thrill to hear the word Yukon. And to breathe this air. He shrewdly suspected Wilfred was right, they would never come back.

"You tell me why I am losing weight, sitting in the truck all day and eating junk food."

"Spending nervous energy living with me."

"Nervous is right. Wondering who you are going to be tomorrow."

"I don't like the way you look at my horse." Put together with this talk of pants it had him worried. Bread and cheese and creek water, they were feeding themselves along with the nags.

"You don't know that I had a pony when I was a little girl. You probably can't imagine that I ever was a little girl! And when I was a teen-ager I had a bigger pony, really a small horse, a paint, brown and white, his name was King. I used to ride with the Parishville Rough Riders. You remember Per Hinman and them? No? They was rough all right but on their manners with me. I was a barrel-racer. That's one of many things you never asked, horseman. Had to listen to you thinking out loud about them pretty barrel racers back at the rodeo we went to. I used to have a set of barrels of my own in the pasture to practice on. King was the fastest horse in Parishville but he was an awful one to gallop for the barn, it was hard to make him go away from home. Many's the time he just took me home at a gallop, nothing I could do, I would get so mad at him, I'd yell and swear and I would beat him when we got back, just beat him, with a plank! I means it Clarence! It didn't do no good. Oh, that King! He died eventually. Not of all my beatings. I couldn't kill him. I tried. He used to make me so mad."

She stopped at last. Way back in the middle of it he got confused between listening to her and wonderment at what she had already said. At his own never asking. What little he knew about her
earlier life she had volunteered, all surprising.

"How old might you be?" he said. Making a try in unfamiliar
territory. Other person's story. He hardly moved his lips.

He never knew anything about her until that spring he boarded
his horses with Wilfred and they gathered sap with them, and skidded hemlock logs when the sap didn't run. Took his meals with
them then and learnt that she could cook but talked a blue streak
not all of it good-tempered. That was when she almost got her
clutches into him. Now I know that that wouldn't have been so bad.
Better late than never. He checked his mouth, still closed, good.

"I have a closet full of ribbons that we won. Had, I guess I
should say. King loved the barrels. He turned real well, kept his feet
under him, kept low. I had to swing my inside leg back or else he
would knock the barrel over with my knee. That smarted, when that
happened. Then how he would dig for the next barrel! Anybody that
didn't know him would go over backward, but I would put my arms
right around his neck and hang on."

This same person? Well I'll be a—I don't know what. If croc-
odiles can fly what was to keep her off his new horse? Look down
the brook there, that game trail going out of sight behind the slope.
He imagined Merlin with that load on his back disappearing around
the hill there, going too fast, losing his footing and capering among
the boulders, all legs broke, his cook in the river and himself ascared
of water.

"I think that old cavalry saddle would hold me in good while I
get used to riding again," she said, chomping on her bread and
cheese, crumbs falling on her bosom to be flicked aside. She smiled
at him. He knew how to see her eyes through them coke bottles now

and they were smiling certainly. "I like these kitchens where you don't have to sweep the floor."

Eleven

THEY BUILT THIS ROAD IN A HURRY during the war, took only one year to do it, right through the wilderness and have been repairing it and straightening it since, still a lot of construction on it and here where it crossed the Kiskatinaw River they were building a new bridge. The old one was wooden timbers only, thirty years old and seen a lot of heavier vehicles than it was built for. It was a long way across and very high above the river. He said it was like the Grand Canyon, never saw the like, the other one couldn't be no grander. "This is a grand enough canyon for me," he said, and she said, "Land sakes I should say so." It was good to have a home town girl that used an expression just like his stepmother's. Land sakes. Those old people must have thought saying Lord's sakes was taking the Lord's name in vain. He used to think he was clever to say that taking Hester off with him was second best to not leaving home at all, but it was better than that. He looked forward to dressing her up like a First Nation resident and seeing what pointy-framed glasses did for her round face.

The bridge-builders told them it would be a long wait, and so although they had just started, they got out of the truck and worked out how to say it, kiss the cat, while they sat on the guard-rail looking at the wide deep canyon which it was hard to believe had all been eroded by that thin braided river running along in the bottom of it. On the top of one side, hundreds of feet higher than the river, green stick-timber; on the other, a barren slope far higher, layer after layer of gray sedimentary rock. They had to wait so long that they scrambled way down to the stream-bed and out onto a pointed bar of white stones. Clarence had quit thinking she couldn't walk, crawl or climb like anybody else. By now if he handed her the revolver he would expect her to hit the bull's eye. Under the clear glittering water, if you looked closer, stones with more colors than the rainbow in them. Not every one but an occasional one, polished, so much whirling marbling of color in it that some people would want to take it home and put it on the table. "Nice place, shall we leave it here or take it with us?" You could have called this the Peace River, peaceful enough today, but it wasn't, it was the Kiss-cat-inaw and inspired inane remarks by showing you how much anything matters except taking it in.

Up by the road on the other side was a memorial of some kind, looked like a poor sort of totem pole or a scarecrow with tattered things hanging from the arms. Clarence scraped what manure there was out from behind the skins onto the ground, and they were in the truck and on their way again without looking it over closely. Couldn't study everything, you wouldn't ever get there. If it was something sacred it would be wasted on them, none of their business.

That day they came to a reservation. They saw it on the map ahead of time, and he knew what she was thinking as they come along these straight stretches, long slopes, then a turn that didn't look like much on the map, seemed more on the road, a new angle, the right of way cleared high and wide here and the roadway built up, so as to drain in a wetter season. Just here, no farms, but woods both sides and far ahead, the mountains further away than they were yesterday. Hand-painted signboards. Sure enough they wanted you to stop, had a sprawling low-roofed store right beside the road. Nobody else was stopping but he didn't wait for Hester to say anything, they were in agreement about this. You couldn't go wrong dressing the way the natives do, they know the territory.

Clarence went inside with her and come right out again, not comfortable with that many Indians all at once or maybe because they was all ladies. Stayed long enough to see Hester right at home where he wasn't. She looked around at the shawls and dresses and said she wanted this, wanted that, and Clarence was the sugar daddy. So self-conscious about it that he didn't notice much except that the Indian women did not smile, but Hester did, and they did not talk, but she did, babbled on to them like a younger girl than she was, as if she never had been on a shopping spree which was probably true, she hadn't. He couldn't imagine Wilfred Gonyea taking her to the Empsall's in Malone and giving her her head like himself. Back in the truck he waited and when she come out wearing her new mukluks right up to her knee, a nice fit because most of them Indian women were built just like she was and had round faces like hers too, he liked them so much he went back in and braved the impassive women and got a pair for himself. Weren't they on a spree! Back in the truck with his revolutionized sweetie he got a peck on the cheek and she said, "These mukluks will be good for ridin'."

"They're to keep your feet warm in the winter," he said. Though it didn't seem to him they put much between you and the ice. But the ladies said they was wonderful warm if you also bought these felt liners.

"Well I wasn't lookin' that far ahead."

Provincial Park for the night. Stop early and see about this riding. Clarence found himself open-minded about it even though it was hard to imagine her getting onto a horse of sixteen hands. Strange horse that might be stranger than they knew.

But next thing she was up there. Got up on the picnic table first. Merlin become a different animal than he looked when once you threw a rope over his neck. You wanted to keep it there or he would walk away a step or two, and once he realized there wa'n't no rope, went a few steps more and pretty soon, trotting away or loping. After that, wait until he's hungry again and comes back for a snack. They had bought a good supply of sugar cubes and carrots. No horse-cakes at the last feed store. "Lord I feel high up," she said. "It's a long way to the ground. And I's out of breath. Let me just set here a minute."

"All right. Merlin don't mind, do ye Merlin." He was not sure Merlin didn't mind, could see Merlin thinking.

"When did you quit shaving?"

"You just noticed?"

"Yes. I just noticed."

"Hnn." Went around and fixed the other stirrup. She had chosen the saddle herself, high wooden cantles front and back.

"Well, let's try and go a little."

"Keep a close rein."

"Don't worry. I had to do that on King."

"We don't know where the barn is, with this one."

"Oh Lordy am I ready for this?"

Merlin shoved him away with his nose. This was about as crazy as I don't know what. They walked around in a circle in the park loop road and came back. Merlin took in a deep breath and groaned. "You know what, he filled up before we tightened the girth." She stood up on one leg and the saddle went around. Got it centered again and he re-did the strap.

"Now in a minute we'll try jogging. Once I get my breath. I hope he's got a smooth jog."

Clarence's mind went back to the day he gave up courting her years back, when she fell out the truck door almost onto him, how he used to tell the tale. Used to think that was funny. If she fell off now, it wouldn't be no rolling down the driveway unhurt and too late for flight on his part. Time to call the Rescue Squad, only there isn't any. Now, looked surprisingly like many another female rider who could hold a horse to the ground. Merlin's jog made her chins jiggle that was all. She got up the road and back in one piece, flushed, breathless, ten years younger.

He held the horse and she got off on the picnic table, sat down on the edge, squirmed down to the seat, stood up on the ground, her thin wiry hair when she took the domed hat off to wipe her brow no higher than Merlin's shoulder. There were trails up the river from the campground. She said next morning after they took down the tent, he could wash the pots and she'd go exploring. But in the morning the insides of her legs were lame, also her sit-upon, and it was cold. "These mukluks are cozy though, en't they?" She decided against it and they were on the road again with the heater on, still breathing frost for many a mile, bound for Watson Lake, Mile 635, what—two days away? It didn't matter, there would be gas and grazing in between, probably not new glasses. Trip was now out of control, had been ever since Merlin stepped into the trailer and wouldn't come out.

"I used to wonder why you insisted on shaving."

"You did, huh?" He was looking at himself in the rear view mirror, which he reached out and turned inward for the purpose. Every day except lately, used to scrape his jaw looking in that mirror, no mirror in their camping gear. Now studying to get the beard to grow faster.

"Yes. I might like you in a beard. You haven't got that much of a chin."

"Summing wrong with my chin, sister?"

"No. I used to cook in the sugarbush. Also in lumber camp, which you didn't ever even know, did you? Well I did. I saw a lot of mens with beards and longish hair too. Them was the days. I was the Supreme Court in lumber camp. I could have told them to shave or not come to dinner."

She got to reminiscing.

"You didn't even talk to the cook. First thing you learn, you do not speak to the cook. You treats her with reverence, and she judges every man. That's the way I been ever since. Handlin' one man is nothin'. One man is not enough!"

"I'll remember that."

"A full camp, and ever one at my service. To haul water, peel potatoes, wash pots. What're we goin' to do when that bankroll runs out? I say we head for the lumber woods."

"If I ever see a tree worth cutting. I am not interested in match-sticks." You're full of surprises today. Also, when did I ask you what we're goin' to do? Let's get there first.

Little burst of conversation, then twenty miles of looking at the scenery. Might have seen the last of farms, don't care if he never see another. Get full of landscape and then say something again. Some reason, talking with her tickled him in the pants.

Rattles and bangs, stones flying up under the truck, over that the steady stitching of the six-cylinder hauling up a long grade. Gravel now, ever since the first eighty-two miles of the Alaska High-way, that was all that was paved.

"Alaska, you know, one big lumber camp. Biggest trees in the world." I'll show you a piece of timber tonight.

"I'm serious. What you know how to do besides lumbering back in nineteen twenty?"

"I just need a clean start where nobody knows me."

"No use talking to you!"

After looking out the window ten minutes, it was her this time. "What if they isn't any horses in the lumber woods?"

"We're bringing them." He was stiff as a flagpole just talking to her. What she called his big red eraser on the end of it. Here he was, plowing up the fur of the Alaska Highway like a ship with a bowsprit.

"Anyways, it's still a long ways to Alaska and a long summer ahead of us and it wouldn't bother me none if we looked to stop in Fort Nelson or Whitehorse and try what we can do. Give this old truck a rest. Let the horses stand on the ground a bit. Them's the last two places any size before we gets there."

"When I worked in the woods, the only thing the cook run was the cookhouse. I would have to think you was scared of Alaska."

"You said that before and I might be. I am scared of the end of this trip."

"I am not. I have put flat land and small mountains behind me forever."

"Well the Rocky Mountains are beautiful at a distance but we haven't had to go over any yet. They worries me."

No campground that night when it come time to stop, just God's country wide open for them to use. Natural meadow by a stream, could almost have been the Sabattis down behind Nellie's farm, only clear water, no tannin in it, drier air just like champagne, no maples, only aspen which we call poplar to-home. Clarence thought of his fishing equipment still back in his cabin on the Project in Sabattis Falls, son of a gun! Fly rod that he didn't use for flies but worms with a bobber, to get more reach. It was not a wonder if he didn't think to load that rod and tackle-box but it would been a lot handier than this gas cooker he was still hauling, good for nothing.

151

Let's sell that thing. If can't, give it away. See if she'll let me buy a new rod and reel. Did I say that?

Let's see about this pack horse, if I can rig it. Pack-saddle is simple but how you lash things on, some knots I never learnt, others I might of forgot.

"Yes and I better see if I can get onto Merlin from the ground."

"We need a name for that soldier."

"Buck. Short for Buckskin."

"Good enough for me."

"You also ought to trim their feet."

As if nobody had just told him something he ought to do he said, "They wasn't as grown out as I feared and I know why, just come off a winter pawing through the snow for their feed. Wish't I'd taken that fellow's nippers, now. I didn't know what the future held."

No traffic at all. Silence and grandeur when you stop. All this and sixteen hours of daylight, twilight through the tent for love.

Twelve

AT LAST! BEARDED MEN WITH PISTOLS on their sides and this new Clarence follows them into a bar in Whitehorse, Yukon Territory, leaving Hester on the street to find something for herself to do besides follow him around. They used to have special rooms for the ladies but no more and did they let squaws in anyway which is what she looked like? What's he goin' in there for? she wanted to know. What'd he unwrap the revolver and put it in the holster for? Well, branching out. Drawn by the gathering of men with guns of which he counts himself one. This has been a long time coming or didn't you notice. He's wearing a good salt-and-pepper whisker, shaved under the chin and on the neck where his red bandana is casually knotted, not spread out over his shoulders in back the way he used to wear it. His revolver is inconspicuous, not as low as some and on the opposite side with the walnut-sided butt forward, the holster so worn, dark and polished with use. Straight leg jeans she has been rubbing on stones beside creek-beds ever since Watson Lake, long enough to get the indigo partway out of them. Enough wear and grime on the straw to pass. You wouldn't think he was a dude at all, and he'd never tell. He was a man with a past like anybody else who would show up in this town and ready to find somebody to share a sarsaparilla with. The mukluks a note of individuality and if anybody looked out the window and saw his shotgun waiting stoically for his return, they might say he'd gone native.

Which they certainly did, one of them fellows standing right beside the door inside, looking out, a long-haired fellow, took him and his girlfriend in, maybe the rig across the road too, summing you don't see every day in the Yukon Territories, in all likelihood, and nodded silently to him on his entering, respectful, as expected.

Jack Daniel's his drink in a shot glass and a beer on the side. The place reminded him of Rule's Roadside Restaurant, across from Gene's Shell to-home. Elk and moose heads instead of deer heads and bigger fish on the boards but same Canadian beer, just what the doctor ordered, Carling's Red Cap Ale. It was hours until evening, nowheres near time to make camp, but this was Whitehorse and the lady wanted to come off the road for a night in a real bed. Maybe here. Like Gunsmoke, she said. He sniffed the air.

The longhair came over to sit a stool away from him at the bar and there were two others at a small table under the railing of the stairs to bedrooms above if the place was as like the Union in Tupper Lake as he thought. He'd be right at home if there was any other woodsmen rooming here but it didn't look it.

"Can't quite figure you out," the longhair said. "You're a walking set of contradictions."

English accent. Clarence chuckled, flicked him a glance to see he was taking his confusion well.

"You certainly are not a cowboy."

"No," Clarence allowed. "Team-es-ter."

"Tea—teamster?"

"That's right."

"Oh, I don't think so. Not a union teamster at any rate."

"If you mean truck driver, which I never liked them calling themselves team-es-ters, no I am not. Means what I do is drive a team of horses. Or did when there was work for a team. What I've got in that trailer, not no sort of a team. A mismatched pair of skins

154

that washed up on shore. Where I'm bound? Alaska, in the long run but in no hurry."

"Looking for work?" somebody said.

"Not 'til I find paradise."

"Independently wealthy, like us?"

"Have a grub-stake, that's all." He was proud of that roll which wasn't a roll and this was an unguarded statement he would have taken back if he could.

"That an Indian woman? We saw her out the door."

"No, a dairy-farmer's daughter from home. She likes the fashion."

"Might have Indian blood, I was thinking. You might yourself."

"Not I know of." But Clarence kind of blushed. What was he indeed? Scotch-Irish, French, never knew anybody in the family that could speak French but the name might be the French word for champion or champagne, good name either way.

"Well..." They had reached sufficient acceptance to introduce themselves and shake hands all around. Clarence remembered only his own name when they had gone around, and the bartender's which he remembered because it was Sylvia and Sylvia was a pot-bellied older man in a cardigan with white hair in a ponytail, looked like Ben Franklin on the nickel. Everybody at the bar now, one to his left, two to his right. He had tried to get a look at their side-irons but only confirmed that they were there, worn so naturally they seemed forgotten.

Where was home and so on. Found himself wanting to make the home territory as remote and rugged as possible so he allowed it was way up north, north of the mountains, a part of New York State not widely known to exist, along the border with Canada. Himself he painted the way he wanted to be painted. Forced by certain circumstances to do summing made him unpopular there, a pat on the grip of the revolver his only explanation. He saw a smile or two turned away toward the television. Went on, "So, made a quick visit to the bank and the dairy-farm to get the cook and here we come." Another unguarded item about the bank but he did not mind conveying substance.

"I liked the look of that girl," the Englishman said. Went back to the window looking for her.

"I have had many a compliment on her along the way."

The Englishman shook his head once in emphasis and his curls flew around. "Yes, I could go for that. Gone up the street now."

"She can cook. Used to cook in a lumber camp, if that tells you anything. Plus she's the one that rides the quarter horse."

"He better be a big one."

"He is."

"You follow baseball?" A game on the screen over the bar. Fellow who asked had on a army jacket.

"No, sir."

"What you plan to do in Whitehorse?"

"Check over the vehicle, if you can recommend a Ford garage. Get some fishing equipment. Which I left mine to home in my haste. It wasn't season yet. She would like to stay a while."

"Though you was waiting for paradise."

"This might be it."

"Oh no it ain't. This place is empty, man."

"Don't tell anyone you're bound for Alaska. There's work, exactly because nobody wants a job here. Everybody's waiting to go there. Starting up the pipeline."

"Everybody's evacuated here but us drunks that have no use for money." That was the British one. Doing most of the talking.

"Funny idea," the veteran said. "Wait to find work 'til you get to paradise. I thought paradise was where nobody has to work at all."

Did I make myself a trap? He puzzled over that idea of paradise. "I love to work. Work with horses, paradise to me."

The veteran said, "Walking around behind some horse's ass all day." This was unnecessarily offensive. If you liked horses, nothing wrong with the back end of one. Besides, not walking, riding, holding the controls.

"Get to Alaska, you'll find there is no room."

"No room in Alaska?"

"No rooms in the boarding houses."

"Like this town when they were building the Highway."

"You here that far back, Sylvia?" the nameless one said.

"That's not so long ago," Sylvia said. He was an unsmiling person, behind the bar, purple sweater that buttoned in front, modest, busy with nothing to do.

"Been here ever since?"

"Been here since the gold rush."

"Yeah, me too."

"And this is all I got to show for it." By "this" Sylvia seemed to mean his customers, them. Clarence couldn't tell what he was intended to believe and what not.

The other nameless one said, "You hauling that trailer to Alaska you should buy a bigger truck. Four wheel drive at the least. That's what they'll tell you over to the Ford."

"I think you'll be the only horseman they've got up there. You may be the only one in this wretched outpost right now. Indian wives don't go down too well either."

"Speak for yourself, Josay."

"In general."

"His is Chinese."

Clarence said, "There's a place for a horse everywhere, my firm belief. Best power there is, many types of job. That's because you

157

can talk to them. When you can get a machine to do what you say, then maybe the horse is obsolete."

"This is a character, boys."

"He's tellin' us a lot of shit."

"There ain't no such place as he says he comes from. Not in New York State! Who does he think we are?"

"Let's we buy him a drink. Set 'em up, Syl."

So Clarence was feeling no pain when he went out again to reconnect with Hester. Said it to himself, no pain and unsteady of foot, whoa there. Once in a while it was good to socialize. These boys called themselves the Jesse James Gang and they was feeling no pain also by the time he broke loose. Lived together in rooms over the tavern and highly recommended Clarence and her should do the same. Take a break from the open road. Had something good to introduce them to.

More than one compliment to his wife or whatever she was. The Brit in particular had a taste for a pretty face like that, he said. Clarence had wanted to tell them how good she looked with her glasses off, but when that impulse came he recognized the temptation in time. Now where in the world had she gone? A real Indian would have had the patience to sit in the truck and wait.

Since she was not in sight he swung up into the truck and eased the rig out into traffic without his usual hesitancy and study of all mirrors. The very thing that had him worried showed up on cue. Let the clutch out ever so careful but still, had to give it the gas and let it spin or else, 'twould nearly stall and buck the rig, jerk the horses back there off their feet as it did now. He did give it the foot-feed aplenty but it jerked and jerked instead of taking off smoothly while he let the clutch out the rest of the way, the trailer coupling banged, he could hear the hooves thumping and once a pistol shot where Merlin let fly against the tailgate in anger. That was a horse ready to blame you for anything. But there where they said it was was the blue and white oval sign, Ford, with the wavy underline Fords had had all his life, the one thing that kept him loyal.

Maybe Hester would see the rig moving along the street here and come on over while he talked to the Ford man. Wasn't a very large main street for the capital of the Territories but don't forget the long dark winters, that will separate the men from the boys. One sure thing, he would see her if she come out on the sidewalk. She would stand out wherever, just see how the Jesse James Gang took note of her. He'd find her if she didn't get kidnapped. That British one with the blond locks looked capable of it, Clarence knew green envy when he saw it.

"You'll have to unhitch that trailer," the man said, had that Ford emblem on his shirt and the name stitched beneath it, Buzz. "Anything in it?"

"Well sure, two horses." What did he think would be inside of a two horse trailer?

"You know we'll be a while if you need a clutch. Prob'ly don't have the part. No, surely don't have the part. Maybe you want to leave the trailer where you're— You camping?"

Buzz was a nervous, worrying type of man, reminded Clarence of Dagwood Bumstead in the comics. Fretting over my horses like they was little children tied to the railroad tracks. Said "You camping?" like he was going to cry if you said yes.

"Maybe you could let them out in somebody's pasture. I haven't got any place for them, or I would offer. Somebody might let you. Let's see—"

"Goin' to Alaska," Clarence said. "Want to be forehanded."

"You'd do better with a four wheel drive."

"Once upon a time they wa'n't no such a thing."

If people could get across the country before there were four-wheel-drives, so could he. "I thought this ought to be enough to haul two horses."

"And it is, 'til you get stuck. You'd do better with a automatic, too."

"When did automatics come to be better than a stick shift?"

"Didn't use to be but the thing is, they don't need a clutch. You can't burn out a clutch you don't have. And yours sounds burnt from what you say. Surely will go out once you get to the mountains. You don't want to break down up there. Oh dear, no. Not up there near the border."

He didn't want to say to the Ford man, "You trying to sell me something?" People had said that too many times to his father. "John Shampine, I know why you try to farm this rock-garden. You just setting here waiting for people can't get over the last hill before the Lake. Hitch your team to their bumpers and haul them over the top for fifty cents. Then you can rest for a day or two." Not Mrs. Bryant, Sarah Weller Bryant. She would scoff at the fifty cents he asked for, make him take twice as much.

Also the same lady that would make Clarence when but a boy pile her firewood bark side up even under a roof. Didn't make no difference and she knew it, but the principle of the thing. That was the Wellers.

Buzz didn't seem to be looking forward to the job. "How much would this be? Oh, geez, whoo! I got to take down the shaft, pull off the bell housing. I probably have to wait a day for the part. Then get it all back together. Criminy! You're talking real money. Oh dear. You're out, you're out of a truck for a while. Leave the trailer right there if you want to. But I wouldn't know what to do about those horses." And gone. Had a axle joint, tire change, exhaust system, no help, going crazy here.

Say that and leave a fellow standing flat-footed. Well, all right. He got into the front of the trailer and fed the horses and watered them. The buckskin was growing on him, a nice-mannered animal, had a mild eye and a readiness to talk horse.

He found Hester at the soda fountain being flattered by the Brit, turned back to the counter beside her to whisper in her ear. He was making for them when one of the others, the one he called Woolyhead in his mind, name forgotten if he ever knew it, stepped in front of him. "We're making your lady an offer," he said. Very kind round-featured face surrounded by brown wool, hair and beard all the same length all round. Mild brown eyes not unlike Hester's with her bottles off. Or the Buckskin's, Buck's.

This was inauspicious because as Clarence now remembered, slightly clearer of head, while they were drinking shot for shot the Gang had told him they were planning to rob a bank out of boredom and wanted to know if Clarence went in for that sort of thing. That Colt's was what made them wonder, they said. So he had told them of the dead man's switch and after that how he had cleaned out the little brick bank back at home without no iron at all.

The Brit had said, "You get crazy in the head after a while up here if you don't have work. Work's the only bloody salvation, wasn't it you who coined that phrase? Look at us talking of robbing a bank. We're a dismal lot. Clarence actually did it!" Tipped his glass at Clarence and took a good swallow.

Modestly Clarence had told them that he had not. Just stood there watching the fellow blow himself up. Would have given him what money he needed, had it ready in his hand to offer. The other place, it was his own money he took out, the savings of a lifetime. That was another slip, one after the other, might make them think there was something besides a bank to rob, much safer. "Oh, a storyteller," the Brit said. "Which is it, God damn it. Don't play with me!"

"Easy, there, Colleen."

"I'm so sick of whimsical jokes," the man said. Something truly dangerous about him, Clarence had thought, his moods switched so quickly; and now here he was talking to Hester. Offering her a deal.

What kind of a deal? Over at the Ford, where he looked out the drug store window, his truck had been detached from the trailer and taken indoors. Out of sight, anyway. He pictured himself and Hester leading the horses down the street looking for a pasture. Or Hester riding and him leading the buckskin. And tonight they'd as likely be in the flophouse with these birds, horses hitched to the rail only there wasn't one. Where would they be? Where did he go wrong and was there any help for it?

Coming by him, leaving Hester with her sundae at the black counter, the Brit said, "The situation is fluid."

She was happy and had no glasses on. She turned her mild cow-like eyes on him in case he hadn't noticed. Have to be blind himself not to, the difference it made. He could tell that she was not seeing him clearly until they were up close, didn't think that was a bad trade-off. She in fact pulled him onto a stool next to her, still warm from the Brit's bony bottom in what looked like leather pants, and spoke eye-to-eye. "In the eye-place they agree with you that I have nice eyes. Still think so? Guess what?"

"You didn't order contact lenses."

"Yes I did."

"We would have to wait for them."

"Not very long. They fly them up from Vancouver."

"When the clutch is fixed this boy is heading out of White-horse, contacts or no contacts."

"I needed new regular glasses too, Clarence. They've got the prettiest frames. They take just as long to come. I figure we got to do these things here, last outpost of civilization. Said Got to, didn't I? Same as your old clutch. I think you did right to get that looked into. I could tell my own self that wasn't right."

"We can have them glasses held." Really wanted to ask her how much they cost. "Send them ahead when we have a address."

"That's right."

Truth was Clarence never pictured having an address in Alaska. Shouldn't have no need of one. But at the rate the world was going this wasn't the last outpost of civilization. There was probably civilization in Alaska even. If so he would be disappointed. Look at this around here, not different enough from Massena, New York. Truth was Clarence had left the clutch until he thought it was too late. Just kept putting it out of his mind. Thought they would have left civilization many degrees of latitude ago. Longitude too.

"Maybe I should marry you so you know who's boss and don't go off independent like this."

"I might have another offer," she said. Never saw her arch her eyebrows before. It made two out of the one, not bad. "Have a sundae yourself. I got more to tell you."

When hell freezes over, but the chocolate syrup from her plastic spoon burst on his tongue like childhood come again. Hunched over his own beside her he said, "They're up to no good, you don't have to tell me that. The Brit is a sly devil. Woolyhead is a draft dodger. The other fellow the opposite, fought in Viet Nam. The three of them more than a little crooked but that is what you expect, desperate characters. This ride has been a picnic up to now and you didn't know it sister but all the while I have been looking for my own kind."

"I'm scared of them," Hester said. "Especially the English one. He says he goes for me but I don't believe him somehow."

Noises outside. Other people in the drugstore turning to the street and thinking of his trailer and horses across the way Clarence was striding in that direction with his hand ready to cross his waist in the practiced backwards draw. Outside there was a scuffle. The Brit was down on the sidewalk, skinny legs kicking out from under two other boys and a big fellow with hand-squeezed clippers was mowing off his hair. Or trying to. Woolyhead was securely held from rescue by a circle of men and boys grinning and laughing. Somebody took ahold of him before he got the pistol out, then let him go, so Clarence finished the draw, thumbed the hammer back and fired straight into the sky. The noise made him want to hide and say he didn't do it. The Jack Daniel's was suddenly atingle in his wrists and everywhere else. The fat man was off without his clippers down the street. Friend and foe thought that was funny and Clarence had to blush, putting the Colt's back in the holdster and thinking he'd better look innocent for the RCMP which was sure to be coming around the corner. Instead, the Brit took a hand from Wooly and bounced to his feet, disgusted with the mess of his hair, which he checked in the store window. Two-thirds long and the rest every length down to scalp. Hester tugged at Clarence's to let him know she was behind him. Things needed to slow down, breathing first. Slow down. Slow down. She reached the other way to tug at the Brit's elbow. "I'll even it up for ye," she said. "I've got my own shears."

He was jumping up and down in his own reflection crying, "Look at that! Look at that!"

Thumps from the trailer. No wonder, he thought. Suppose you was a horse and you heard that shot, couldn't see where it come from or what 'twas about. While he strode across the wide street he admitted over his shoulder to her, hurrying along behind him with quick short steps, "Wouldn't of done that but for the whiskey."

"I know it," she said, panting. At least she wasn't telling him he shouldn't have fired.

"I used to have a pair of clippers like that," he said, "needed no electricity. I cut my own hair most of my life." They leaned on the trailer for breath. She showed him what she had in her hand. She had picked up the hand-clippers. Squeezed them experimentally.

"I'll cut it for you from here out. I always cut my Daddy's."

"He looked it," Clarence said. Like straw sticking out of a scarecrow's hat, only the color of cast iron. That old engineer's hat so many farmers wore, black with grease from the flanks of the cows.

"I'll let it grow some more first." Her fingers twisting what there was at the back of his neck. Come to think, when was the last haircut he'd had? Not on this voyage.

The animals calmed down hearing their voices. "It's all right, Merlin, all right Buck." But Clarence was thinking, We got to get them to some roughage. Or, used to be, there would be a stable behind the tavern, well known from many a Zane Grey story. But Clarence was conscious that he was mixing up Alaska with the Wild West. So far the route to Alaska had contributed to the mix-up but Whitehorse was not a cow-town.

"What was the deal?" Said she had more to tell him.

"Well, I don't know now, after... Besides, I's embarrassed."

He knew the Brit liked her looks. Them others said the Brit here went for Indian women but the braves were wise to him and he was a-scared of them. Said that in front of the Brit, laughing at him. Clarence wondered what the local boys had against long hair. Heard somebody in that crowd mention dope.

It seemed to Clarence that the two others, Woolyhead and the veteran, were taking their chances with the Brit. Himself, he would not fool with him. Would not make fun of him no matter how ridiculous he was. It was not ridiculous to be ascared of braves. Once when a boy Clarence had introduced himself to a girl that won the Queen at the Malone Fair. She was from Hogansburg. All he did was introduced himself to her there at the foot of the stage across the racetrack from the stands, and four of them walked in between them where he couldn't even see her. Lucinda Bonaparte was her name, never forgot it. Backed him up clear through the crowd till he felt the dirt of the race-track under foot and had room to scamper. That was one of many incidents that added up to where he quit introducing himself to girls early, gave it up completely. Let the girls come after him, as Hester did. That way you didn't get into any trouble. The Brit, they said, was getting sore from waiting for it. Wouldn't be content with nothing but what he couldn't have and all he wanted was trouble. Sometimes they called him the Philosopher. Anyway the Brit looked awful mad after he got his hair cut, watch out for him tonight.

Well, all right. The horses. Here comes the fellow from the garage.

Buzz held out a set of keys very like Clarence's own and pointed to a blue pickup out back, same vintage Ford but up high on knobby tires. "That's got a hitch. It's a automatic. You can borrow that to get them horses to some grass. We got yours on the lift. All right? You just use that'n for the night, no need to bring it back until tomorrow. I would go out east along the river, somebody'll let you put them out. Make sure they got good fences as not all has. Would you want your tent? I see you got a tent, and things. We'll help you shift them into the loaner."

Clarence found that he did not envisage tenting with the horses the way they usually did. Wanted to see what credit he got for firing his revolver, saving the Brit's gold locks, some of them.

"Ask him if the Ford's safe in his garage."

"What do you mean?"

"Overnight. I thinks they mean to look for your bankroll, CW."

"What?"

"You want outlaws, you got them. They've got ideas about your money. Our money, they call it. Want it for a investment. They could double it for us real fast, they say."

"Thought the Brit wanted you."

"That's how they get the money."

"I don't get that."

"Oh they's got more ideas than you could shake a stick at. You'd buy me back, wouldn't you?"

"What?" That would be a good question, that would. If she went off with the Philosopher.

"Anyways they won't get it. Neither will you without this." She held up another key.

"I don't like too many keys," Clarence said. "I would get confused where things was. What's that for?"

"That's for a safe deposit box in the CNB over there. Canadian National Bank. I put the envelope in there, for safe-keeping. Once I saw the kind of people you was associating with."

He took a closer look at her, maybe the closest one yet. "You done what?"

"Don't you feel better that way? I took out five hundred dollars and changed it into Canadian, because it looks to me like you is fixing on a spree. We can cut loose here in Whitehorse. I like that Brit, he's a devil and he's cute. Bald head would be interestin'."

"This ain't the trip I was on, a little while ago."

"Well I never been flattered before and I likes it. Anyways we got to wait for the clutch. And the contacts."

167

He had the key to the safe-deposit box in his hand, irresolute. "Who's supposed to carry this?"

"You! I might get pawed over."

Thirteen

ON THE WAY EAST ALONG THE RIVER ROAD in the high blue Ford—four wheel drive, V8—with the trailer behind, they were passed with great suddenness by a speeding car and saw something fly out the back window of it as it swerved back into the right lane. Clarence hardly had time to utter an exclamation or review his own speed, very slow, when another speeding car, painted red startled him the same way, like a blast of wind, not seen coming, RCMP. They watched while RCMP caught up and tried to pass the first car but the first car shifted to the middle of the road, whichever way the Mounties went, gave them no room to pass, siren now high wailing high and low. Clarence expected to see pistols held out the windows but the two speeding cars were getting farther and farther ahead, around the flat curves next the riverbank. They'd see the police try to pass, then the brake lights go on, back end lift, swerve. On around the next bend and out of sight.

When Clarence and Hester came along at their slow rate the police had the veteran up against the car. Recognized his camouflage jacket and earrings as they went by. Clarence would have liked to rescue that fellow the way he had rescued the Brit, with a timely discharge of his revolver but didn't see how to do it. It would have put him in good with that the Jesse James crowd for certain but not too good with the RCMP.

"I'll say not."

It was not long before the police come after him anyway. They were stopped alongside the road looking over the meadows along the stream to see if there was any place to get the horses down to the good grass along the river. Neither one of them was for tenting tonight but the horses needed to graze for an hour. Clarence had a yen for more dark tavern interior and serious male company and Jack Daniel's, nothing to worry about if he got tipsy, because bed would be right upstairs and his woman was the envy of the company. He wondered if he had become such a bad man that he would leave the horses standing in the trailer all night, he might be in conflict between new man and old. Along come the red police car, and the trooper getting out of it and coming to him in the mirror.

"May I see that sidearm, sir?" he asked.

"Well, I guess so."

The trooper turned down his head to sniff the barrel. That was as good a hat as his own, with a leather band he did not have, that gave it extra class, and he wore it straight, very stylish.

"That was you, then," the Mountie said.

"I stopped a riot with that iron," Clarence said.

"I don't doubt it. Did you know that it is against the law to discharge a firearm in the city limits?"

"I did not. I thought I was in the Yukon Territory."

"You are." He looked over the truck without comment, and the trailer with attention to its contents and the plate. "I always thought the Brit could do with a hair-cut and you interrupted that." Before Clarence could say anything witty he added, "You have a trailer from Saskatchewan."

"Yes and a truck from New York State which is in the Ford garage."

"Um-hmm."

Clarence handed him his license from his wallet, on request. A picture that did not flatter him, in which his mustache looked like Hitler's.

"Mr. Shampeen, is it?" the Mountie said, handing the license back without much looking at it. A short glance at Hester. "Ma'am." He stood straight. "Did either of you see anything fly out of that car that passed you?"

Clarence had experience answering questions like that. "No sir we did not," he said, very promptly. You don't want to get mixed up in this sort of thing. Hoped his consort would get the message in his lack of hesitation.

"You, Ma'am?" Taking off his hat and bending again to look across the cab.

"I don't know what you're talking about."

"The speeding car that passed you. I asked if you saw them throw anything out the window."

She shook her head slowly, wonderingly, looking straight at him.

"All right, then. Sorry to bother you. If your memory changes, just call the RCMP. Sergeant Campbell." He saluted them and backed a step. "That revolver," he said.

"What?"

"Colt Forty-Five. The Peacemaker." Ducked into his vehicle and backed away.

Slipped Clarence's mind they called it that. Peacemaker. Also, it came to him now, the Frontier Colt. Made in three different lengths of barrel. Sorry to forget those names so long and grateful to the Mountie. That much prouder to pack it.

Clarence explained this to Hester while they let the horses browse along the stream, good nutritious hardy grasses amid such wildflowers, not all unfamiliar, Indian paintbrush for one. The two of them sat in their folding chairs and Clarence had a sniff of the cork of the Daniel's. That deal with the Mountie took him very clearly back to one morning hunting with his brother-in-law and the crew from the Hotel. The night before, planning, Morley ridiculed every other man's suggestion including Clarence's about where they should hunt that morning. "Most days, he had to go out to his insurance office to Malone, but this day," he told her, "though it was a Tuesday, he would take the day off, hunt with the crew. 'You can't get no deer without me,' so he said. Insisted we make a long drive way back in on Rocky Brook Club land, which is trespassing plain and simple. Johnny and I, we objected, but he wouldn't hear none of it. Said no one would know, nobody of Rocky Brook Club would be back in there on a week day. Watchers had to go in before day light, he said. Drivers could go across the lake in boats, later, and cross to the Rocky Brook line from Furtaugh's camp. That was the shortest route. He'd take the watchers in himself, the long way, nobody else had to do it. Yes we'd make tracks in the snow but so what.

"And wouldn't you know, we hunt all week and come up dry, he comes with us this one morning, and takes the last stand in, shoots a buck. Six-pointer. He couldn't see no horns but he's up on the back of a doe on that ridge, so Morley shoots him in the act. Turns out to be a six pointer. Well, I'm hauling on one horn with Leo Weller on the other, skidding him out the trail, out off of Rocky Brook Club land to the Furtaugh Camp trail to the Mud Pond trail, then to the lakeshore, and who's standing by the trail but George Berry, a member of the Rocky Brook Club and a stickler about property. A surveyor. You know him, or your father does, from Risdonville. Well this is Lucky Club land now, almost to Morley and Corinne's property, legitimate for us to be walking this trail because by right of way, it's the way to Mud Pond which Corinne owns. And

George Berry knows exactly where we been that morning, saw our tracks going in. So he says, 'Where'd you get that buck, boys?'

"Well, same principle as this Mountie. I said, 'We got that buck, sir, on Flowers Hill Club, now step out the way, we're dragging him home.'

"Morley come along and they had words. Morley told him he could go back along their tracks and find the guts if he wanted to, and George said that's just what he intended to do."

"I don't get what that has to do with today."

"Well, same principle. When I said 'No sir I did not.'"

"Did you?"

"Yes I did."

"If you was really smart you wouldn't tell me neither."

"We both saw it, we spoke about it."

"I don't know what you mean. What same principle? I don't get it. I didn't see nothing! Ha-ha!"

It was late afternoon when they loaded up the horses and headed back, beginning to feel like natives for going over one stretch of road three times. The two of them were in agreement about staying the night in town though they still had to find some place to put up the horses. Clarence had decided he had run from human life long enough, the Old West-style tavern with rooms above and outlaws at the bar called to him and Hester was subject to a new lust for flattery.

"Oh look there."

Not one but two cruisers, parked along the road, and three Mounties were searching in the brush along the guard-rail as they went by. Clarence kept his eyes straight ahead, steering two handed hunched toward the wheel.

They were well past when Hester said, "They's looking in the wrong place. There's where that tin flew out of the car, right there."

173

They were passing a mile marker on the Alcan Highway. He didn't catch the number.

"What tin, ha-ha."

"Don't you stop now."

They parked the rig in the empty herringbone parking in the center of the main street where they could use two spaces. No sign of the Mounties. They crossed to the tavern. Sylvia was tending the empty bar and Clarence ordered a JD boilermaker as before while Hester asked for a Coke and sat at the small table under the stairs. Clarence took a small sip of whiskey, a larger one of Red Cap, and eyed the host. "This place been here a long time, I would bet," he said.

"Since before the motor car, you're thinking," Sylvia said.

"Yes and so there used to be a stable out back."

"Still is."

"Once upon a time you boarded horses here."

"I'm sure of it." Polished a little piece of the bar, then threw the towel in the sink. "The place is full to the rafters."

"What's it full of?"

"Full of old buggies. Old forge. Chicken feeders. Such-like. It's a regular museum."

"Well all right. Suppose we pull them buggies out and make room for my team."

"I knew you were coming to that. That would be a pile of work."

"Work, that's my religion. We get the Jesse James Gang to help."

"That itself would be a pile of work."

"No it wouldn't," Hester called from the table. "They owes us. He there saved the Brit his scalp."

"I heard that." To Clarence, "You think that's how we do here? This isn't Yellowknife."

Clarence drummed the counter. Hester said, "If I and him are goin' to stay here, we got to find a place for them horses. Do you own this place?"

"I don't own a pot to piss in or a window to throw it out of. But I run it. A pile of work and all to do over again when you move on. Probably somebody outside of town with some fenced acreage would let you pasture them."

"Everybody says that except some'n who's got fenced acreage outside of town. Besides I don't let them that far out of my sight."

"Well the boys are off making a delivery."

"I think they'll be right back," Hester put in.

Sylvia looked at her curiously. Went out from behind the bar to look out the window at the street, this way and that. Then he turned back to Clarence.

"What you need? Box stalls?"

"Don't have to be box stalls."

"Two, I suppose."

"One space, if big enough. They won't kill each other."

"You'd probably like sawdust too. You think this is a regular horse hotel. You know the last time anybody showed up here with a horse? Wasn't a horse either, but a burro. Some coot who thought he was going mining. Read too many books or saw the Treasure of the Sierra Madre and mistook the direction to head in. They'll find his skeleton some old day, his and the burro's."

"A man that grumbles like that is about to do what you ask," Hester said.

"It ain't no skin off my teeth except I'll have to supervise. I don't know what isn't piled around those buggies. And you'll have to put it all back. That's a lot of supervising for me and I don't supervise

175

for nothing. Fifty dollars. You don't want to spend that much I hope."

"She'll say too much but it's a deal."

Sylvia led them back through kitchen space behind the bar where a woman working blew the hair out of her face and put her fists on her hips until they were by, and found a Carhartt jacket on a peg, and an engineer's cap like Wilfred always wore. His white-blonde hair stuck out over the corduroy collar, much like a girl's, which went oddly with such a pronounced pot belly and ancient maroon bell-bottoms very skinny at the knee, sandals with white socks on. Then out to the alley where they were faced with a tall gambrel-roofed building, sheds under the eaves both sides, timber weathered beyond anything and a two-pitched roof but three-piece cornices and fancy window casings. Clarence surmised there would be some dusty old hay up there in the loft, good for bedding but the animals would probably eat it and get the heaves. He took the accommodations of his team very seriously although this whole deal tickled him. Kept calling it a team which it wasn't.

While he was standing there with his hand on the door, reluctant to open it and face the museum, Sylvia said, "You know, Robert, those three boys are no friends of yours." Clarence ducked his head. Hester right behind, she heard that. He'd forgotten he'd used the outlaw's name, introducing himself, earlier in the afternoon. A impulse, no other reason. He'll hear about it now.

"The one with the Afro has a Chinese wife that owns two businesses and three daughters all either musical geniuses or ballet dancers or both not to mention pretty as dolls. All of them are gone right now to Vancouver for a poker tournament, wife's little hobby. Robby runs her two businesses, good at it, a hair-dresser's and a laundromat. But he doesn't have any time to fuck off, so no sooner than his wife and kids are away south, he's hanging out with the Brit and Donnegan there, being a damn fool."

Much of this went past Clarence but Hester said, "I's working on a deal myself."

He turned around to face Hester. "It wouldn't be a small amount. What made you say they'll be right back?"

"We has a date," Hester said. She held up the clippers from her purse.

He turned around again and leaned way sideways, dragged open the sliding door of the barn. Workbench down the left side, chicken coop on the right but just enough room between to roll back the buckboard and see what's up in the other end. Another two big-wheeled horse-vehicles side by side which Clarence would have loved to have the right horses to go with. Two stalls beyond, partitions cribbed half away, but the same kind of roundwood mangers Millard Frary had, that tip into the stalls from the outside, and hatch-slides to the mow above them. Stalls full of chicken feeders and waterers and cardboard barrels probably full of crockery, by the look. Hester right behind him said, "He called you Robert."

"That's me. Robert Sochia," he whispered.

"Why?" But she clapped her hand to her mouth.

He'd identified with Robert Sochia when he was searching for him, just like he imagined the life of a deer he was following. And now, taking up outlawry after him, it seemed natural. So what?

"I hope you told them I'm Rita Hayworth."

"So." Sylvia said. "Won't hurt these wagons to stand outside a night or two. All this loose stuff can go to one side. It isn't that bad. Do you suppose your nags would mow my lawn in the morning?" He pointed beyond the alley to a patch of green grass, gone to seed in front of a weathered gingerbread house.

Where was the gang, they wondered. They got their room, washed up, had a tavern supper, meat loaf and mashed potatoes and gravy, and went for a walk around the town at Hester's suggestion, so they could talk without anybody hearing.

"I know right where it is," she said.

"If that is what I think it is, good enough. Leave it right there."

"I would like to get it."

"You would, huh."

"Somebody else will get it if we don't."

"What would be the good of us having it?"

"Worth a lot of money. You want to pan for gold. This would be better than gold. Besides."

"Besides what?"

"Being able to decide."

"Turn them in or not?"

"I wouldn't turn them in. Try it! Or not."

"Not me."

"I would. I would just like to try it."

"I would not know what it is or how to try it."

"It's dope!"

"Well, do you know what dope is? I don't. Just means drugs to me. They's different kinds but I don't care what it is. Nor would I try it if I did know how."

"Well I know right where it is. Milepost 912. We could go get it."

"Look good if we got caught doing that, by either them boys or the Mounties. Forget it, sister."

"I wonder what it's in. Some kind of a small box or package. A little tin. We could stick that in the truck somewhere, hide it away and forget about it, take it to Alaska with us. I ain't sayin' what we might do with it. Just have it. And we could just try it, you know, someday. Wouldn't cost us anything."

They heard a crash right then, a dullish sound of breaking glass. Then smaller sounds, over in the town, but no yells or voices or cars moving fast. Some cat tipped over a garbage can. Made them stop and wonder, anyway, and they turned around.

After a minute she said, "You said your world come down around your ears back home. You said you was going to light for the Injun Territories, and live outside the law, just like the song. Seems like it's turning out just that way and you are afraid to do it after all."

"Yes I am."

"Stole a gun, stole them horses. Started drinking whiskey like a fish. And now you won't just see what other people been experiencing."

"No and I am surprised you would. I never give up all my principles." It was the money that interested him.

"It's not unholy murder. We're in another country, nobody knows."

"I'm going straight."

"You can't go straight, Clarence! You're a horse-thief, and so am I!"

"Well, I'll carry that on my conscience since I have to but I'm reforming, as of this minute."

"We'll reform when we get to Alaska."

"Hnnh."

"Right here, this one night, let's just see what happens."

"It's going to stay right where it is for all of me."

"Wait till everybody's asleep."

Not listening, either one of us.

If they were expecting a lot of excitement in the Last Chance Saloon early in the evening they were mistaken. It wasn't until midnight that the Jesse James Gang showed up and then they were like strangers for half an hour until Hester took her new clippers out of her purse and stood beside the Brit at their separate table. He had his remaining hair stuffed under a floppy felt hat, the kind you can fold and put in your pocket. She held up the clippers in front of his face and squeezed them.

"Look what I picked up on the sidewalk."

"There you go," said the veteran. He was continually wiping his hands and looking at them. Something seemed to irritate him, up his sleeves, around his neck.

Depressed, the bunch of them. Clarence didn't like the deal, Hester messing with them three. Heard her say, "Where you been? Court?"

The veteran was talkative. "Robby got a ticket. Five different things. A hundred and ten in a seventy km/h zone, failure to yield half the highway, failure to obey police instructions, possession of a controlled substance seventh."

"Which is what?"

"His weed."

"Our weed," Woolyhead said.

"You forgot open container," the Brit said.

Nobody mentioning what was throwed out the window during pursuit, Clarence noted. Good, maybe it was her imagination. Except he saw it himself.

"How come they didn't lock you up?"

"I'm a respected businessman," Wooly said.

"Yeah, when his wife isn't away."

"What about it, Brit?" Hester waved the nippers at him again.

"No barbering in the bar," said Sylvia.

"Come up to my room."

The Brit perked up at that. "Will your husband allow it?"

Clarence had no say. Didn't own her.

"Robert Sochia there? We en't married. We's just travelin' together."

"Oh man. I don't want to cross him, with that forty-five."

Robby said, "I'd do it, Brit. You got a good shaped skull."

Hester peeled off the hat and felt of the skull. Seemed to take a liking to it, rubbed it all over.

What's my act, Clarence thought. Had another sip of his Daniel's, another sip of his Red Cap.

He'd fired that pistol in the air and sent the fat man trundling. They didn't know it, but they owed him double, he denied seeing anything thrown from the car. Now, too big a man to get nervous over a girl. Had all I want to drink, headed for that bedroom myself.

But when he stood to follow Hester and the Brit up the stairway, the veteran rose from his chair and hardly looking at Clarence at all took two steps up ahead of him, turned around with a bored look on his stubbled face and had the Colt's revolver out of the holster before Clarence saw his hand move. Shoved him backwards so that Clarence tripped and turned around and trying to keep his feet went all the way to the bar before he caught himself up against it. Now, too far away to tackle the man, and Woolyhead had him by the arm, helping him to straighten up and walk back to his table. His and Hester's a minute ago. "What—?"

"I just want you to leave them alone," the veteran said. "Here. You want this?"

"Yes, I do. But I will go right up there and watch this hair-cut."

"No, you won't, that's the point. Set down and have another shot, and I'll put this on the table. My table, not yours. I could just take it but I will give it back to you if you set there. Come on now. Robby will sit with you and explain." Went and sat back down looking at his hands. One side, the other.

"It would take some explaining," Clarence said. "I have helped you fellows."

"We don't need no help."

"That's what you think." But stopped himself. He had come this close to telling them he knew where their drugs was. Hester would not have advised it.

"If those two get it on together, that's what should happen, Robert."

What that means I think I know. That's your philosophy, is it? Robert Sochia wouldn't just sit here like this.

"But maybe it's a hair-cut, is all it is. The Brit he likes your wife."

"She en't my wife."

"So then what's the trouble? She thinks he's cute. He'll be even cuter without those dirty dreadlocks."

"Well, I'll agree to that." Though he never thought anybody looked too cute with a skin-head, either.

The veteran went back to his table, shaking the sleeves of his frayed fatigue jacket. Something fell out of one of them, like a couple grains of rock salt. Hit the floor so you could hear it but Clarence couldn't see it, to tell what it was though he had the tail end of an idea from the sound. Woolyhead brought over his pitcher and glass and sat down with Clarence. Hardly room for the both of their elbows and glasses, and the tabletop had gotten wet somehow. In spite of everything Clarence was sleepy and wished to be up in the room abed.

The deal upstairs? Clarence did figure out this much. These boys need money. Had a deal cooking before, it's out there in the

sage brush by the river, now who knows? Sure could use a new partner. Brit there, he'd be buttering up your sweetie. What Robby did
was drink, that and cry in his beer about his own troubles. His wife,
Subie, what she'd do when she found out. Chinese people so moral,
man. Hnn. Good people but awful strict, man. Yes, well, so I hear.
Her father made money and left the Territories, now Subie thinking
of doing likewise. After this fuck-up she'd do it, man, take the girls
and go south. Her little trip to Vancouver is one thing, man. Moving
to San Francisco is another. That's where her father went. Fine for
her and the little girls, but Wooly, soon's he sets foot in the US,
man, he's a criminal.

Just like me, Clarence thought.

"I fucked up, Robert. Those kids, so nice. Love them so much!"
Threw away fourteen thousand dollars of her money. "I fucked up,
Robert." Clarence wished he would quit using that word, ugly
sound, spoils the fun of the act which should remain nameless. "I
fucked up." Well, that's about what Sylvia thinks you did too, my
boy. Good time to cry about it, after it's done.

He dozed a little bit but before he dozed he thought clearly, "I
have got to drink these two bozos under the table. That's summing
I know and they don't."

He did not see every intervening detail but the place had emp-
tied out, the veteran was asleep and Sylvia was closing up. Vaguely
remember Wooly saying he was going to bed, too good to be true.
Or was it the loo? Sylvia stopped at the table, gave him a shake not
necessary, said he could have another room with a bed, no charge.
"Leave the lovebirds in peace." This was a shocking consideration
but so were many. Gave him the key which Clarence absentmind-
edly pocketed, immediately forgetting what it was for. Clarence took
the pistol off the table and pointed it right at the veteran's head,
which he lifted to stare into the muzzle. "You old fart," he said.

Ought to tie him to his chair and gag him but I take that back, he fought for his country though Clarence didn't know which country it was. Robby was American, a draft dodger. No hard feelings apparently in spite of different points of view. That war, Clarence would been scared to fight. Walk down a path in the jungle, whoops nothing under your feet and in the bottom of the hole, sharp sticks with poison on the points. Anybody wonders, I am going for a walk.

He would need a flashlight, so he unhitched the blue Ford and drove first over to the Ford garage where they had rolled his red truck outside until the new part came. Forgot he didn't have the key to that but before he went to dig it out and found this strange large new key in his pocket with a wooden tag and another one besides, he saw the driver's window, said "For h-h-heaven's sake" as if it was news. Remember the cat tipping over the garbage pail? That was this. Safety glass, breaks in a thousand pieces and stays right there, plastic in between two layers, but they had pushed through it in the center and reached the door handle inside just as he now did, didn't need the key.

Everything turned upside down of course looking for their bankroll and he paused to think well of Hester despite her infidelity. Worth her weight in gold, that cookie, she took the money to the bank for safe keeping. Difference between a smart person and someone like himself, just average: she thinks ahead. See if the flashlight is still in the glove compartment, they would have no use for that, operating in the dark. There it was and the batteries were good. Shut the door quietly, no matter if it isn't double-latched. We'll talk to them perpetrators tomorrow and may be to the Judge. But no, never mind the Judge. Same reason I didn't buy the Colt's, would just slow you down. Don't forget Alaska.

Now he finds himself out on the highway east along the river trying to remember the mile post number, what the bend looked like, what it can have been that Hester remember it by so clearly. Did she say? Mile post. What were the numbers? Everything looked so different, dark night even if star-lit. When was the last cloudy day they had seen? Never so much sun in all his born days. Don't go too far you'll get confused, look the first likely place and that will be it. That's what confused the police, they were coming the wrong direction. He stopped, convinced. Saw the post, the speeding car pass, the object flying out across to the inside of the road, how far? Not far. And what was there to hide it? Nothing. A gravel bank and in the bottom running water to a culvert. If 'twas under water, if 'twas white powder as he thought, gone. The trout in the river doing cartwheels. Unless the tin was tight enough which I doubt.

He shone the light at a low angle, swept it up and down the gravel banks of the ditch. If not here, turn around and shine the other way. The box would stand out, make a long shadow. His impression, long and shallow, maybe four by three, an inch thick. Make sure, then go ahead thirty feet and do the same. Meanwhile, walk the ditch, no matter if your feet get wet. No, first go back thirty feet, to be sure. Assume that it is here, just as you assume the buck is there, because if you don't, you get careless. You make a sound or go by the hiding place, you will never know it. He'll be gone. He lives there and you don't and likewise that box is where it is. If you miss it, too bad. Won't jump up and blow at you. Stamp its foot. If you are not in the right place, that's a different thing. You will also miss it if you think it looks one way or is one size and you are wrong, it's different and you didn't allow for that. Or you mistook the background. Don't make no other assumptions except that it is there.

Felt various things with his foot, carcass of a bird, cardboard six pack half full of cans, and then in the second thirty feet, third if you counted the insurance one he covered backwards, something different. It kept moving ahead of his foot, trying to escape. Once it

185

gets to the culvert, gone. He quit toeing it and let it drag in the grasses and stop, felt for it and brought it up.

Smaller than he thought and plastic not metal so why did it sink? How tight the cover? Well, he had to sit down with the flashlight held in his armpit and open it with two hands, feet still in the crick. Two little latches one side, two hinges the other, hard to tell which is which. A good tackle-box this is, for streamer flies, and not a drop inside, the white powder dry and plenty of it. Nobody said how much but it doesn't take much, enough to send a boy to jail.

Not Robby that broke the window. The vet. That was glass, fell out of his cuff. Did it on the way back from Court. I could take you right back to court tomorrow, boys. But that isn't my game. I think my girl will come back to me if I have this, and that's my revenge. I don't ask for no more. Why did it sink, there's your answer, two lead sinkers. Lucky throw to hit the creek but if it did, nobody that didn't wade the creek would find it.

Fourteen

"OH THAT'S PITIFUL. THAT'S PITIFUL, THAT IS," said the Ford man, Buzz. Ford on his pocket and Ford on his hat. "Gee whiz, golly, that's pitiful. That'll take another two days to get the glass and fix it. That is pitiful. This doesn't happen here. I'm sorry. I can't tell you. Aw. Aw. That's awful."

He was a nervous man walking around in circles complaining. What was the wife's name? Blondie. Dagwood used to make three layer sandwiches, in the funny papers when he saw them, young, not every Sunday. Look like everything worried him. It was nice that he took it so bad since it wasn't his problem, it was Clarence's but Clarence didn't care. It was summer. He wasn't waiting two days for glass. The clutch had come first thing in the morning, by air, how could that be, and would be installed by noon.

The pilot was in the restaurant where they had breakfast. He looked about sixteen years old. Hester said she wanted to take him on her knee. What about the key, Clarence said. He had it around his neck, she said. News to him that he ever had it around his neck but there it was, on a leather string.

They tried the bank but the bank was not open yet.

He said, "How did this get around my neck?" Large blank periods last night including going to bed. Woke up in bed with her in the extra room.

"Who's missing a boot-lace?"

"Colin. Who left it in his pants, hung on a chair?"

187

"Did I do that?"

"You don't know what lowlifes these is, the vet in particular."

"I forgot all about it."

"Don't worry, even if he'd got it, he couldn't get into the safe deposit box. It takes signatures too, and the bank's got another key."

They were not looking at each other. She had something else on her mind and he did too.

"You know you said you was taking a good look at every female that you met on this trip Indian or white, said that in front of my daddy. How do you think that made me feel?"

"Sharks," he said. "I caught a big fish and had it eaten by sharks before I got it home."

"You talked about selling me! How do you think that made me feel?"

"I was planning to buy you back this morning but there you was, in bed."

"You ought not to ever said that."

"That was in another country."

"I wouldn't go, whoever bought me."

"You don't own me neither. Remember that."

"I didn't say I did, but don't I?"

"You don't know 'til you get a offer."

Some men would have to give a performance but the fact was it didn't seem to him that there was a big wall between before and after. The molecules remain the same, what people are made of.

Behind them six different door-locks clicked. When they came out, the envelope stuffed in his shirt, Clarence looked sharp for the Gang. She said, "Guess where they scored the cocaine? The child pilot."

Gang nowhere to be seen and that's where he wanted them. Wanted to be nowhere to be seen himself. His problem, time to kill.

She snapped a brochure open before his face. "I read your mind," she said.

"What?"

"Museum!"

It was a grievous disappointment to Clarence Shampine to learn that horses had nothing to do with the gold rush. He nosed through the old photographs in the Museum of the Klondike, searching for horses. There was one photograph, in color so he knew there was something fake about it, of a plump RCMP in a red jacket prancing around on a black horse with white fetlocks in front of another museum in Dawson City, another good name. They'd already been through Dawson Creek, Mile 0 of the Alcan Highway, but this was the gold rush one, near Klondike Creek. That was further north up the Yukon River where the gold rush really was. Not up, down. Further north, down the river and not on the Alcan Highway which was going west again though he would be glad to go through Dawson City if he could. He pieced together from the maps in the Museum that Whitehorse, then called White Horse, had been an important transportation and supply center on the gold rush or the Stampede as they also called it. Sam McGee was on the Stampede, got cold over the winter of 1887- 88, just north of White Horse on this lake here on the map, Lake LaBarge.

All right, smack on the gold rush route, why not a horse town? At least there was a carriage barn at the saloon, and buggies, but that all come later. How in the world did the gold miners do without horses and even if you could, why would you? The absence of horses stunned him. He was bewildered by it. He needed to be shown the reason.

The photographs of the mines and the camps were familiar to him. Must have seen ones like them somewhere, in school history books or some magazines. Sure enough there was all these men in black hats and vests, smoking pipes, working away with picks and shovels and building sluiceways and wooden boxes with screens and running wheelbarrows up narrow planks from the cobblestone riverbeds. They dug up the riverbottom gravel and carried it up that way, wheelbarrows, then sent it down these trays and troughs, shaking it and rinsing it with water that must come from a spring or a stream, or melting snow up on the mountainside.

Hardly a woman to be seen, understandable, no place for a woman. Do without women all right. But the men themselves was all the beast of burden they had. Goodness, if he had known, he could have been a great help to them. Oh how he would have loved to been there with a good pair of Belgians, his favorite breed. Light ones, didn't have to be heavy. How come these miners to be so ignorant?

He pointed out the tents to Hester, very similar to their own, fifty or a hundred in one photograph, whole towns and villages of them, set every which way, close together with no streets, there in the midst of such scenery as they had been driving through only more snow on the mountains, and ice on the river. All wooden catwalks and cribs and troughs to carry water and not a single animal to carry the load. They had boards. They had plenty of roughsawn lumber, so, stands to reason they had a sawmill to saw them. No horses to draw the logs, the loads? These was not lumberjacks, they was not the men to make lumber with a pit-saw or a adze. So surely there was horses to draw the machinery. But he could not see a team nor a stable nor even a donkey, not in the Klondike. Not in these pictures in the museum, and they was good pictures, put you right in the middle of the gold rush, sharp focus, see these men clear as your neighbors.

Tent villages all around the creek but then some of them built log cabins, long low ones, the logs not very large but certainly long, and straight. And the firewood they piled outside the cabins was roundwood, smallwood, you wouldn't even call that firewood to-home. Here and there what looked like a black man but probably a Indian, and those would have their women of course, standing outside the door when the picture was took. Often looked not unlike his own woman, if he could call this one his own, guess not but still here beside him. Children too. That firewood, you wouldn't bother with limbs that size to-home. Leave such small stuff to rot down and replenish the soil. But you could see on the slopes, all around, what they had to cut firewood from, hnnn. Softwood, no maple, no birch or cherry. Tough work to keep warm with that stuff, and besides, didn't look to him like they had enough put by, no not near enough. They would have to cut wood all winter, burn wet wood. Nn-nnh. And in the very first winter, he could see, so many tents and cabins, smoke from every one, a lot of wood being burnt. Come a second winter it would be gone, wouldn't be any firewood to be had for miles up the long sides of the granite slopes, in every direction. Already looked poor and thin, those forested slopes. Why Sam McGee crawled into the stove.

In place of horses, dogs, my goodness gracious. In one picture, two fellows walking debonair across a low plank bridge over the Klondike stream amid two lines of dogs with saddlebags across their backs, caption said dogs carrying provisions. Looked like about ten pounds of flour each side, or sugar, coffee.

And this was interesting, a dogsled in the snow, ten or twelve dogs out front of it lying down, some standing, and the men, and on the long sled, two bighorn sheep. Somebody's a good shot.

Should say "Look here" to Hester and look at this along with her but they were awkward now, his good resolution to think out loud to her was weakened.

It was interesting and it thrilled him deeply to see these images and he would have loved to be there but no horses. Why would such a thing be? It was the nineteenth century, long before he was born, a time he wished he had been alive, for the simple reason it was the time of the horse and yet here no horses.

And such a awful lot of men! Just masses of them all close together in such a huge space, he hadn't pictured it like this. He read that they were educated men, accountants, lawyers, teachers, up and left home to go halfway around the world and up into the frozen North and dig for gold. A lot of people not qualified for such a adventure. Or just for the idea of it, and most went home poorer than they started. Working men or woodsmen or farmers would have had the sense to bring a horse along.

The clutch took longer than expected. And with the fly-box of cocaine in his breast pocket under his jacket lest somebody delve into the glove-box for his registration or the truck's serial number, he told Dagwood Ford to go ahead and put on four new heavy-duty truck tires. Dagwood was so worried about that truck in Alaska, already taped plastic over the window, pleaded with him at least put on good tires. All right, with the cocaine in his pocket plus the envelope he felt rich enough to say go ahead, put them on, though Hester wondered at him. While waiting, he wanted to go back to the Museum, wasn't done there yet, still mystified. Besides, her contact lenses, she didn't have them yet either. So they had a sundae at the fountain, fed the horses Sylvia's grass, and went back.

And here it was, the explanation, simple when you started at the beginning and didn't just scan every photograph for nags. The people came mostly by ship, from the east or west, around Cape

Horn South America if they had to, or walked across the Isthmus of Panama on foot, they wanted the gold so bad. Forty thousand of them! So many they had a famine up there in Dawson City the first year, and to keep that from happening again the next winter, the Northwest Mounted Police stopped them at the first pass, would not let them into Canada unless they brought a ton of provisions. A ton! And still no horses?

Yes because as he explained to her, here's why, they come by ship, mostly. To Skagway, Alaska, south, here. Showed her on the map on the wall. It was almost due south of where they were now, in Whitehorse. From Skagway, where they got off the ship, they had to climb up over the Chilcoot Pass, which was a glacier! Look! A wall of white ice. Too steep for horses. They looked with wonder on a picture of a thin line of black figures one after the other climbing up this snow ravine a thousand feet to the top, which was just a notch in the white mountain, too steep even for humans to climb. "Those people are climbing in steps carved with a axe in the ice," he told her. No horse, no donkey could go up that angle. Get up there with one load, had to come back down for the rest of their stores, how many times for a ton? Now here's a picture of a huge piece of machinery, kind of a winch, they eventually put at the top, tried to haul that stuff to the top of the glacier with that.

And as if that wasn't enough, look the other way from the pass, look north: a huge long lake carved into the mountains, mountains plunging into the water, bay after bay twenty miles north from the photographer's feet: that lake was the beginning of the Yukon River. "That's what they clum that pass from the coast to get to. A lake and a river, not a road. This is still a hundred miles south of where we are, Whitehorse. So you see the next pictures. Tent cities in a valley by the first bay on that lake, and what are they doing all around them tents every one?

Talking to her without thinking about it now. "They's building boats." Amazing to see, never heard of before, Clarence numb with surprise, they were building boats. A boat beside every tent. Tents and boats crisscrossed all up the mountainsides around that lake. Boats that looked to Clarence very much like log drive bateaux, flat bottomed, slant sided, only usually not pointed at both ends like log drive boats but square at the back. Big boats too, he would guess twenty-five or more feet long, some larger. Made very long oars to propel them, steer them. Sometimes built their houses or pitched their tents right onto them boats. No horses to be seen on these boats, or pulling them. This is not the Er-i-ee Canal. These boats, he began to perceive, would carry the miners downriver, just float-ing, right through White Horse and the lake where Sam McGee warmed up, all the way to Dawson City, eight hundred miles or more. The river is mostly thin, braided water flowing in a winding, low-gradient cobblestone bed at the bottom of wide, wide valleys. Just like the Kiskatinaw, serious rapids only a few short stretches. Or another river going the long low way to the cold ocean of the north, the Peace.

And as the photographs go on to show, they will then turn them up the Klondike River, faster, shallower, they will lift, drag, and pole them up that river to the different creeks where they had found so many nuggets in the gravel. And the lumber for all those cribs and sluices come the same long route, far as he could see, or else they tore apart the boats. Then how did you get home, my boys?

Clarence felt bereft. Boats had taken the place of horses in this old story, and him a man ascared of water, always was. Before he quit repeating all his old sayings, he used to say he couldn't swim no more'n an anvil. No more'n a cookstove. Which was true but if he had been there he would have done no worse than the average man. He would have gone in the boats and done what boatman's work was expected of him, steering with one of those long oars, only knowing that to fall overboard into that cold water would have been his last laugh.

Funny thing to call a Stampede when once they got their boats built and shoved off they just drifted down the shallow river, so far, a thousand miles of low-running river, with a thousand pounds of supplies per person, floated in flat-bottomed boats to the far country.

Well. What do you do after you learnt a thing like that? Very like having your girl taken from you for a night, things won't ever be just the same but it won't do no good to be hard hearted, or disheartened, either one.

Fifteen

EVERY NIGHT NOW, WHEN THEY HAD STOPPED in some over-whelming sunset scene with the mountains rising up to meet the setting sun and the distances throbbing in their breasts, they baited the horses and built their tent and washed and cooked and ate, and sat in their folding chairs wrapped up against the cooling but always comfortable air, and Clarence with his whiskey warm behind his breastbone thought he might reveal to her that he had recovered the tossed cocaine. Separate but confident now, in themselves and in their tires and clutch, they still had not had to climb severely, and they did not attempt long mileage tallies for the day. Three hundred miles was enough. Whitehorse was Mile 918. The first night they were not far past Haines Junction, mile 1016, after the late start. Then more northerly, across the stupendous valley of the White River, low and wide and braided but in flush now with the melting like the Yukon to which it flowed.

The first night he heard her turn over suddenly, whump, over and over, silence between. Second night he thought she shed a tear.

That was too bad but he couldn't help her. There was a difference after all. Still had plenty of skin contact and time heals all.

The third she said, "Know what bothers me? You haven't said anything about my eyes."

"I haven't looked at them." Don't want to soften up too quick. Trying to show you I'm wounded. Besides, contacts: big ceremony every morning now, putting them things in. What's better, all that rinsing and fuss, tiny things you couldn't find if you dropped them, or something that hooks on over your ears?

Still it appeared to him it was time to put the flybox on the cooler, which they used as a small table between their chairs. Sparkling brook, chomping nags, full stomach, JD, the usual paradise. Unfolded the flap of his pocket, of the shirt under the wool jacket, and tossed it like a pack of cigarettes on the cooler. And that stopped her act if that was what it was. Never wanted to be moved by a woman's tears, too hard to believe them if he was supposed to think himself the cause. She leaned right up at some cost to the canvas under her which begun to rip and so she set back.

"You went back there."

"Yes since they knocked me down when I started to march up the stairs, and took my side-iron."

"Well if you was being such a fool I am glad they did."

The thought apparently flustered her. She made as if to fan her breast.

"Luck'ly, you was right. Mile 912."

She gave a cheerful peal of laughter, made Merlin raise his head. "You know I learned what you do with that," she said.

"Did you."

"Yes I did." She looked at him but he showed no curiosity. Neither did he say otherwise. "Best have a plate of glass, like a glass table-top, something smooth. And a straight razor blade like you use on your neck. Sprinkle some on the glass and scrape it into little rows, which they calls lines. Then you use a straw, or make a thin tube of paper, and sniff it up."

"Now that would just be humiliating, to me."

"Well I wasn't too proud to try it."

Clarence did not see any future for them. The future of the two of them just seemed to go off like a will o' the wisp down the White River Valley, should have abducted somebody else or nobody.

"I think you's wonderful for getting this. If them boys knew!" Her laughter again, and Merlin lifted his head.

"I also learned what they think that tin is worth. Do you know what that is worth?"

"Not worth going to jail, that's what it's worth."

"Six thousand dollars Canadian."

The Philosopher lied to her, surprise.

"What did you say?"

"I said, Good for somebody." He reached over, picked it up, took a look inside, sniffed close. Shut it and put it back in his inside shirt pocket.

They were almost in Alaska now, a big deal only Clarence didn't rightly care because he didn't know who he was traveling with. Even the horses didn't make sense any more. The country just shook him and he told himself this was what he came to see. It was enough. You could start out for Alaska and never get there.

"We got to sell that in Canada, CW. We can't cross the border with it. There must be customs at the border, same as anywhere, and they might search us good."

Not talking on that subject.

"I don't know what we could get, not knowing how to deal. Three thousand dollars, say. That'd be nice. We has to stop again and stay in a likely place."

"No place left."

"Or go back, even."

"Hnnh. We could throw it in the river too."

"No-o-o! You went on a spree there in Whitehorse, tires and all. Contact lenses too even if you won't look at my pretty eyes. We

198

needs every bit we has left, to set us up in Alaska. Admit it, why was you so carefree if you didn't intend to cash in this stuff?"

Carefree was I. Bought tires, which we needed. Who was carefree, didn't care what she threw away. He'd done talking about it. Tried to have good thoughts and not to care about spilt milk but there it was, he wasn't that good a man. He was living on the scenery which was really all he needed, said so to himself, filled him to the brim and even above the brim all day every day, and the stars did the same every night while he shut out the thumps and the sighs.

All right, here they were, one step from the border and stopped early only because this matter wasn't settled and in a way the trip would be over or culminated when they did cross the border. Did not know what to expect at the crossing now except a letdown, going back to the United States. It would be different if anything had been what he expected but he still had that image in his mind of that long line of people climbing the ice steps in the snow of Chilcoot Pass. If that was the Klondike Gold Rush and if the Jesse James Gang was dealing cocaine and Alaska was building a pipeline for the oil business and his girl wanted to become a dope addict he didn't think that his effort to become a outlaw had been a success and besides, look at the colors on the map, all downhill from the border. Nothing was as he'd dreamed. Mistake to dream all your life and then go pursue the dream so late when everything has changed.

So, one of the most beautiful camp sites they ever had, no, call it what it is, the most perfect and delicious place for the horses to feed and them to cook out with the tent pitched so the morning sun would tiptoe in between the flaps and wake them up. Most postcard-perfect peaks to the west and most perfect trout stream below, a good place to rinse the pots without getting your boots soaked, everything fine, just fine and a pair of elk there that you would catch with your back-cast if you was fly fishing, no more bothered by people and horses than that. What is more, hot baths up the trail. Somebody had walked that shore line and come to this steaming spring of hot water, gone back to Los Angeles, so it said in carving on the side of the shack, and brought back boards enough to make the shack and a wooden bath tub and a big wooden plug to stamp into the drain. It was filling up right now with water almost too hot to set in but you could temper it with potfuls from a spring stream right beside it. Hester and he were going to bathe. He was having an early drink and so was she and nobody had mentioned anything for some time, so maybe they would be on an even keel again by the time they did cross the border. Tonight might tell.

Trouble was, that little box on the cooler. He set it there again in this last camp site and there it was. What are you going to do about that, sister? Or what am I? He didn't know about either one of them.

Come a very big racket up on the road, up behind them. Long, loud racket, another one of them strings of motorcycles, just battering the air with concussions the way they do. After he had heard it for about thirty seconds continuous he looked up and saw the last few helmeted black-leathered riders, one of them looking down over the bank at their encampment and then putting up his hand, making it go around in a circle over his head. And then up the road a way the battering quieted, they'd maybe slowed down, or what they call the Doppler effect, just lower because now they was going away, not coming.

Their spread there, they had reached by turning off the road up ahead and coming back down a gravel dugway made as if just for them to use, petering out in a level circle where the truck and trailer sat, and all they'd had to do was lug the tent and poles down to a bit of nearly level shelf next to a smaller stream running into the river, what river Clarence didn't know, running north here pretty as a pic-

200

ture, mountains rising right up from a band of stony pasture along the shore.

"Oh my," Hester said. One of them motorcycles coming right down the gravel way toward them. No, not one, a string of them maybe the whole string, as ugly a looking set of hombres as you ever hope to see.

Clarence patted his Colt's. Mental note not get so close to anybody that they could draw your own gun before you could cross your hand over to it.

"Good lord how many is they?"

They kept coming, one after another, pulled up to a stop all around the rig, right to the edge of the level gravel just above their tent, cookfire, chairs, cooler. Clarence went to put the little flybox in the breast pocket of the shirt under the checked wool hunting jacket, which had a second layer of wool over the shoulders. Woolrich, from L. and L. Bean. Wouldn't see the bulge under that. But where was it? She'd already moved it.

He stood up and now could see beyond the front rank of the bikes, husky men and husky women standing off their machines and pushing their helmets off their heads. Women in leather pants tight as skin. He well remembered wearing a helmet himself when on the snowmobile behind that young fellow, searching for Robert Sochia's tracks everywhere in the North Woods except where they were likely to find them. How shut-in he had felt. Anybody that could stand to drive in the Yukon Territory with one of them things on their heads—Well, not all of them did, there was some that had their helmets strapped to their machines, brown faces, dark glasses, hair pulled back in pony-tails. He did not feel threatened when one of them came down the scree, stomping the heels of his black leather boots into the stones to get a grip. Genial grin, big hand, red bandana wrapped around a brown bald head, pilot's sunglasses which he pushed up over the bandana to show his kindly brown eyes. Rest of them stayed up there talking amongst themselves, laughing, getting out their smokes. Clarence surprised himself by saying, "Just the man I want to see." Tongue figured things out faster than the brain.

He did not immediately know what he would answer if the fellow said, "Oh, why's that?" but he had the front end of an idea that hadn't taken shape. Maybe didn't say it aloud. While tugging at his hand the fellow looked around at the scene, the horses, the two elk, Hester sunning in her folding canvas chair under Clarence's felt hat, with a glass in her hand. Took it in, shook his head, then got right to business. "Back a ways a fellow told me about somebody of your description." He gestured with his round bald head at the rig. "Horses, lady, red Ford pickup."

Who was that, I wonder. Didn't say that aloud either, nothing against the fellow yet.

"Colt Forty-Five on your hip. You could be the very party."

"Yes and if I am so what?" Not sure he heard himself even then.

"Nobody to mess with, I hear." He mimed somebody firing in the air.

Flattery will get you nowhere but does no harm either.

"Said you might..." Bigger grin, if possible "...might have picked up something that this fellow back in Whitehorse, he lost." The grin stayed bright, the man waited. Looked like he could have said more if needed.

Clarence took in the bunch up behind him. Passengers included, the riders numbered well over thirty, thirty-five or more. Two to a bike, many of them. Seen several packs of motorcycle riders on the trip, this the biggest. Hell's Angels, for aught he knew. They would make better friends than enemies.

"Something you might be willing to sell. So the fellow thought. If, he said, your lady wouldn't object. Said he didn't know about that."

Well, gracious, he hadn't agreed he found anything yet. Been going to say, What made anybody think—? But among many changes lately here he was thinking his words before he spoke them. A minute ago the other way around.

"Get rid of it is more like it."

"We been watching for you. Thought we might catch up. Saw your rig down here and we had a confab up the road there. We took a vote."

Whether to take over the camp and hold a debauchery on his woman, I suspect. I know what her vote would be. Except they had a nice bunch of blondes of their own. Heard of Hell's Angels taking over a whole town up in New Hampshire. Done it year after year.

He had a plan for the night himself, a hot tub for two, don't tell no one.

"We voted that we would tax ourselves a hundred a bike. That would make seventeen hundred. American. If you have what we're talking about."

Clarence looked sideways. The elk was watching.

"Not as many bikes as I thought."

"Maybe I counted wrong."

"Looked more like thirty to me."

"That would be high. The number is not exact. Twenty-two."

"You ain't goin' through customs."

"Oh sure we are. That's no problem."

"How so?"

"We got a reputation we don't deserve. It gets us free passes all over."

"The fellow back a ways you mentioned. What makes him think—"

"Oh, he's over it. Going to his daughters' softball games with his wife, they just flew home from somewhere. He's glad you found it, in fact. Better than somebody else, if you know what I mean."

"You're not in no cahoots with him. Or them. The three of them."

"Oh, shit no. We was just asking around, looking for a party. We're a fun-lovin' bunch. Doctors, a couple of dentists, otherwise same sort of riffraff, Viet Nam vets, draft dodgers, a bunch of old softies really. Wives and friends. All love the open road and two wheels. We don't deal. We use a little, once in a blue moon. Twice if lucky. You're a quite a big piece of luck, to us."

He went back up the bank. Clarence saw him, the top half of him, going among the people and their steeds, collecting. Clarence kept his eyes off of Hester but looked for the stuff on the cooler, not there, and even with the back of her head to him he could see she had her hand over her mouth. Fellow came back folding a handful of bills. Said, "We lost one somewheres. Loose-knit. Twenty-four?" He gave it an upward tilt, a question.

It was nothing to Clarence, to a poor man what's a hundred dollars one way or the other. He could enter a lot of rodeo events with this.

"Glad if some'n can enjoy it," Clarence said. "Me I'm too old."

"Your girl," the fellow said. "She might be sorry to see it go."

"Might be so but she don't wear the pants. One other thing I should have said before we done the deal."

"I could probably do it."

"Don't tell no one Indian or white. Mounted Police or outlaw. Last people to tell, anybody in this business that they call dealing. This ain't dealing. If you call this dealing take your money back and

I will pour the stuff in the stream. This is unloading something does-n't fit my life style. Or hers after a brief try."

"Right. Right."

Clarence was finished but the fellow was waiting and then Clarence realized he hadn't given him the box. Already forgot it was-n't there on the cooler. Went down to the chairs and took his hat off her head and caught it slipping off the back.

Little thing. Had not looked closely at it since he opened it. "It's a good fly box that keeps out water," he said. He took a look up at the road, each way, what he could see of it. "No sightseers?" He handed it over. Fellow kind of saluted with it, brought it up to his brow and give it a little shake and then a peek inside.

"Fourteen grams, I was told."

Clarence said, "You know more'n I do. I am grateful that you come along. If you ever come across my camp-site again, you are welcome, you and your friends. If I have my gas cooker working, cook us all some steaks or salmon. I would open a new bottle and throw away the cap."

They shook hands. The riders fired up their machines, blasted the air, one and then another and then all, turning one-eighty through themselves and passing by close to the edge of the bank to wave. After he saw the last of them make dust up the dugway, he turned to face what he had just bought himself for all this cabbage.

Did not truly know what it might be.

It was Hester, mad, reaching out to take him by the hand. But then she dropped her hand and just asked him, "You want to come take a nice hot bath with me?"

Uh, well, yes.

"First I wants to make a speech. Sex."

Another word not meant to be spoke aloud.

"Sex is natural, it's necessary, I likes it fine, but it is a form of temporary insanity. It is worse than dope for altering your consciousness. I do not wish to be judged by what I does under the influence. Less said about past and future excesses, the better."

At the Welcome to Alaska sign, at a lookout over the Coast Range, who should they meet but the sweet young thing with two children and the VW bus all painted up ridiculous but funny and amusing that they had run into before but a long time ago, back in endless Ontario, maybe somewhere else, without so much as speaking, hardly, just a pleasant nod in a diner. She seemed to think they was relatives for this reason and come right to him and give him a hug and a kiss. "Excuse my soup-strainer," he said, blushing.

"You've been letting it grow." She said hello to Hester, and they all exchanged names, suddenly less shy than they had been in roadside diners back on the plains. One kid on her hip and the other hanging onto her long skirt, noses none too clean. No man in view but now a boy come out behind the bus, zipping his fly, big smile saying what a relief. Clarence thought he might be inheriting a family without volunteering. Felt to tell her the story about how volunteering went in the log drives, olden days. Call for volunteers: You, you, and you, get your pike-poles and get out on that log-jam. No insurance no social security. But he didn't. Didn't have time.

"And you've got additions!" she said. "We saw, passed you with your trailer once. Never thought we'd see you again. There they are, Luke! How beautiful! See the pretty horses, Julie?"

Hester said "That's Merlin. And that's Buck."

"Aren't they big? I'm so happy to see you, after this long way! We've made it! Aren't you amazed?"

She put down the baby and went to her van for her camera and took pictures of them all with the sign and the skins and the view behind them. Then she got the baby up on her hip again and gave it her breast to nurse while one-handedly digging in the van for more lunch things for the other children.

While that was going on, Clarence moved to Hester's side. Touched her. From where they were, the foreground was a long steep descent of stick-timber and scree with no trails or roads in sight, deep eroded canyon at the bottom, glimpses of a turquoise stream a thousand feet down and away. Said, "I used to picture us breaking down or running out of gas on the Continental Divide here. If that is what this is. Seems like it. Divide between the Arctic Ocean and the Pacific Ocean, may be. Close to it. Well, I didn't hardly think we would ever make it all the way to Alaska without no breakdown. One reason I wanted some horses. Where you can't trust a machine, you want to have summing else."

Took a deep breath.

"So I pictured us stuck here, nothing else to do but leave the truck and go down into Alaska on foot and horseback. Me on foot leading the pack animal and you on the nag. Six ca'ridges to the Colt's in case of bears."

"Oh my land, bears. I never would have come with you."

"Bears everywhere in Alaska. If not grizzly bears, polar bears. We will see a good many before we hit Fairbanks if we ever get that far. If a bear stood up anywhere near us on our way, Merlin will bolt. You think your old King used to gallop to the barn. You better hope you learnt to hang on. Going right through the timber too. But nothing's the way you imagine it. Knock wood, truck still running. Nags enjoying the trip on rubber wheels, just like us."

"Say my name."

"What?"

"Say it!"

"You say it Hester or Hes-ther?"

"Says it Hester, spells it Hes-ther."

"Hesther. Don't seem right. I'll spell it that way in my mind from now on. Might get used to it."

"Well do. It don't matter how you spells it. Say it and I'll forget you sold the dope. I liked that stuff."

"Hesther."

"Every once in a while, throw that in amongst your Cookies and Sisters. I thought you was a man of principle."

"I was waiting for you to either sniff up another whatever you call it or pour the stuff out on the ground. Whichever road you wanted to go down, that would be the turning point. Well, got sick of waiting. Opportunity knocked on my door. Then, I would of give it to them but the money tempted me. And I guess they thought it was a good deal so why argue?"

"Anyways," she said, "that was in another country."

"That's right. Ahead, might be no place for us. Might be just like the gold rush. I don't know what I would have done. All you can say is, this deal, you and me, so far still on." To himself, I wouldn't say so good exactly but good enough.

They looked over to the girl and her children and their VW bus. The girl took the baby off her nipple and put it in its seat in the open side door and didn't cover herself up. Contrary, she took off her shirt over her head and shook it out. Shook out her hair and held her breasts up to the view or else the sun, then gave them too a shake and a shiver. Putting her shirt back on she came back to them saying, "It's a sign, us both being here at the same moment! Shall we go along together for a while? You never know what may happen!" Got between them, turned them toward Alaska, and, hugging them both around the waist, led them in a little celebratory dance. Clarence couldn't get the kick, but he shuffled from foot to foot in time.

Sixteen

THE BORDER BUT NO CUSTOMS. Too far from anywhere, Customs couldn't be bothered. That was strange because back home there was Customs on every little dirt road that crossed into Quebec, even if no traffic, not that Clarence ever went there. Border there shaved bare just like here, a disgusting sight like somebody took the clippers to the mountains. Straight line north and south over hill and dale far as the eye could see, like a power line with no power.

Got a late start with so many people in camp and now a early stop for lunch since here was a lookout with a picnic table overlooking this huge river valley, Tanana, never heard of it, goes away forever northwest, very wide, mountains now farther off not nearer. No need to let the horses out, they are bloated as it is and nothing but stones here.

As I walked out one morning fair
For to view the fields and take the air
Yes I thought I heard my true love say
Oh to turn and come this way.

The boy said, "When we saw you first, you didn't have a pistol."

When you saw me first! A long time ago. "I call it a pistol some-times but it isn't a pistol. It is a revolver."

"Can I see it?"

He laid the revolver on the picnic table. The kid sat on his hands and hung his face over it, looking close. He read off the words rolled into the barrel. "Colt Single Action Army 45."

"Long barrel version. That gun won the West. Some called it the Peacemaker."

"No, the Winchester Model 1873 rifle won the west."

"Well I did not know that."

"Do you have one of those?"

"No I don't. I would like a Model 94, lever action. I do have a Savage 30-30 but that is not as accurate at long range, it's a brush-gun, so-called, because I was a guide, might have to shoot quick, in cover. But I'll keep my eye open for a Winchester."

"Then you'd be completely equipped."

"What do you mean?"

"Well... You know."

"No I don't."

"Well, you didn't have the pistol. I mean the revolver, when you started."

"What do you know about it?"

"We saw you!"

"When was that?"

"Way back in Ontario. The middle of Ontario."

"I don't recall seeing you."

"Of course not. You had your eyes on Alaska. That's what we guessed. We said you didn't see anything."

"So happens I did have a Colt's revolver, just like this, b'fore I left home. I lost it. That's another story. I'll tell it to you sometime, may be."

"But you lost it?"

"Yes and kept the holdster, you see. Wore it too, let anybody think the revolver might be close to hand, watch out."

"How did you lose the old one?"

"Wasn't old, it was brand new. Shot it once in a gun-battle then lent it to a fellow and what'd he do, kilt somebody with it. My fingerprints all over it."

"Who did he kill?"

"Well. I didn't want to tell you. Himself."

"You gave it to him so he could kill himself with it?"

"N-n-n-no. I just had it in my hand. Wanted him to get out the way."

"Why?"

"Had a job to do."

"What?"

"You ask too many questions."

"What?"

"Well, bury something. Rather, put it in a glass jar and push it down in a mud spring. Couldn't bury it the usual way, why, b'cause the ground's frozen solid."

"What's a mud spring?"

"Kind of like quick sand, mud made by a underground spring, very cold water, good place to keep your spaghetti sauce or your canned venison."

"What were you burying, spaghetti sauce?" This made the kid burst out laughing again. Call it giggling. Pulled on his arm and forgot to feed him. Had been putting a piece of celery with peanut butter on it in Clarence's mouth every so often.

"No. Poured the spaghetti sauce out of the jar so's to put the other thing in."

"What was the other thing?"

"Well."

"What? Come on, come on!"

"Not very funny, what it was." He looked over to the mother, who caught the look and smiled at him. She seemed to be saying, "Well, tell him! You started. He's not a boy to be protected."

"Come on, Uncle Clarence!"

Uncle am I?

"Come on. It's okay. I know what it is. What did you bury?"

"I didn't bury it, b'cause the other fellow did. Swiped my revolver out of my hand whilst I stood there flat-footed and took over my job. It was in the pail I carried it in. Well, he poured it out of the pail into the jar. His little baby boy that was born too early. Into the jar. . . into the jar and rolled up his sleeve....Put it down far as his shoulder, very white. Then went up in the trees, other side of the brook near-by."

"You said he killed somebody."

"Yes, and if it had been me, I didn't care. I went down the brook expecting it, hit in the back before I heard the shot. Might very fairly have blamed me, see, for I took his girl-friend from his hideaway and brought her out of the woods, over the lake, shortest way but still very long and the snow on top of the ice, breaking sometimes, very hard going, too hard for her. I did not know she was about to have a baby. Took her to the home place, put her to bed, and that's where Leo Weller found me. He took care of her. I melted snow and heated water for him. Then, when 'twas over, sun-up, most beautiful morning of the year, every leaf and twig encased in ice, my job to say good-bye to the baby...Well, I did hear the shot, and I fell in the brook, but come to find out he missed me."

"No, he shot himself! He was sad!" He didn't laugh now. "He was very sad."

Clarence was very sad too but for some reason he had told the story he did not think he would ever tell.

"You're on the run, aren't you?"

"Well, no, not no more. I think I have escaped pretty well."

"And you got another revolver!"

"That, I lifted. Gathering dust on a store, just like the first one. Nobody knows what them things are any more."

"What about the horses? And the trailer? You didn't have them when you started, either. You picked them up along the way."

"That's what I was going to say."

"I was pretty excited when we saw your truck going along with that trailer and those tails blowing out the back. Boy! I said to Mom, 'You know what, Ma? They stole that trailer and those horses.'"

"You got a good imagination. Think I stole that outfit? What makes you think that?"

"Hunch!"

"How do you think anybody could steal a trailer full of nags and get away with it."

"Show me your registration. Mom says it would be easy to catch anybody that did that. Said you'd better have the right registration on that trailer."

"Well now you're making me nervous."

"You better be!" the kid was gleeful, looked up at Clarence with his face beaming. Clarence could see all his teeth, good ones, tiny but white and even except for eye-teeth like a puppy's, sharp. Prettiest boy he'd ever seen.

"Maybe it was Hesther's idea!" Laughing right in Clarence's face and beaming. The child couldn't sit still, he was so happy. "What're you going to steal next? Steal a Winchester Model 94!"

Clarence thought, might steal you, you little rascal. Have to keep you in the gang lest you sing to the sheriff. Come that near saying so. And your mother. Would that be all I need?

"Pretty soon you'll be a guru!" and still laughing at him. Now Clarence wasn't sure he wasn't being made fun of. If he was it was a mixture of mischief and admiration. Love, he almost said. My goodness.

The mother brought the barbecue, leftover, cold, set it in front of them. The new crew eats very different.

"I'll feed you," said the little boy. "Open!" Laughing, he held a rib for Clarence to suck and gnaw. Which, blushing, eyes closed, Clarence did.

Clarence said, when he had a chance, "Next thing, you'll be telling me where I got all my money."

"Do you have a lot of money?"

"Don't know. Ask her. Had a lot one time, before she took over."

"Sure, you robbed a bank!" More laughter, and now the kid jumped around to sit beside him and hugged his arm with one hand, leaning against him, squirming, feeding him another rib with the other.

Customs, halfway to the first town, was a mere roof on legs, in the middle of nowhere. Border Camp, they called it, a lonely young officer under a roof on a barren hillside. Clarence kept his mouth shut, just answered questions, since it was apparently written all over him that he was a horse thief and bank robber, plus drug dealer and possible bigamist if thoughts was deeds. Fellow warned him a plastic window might not be legal in the USA but he'd leave that to the state police and waved them on preferring to talk to the girl in the Microbus. Clarence had already put his elbow through the window and now tore off the rest while waiting.

Pippa had lived in Canada and had a Canadian license plate but turned out she was an American citizen, all you need to be and the kids get in free. Alaska was a state, not a territory, news to him, but America either way.

"Whew!" he said. Now they felt they had entered the homeland, left Canada behind.

"You people!" Hesther said. "That's the last of oot and aboot."

Now here they were in Tok, 93 miles from the border, all downhill, Clarence feeling funny having passed the only road going north. Had an admirer now, a little devil he didn't want to disappoint. The fellow pumping gas says with a nod at the trailer, "You got in there what I think you got?"

"Well...that depends."

"Don't see horses much in Tok. In Alaska for that matter."

"Did I say I had horses in there?"

"Fellow about sixty miles down the river plows his garden with sled dogs. I don't know how good they are."

"Hnnh." One thing that Clarence had been wondering about was whether he could plow a garden with either of these two nags in the trailer, but he didn't say so. The girls had been talking what they could do in Alaska and Pippa suggested open a restaurant for the pipeline workers, and Clarence was to be the gardener. Another reason he was feeling funny.

"Then there's the fellow who plows his garden with a moose."

Thinks I'll believe anything. But Clarence felt right at home with the character, very familiar, seen him somewhere else.

"Thing about horses, among other things, what do you feed them in winter? Dogs, now, they eat dried salmon. It's easy to feed dogs. If your horses'll eat salmon, you're good."

He switched hands on the nozzle and turned away from Clarence. "No, don't see many horses in Alaska. Want to hear a story about horses in Alaska?"

He said, "The last story I heard about horses in this country was, geez, I think eighteen-ninety or so. They had a lot of miners up north of here at that time, the Franklin strike, thousands of miners suddenly come into that country, no law at all, sent the Army to keep order. Well, the Army thought they ought to have a winter mail run. So they give a contract to a fellow over at the coast, two thousand miles away, Seward. And he started off in January with eleven horses, two bags of mail. Walked into Eagle three months later, on foot, with just the mailbags. Had three letters. No horses left."

Switched hands again. Slowest pump in the world. "What I would worry about, if 'twas me, more than feed, is bears. Wolves and bears. So," he said, "where are you headed?"

"Well, I don't know. Just got to Alaska. Fairbanks, for a start."

"Fairbanks."

He said that word, Fairbanks, with a certain disgust Clarence could see right through his back. He finished up his pumping and hung up the nozzle.

"Now why would you do that, after coming all the way from - " looked at the license plate on the front of the truck - "New York?"

"Northern New York, almost to Canada."

"You aren't, are you?"

"What?"

"Going on down to Fairbanks."

"Well-l-l, the girls think we are."

"You think otherwise."

"Do I dare to? I'm outnumbered." So proud of his two women he could afford to pretend.

That's just what they had been talking about ever since they crossed the border, he and Hesther. Fairbanks, sure, that's where they had been heading ever since they started. It was smack on the Alaska Highway, where else would we be going? But Clarence did not like going downhill. They had been going downhill down this wide flat river valley ever since the border. First he thought it was just a long slope downward, in between long slopes upward, as usual. Give the engine a rest a little while. Well, too easy on the engine, the engine had been sounding like a sewing machine with nothing to do but hum for far too long. Made him nervous until he mentioned it and she, the map-reader, said "Well of course it's downhill, we's going toward the west more now, toward the coast, toward civilization. We's crossed the Rockies."

That was the wrong word to use on the same trip with him, civilization. Thought he had made himself plain many a long mile ago, leaving civilization behind.

The man leaned on the front of the truck. "Let's see your map," he said.

When he got done pointing out the yellow areas all around the circle that was labeled Fairbanks they knew it was overpopulated, expensive, full of trailers on tiny lots, one big slum, that the rivers were fished out and there wasn't any game, and the place was full of oil-company roughnecks, in a word, Texans. He said Texans with a worse snarl than he said Fairbanks.

"All right," Clarence said, "where do you think we should go?"

"Right back here to the Taylor Highway, and north."

North, good word, but that a highway? Clarence followed the man's finger, a thin wiggly line that went up one creek after another, went over almost back into Canada, turned north and west following one gully after another and disappeared in the direction of the Arctic

Circle. One town along the way, called Chicken, no yellow around that, probably nothing there.

No, it didn't disappear, it run into another big river. Very big, running north-west.

"The Yukon," Clarence said, almost breathless.

"No, no, no," said Hesther.

The man said. "That's what you want. You can be independent, up there. Your meat is free, your fish is free, land is free."

"Land is free?"

"Absolutely. Go anywhere you want, pitch your tent, build your cabin. One of these rivers here, coming into the Yukon: one man to a river, take your pick. No boundaries, no taxes, nobody bothering you. Grow all your vegetables."

"Grow vegetables?"

"Oh yes, abundantly. Short season but long hot days, you'd be amazed. For the little bit of money you need, trap a few foxes, lynx, a wolf. Pan a little gold."

"Oh lordy, wolves," Hesther said, almost in tears but she put her hand over her mouth.

"There's the life, if you've got what it takes."

"Yay!" said Lucas.

"Come on into the store," he said, noting the numbers on the pump. "We'll put it all on the one bill."

Clarence was reminded of the Mounties stopping people at the top of Chilcoot Pass and sending them back down for a ton of provisions per person. "You need a year's supplies, two would be better, all but your meat. That, you'll have to shoot. You just let me make a pile and we'll move right along. I have done this before but I have got to multiply for this outfit. Winter feed for the horses, I don't know. We'll leave that for the fall and see if we can get you some hay sent up by airplane. You can get anything you want up there but it's nineteen cents a pound to fly it. If this is a shock, Missus, come over by the woodstove and set down till it passes."

Is your name Arquit by any chance? The same twinkle behind the wire-rim glasses, teasing, making fun of a fellow, only you couldn't be sure and so far Clarence had to be grateful for him taking charge. And Hesther looking at him with her mouth open like the cat got her tongue but she did go set down. Pippa put her hand through his elbow and Lucas on the other side looking up at him ready to giggle. Squirming, pulling on his belt.

"We come to the right place," Clarence said privately.

"You get your wheat in the berry, so you need a mortar and pestle. You need a gold pan. Tell me if you already got anything I mention. Sugar. Beans. Coffee."

The stovepipe went up and elbowed into the gable and there on the wall, a museum of every kind of ancient animal trap ever known to man, up to an unthinkable size, a dinosaur trap, elephant trap. "Traps. Don't confuse me, I'll get to your traps. Next I was thinking of your meat. What's your weapon?"

"What? Rifle?" He wasn't proud of this. "Savage lever-action."

"Oh for Christ's sake. What shell?"

"Thirty-thirty."

"No doubt. Well, it'll kill a moose, if one wanders into your yard. Which they do. It's like shooting your neighbor's cow. You'll need two a year, or three. Two boxes? Five? Take enough, you'll need to scare away the wolves. And what's that?"

"This, sir, is a Colt's revolver."

"Size of the ball?"

"Why, I don't know." He drew, clumsily, across his body, and studied the lettering on the barrel. Luke said, "Yes you do! Forty-five." Oh of course, just couldn't think.

"That your bear-gun, is it?"

219

"Well ... "

"Is that it? You better have something for the women back in camp, while you two are out on the trail."

"Winchester Model Ninety-four!" cried Lucas, gleeful. Duke Arquit the Second tousled his hair, on his way to get the closest thing, Model 70 Super Grade, itself 700 dollars. Hesther still had her mouth open, stuck that way apparently. Pippa in an overstuffed chair, nursing her baby as usual with a motherly smile on her face.

Seventeen

IN ALL MY LIFE I NEVER SET FOOT IN A PLACE LIKE THIS. Left on my own here I'd never last a year. I have lived a long time in the woods but I never set foot in a place like this. This is not even the same as anything I ever knew only more so. We are on a road but we are beyond roads, we are in a country where a road don't amount to anything. It might as well not be here except it runs us further and further into this area beyond anything. What I know don't apply here. I will have to become somebody else.

If I said that aloud I didn't mean to. Two of us fearing this country would be too many. But is it fear? If you were afraid why would you be so glad to feel it?

He wasn't worried about Pippa in the other vehicle behind. That boy of hers was a devil and she was the devil behind the boy. She stayed far enough behind that the dust blew away and she could see the road, which she better watch close, made out of rocks the size of grapefruit. She didn't have heavy duty tires the way he did, thanks to Dagwood Bumstead. Them that said he should have a heavier truck, four wheel drive, V8? They were right but you do with what you've got.

Many things not known about Pippa such as what is she packing for money? Clarence did not care, what would she do with it here? Taking her on with no restrictions. Pippa, another reason no one was going to hear him say I do not know how we are going to make it. I looked to Duke Arquit the Second as if I was made out of the right stuff, well maybe I am. I like the crew with me and I never see such a country to make you want to handle it.

Children, too small. A lot riding on him. Cope with what come, the best I can.

Model 70 Super Grade, not a Model 94 only better. It was all the man had in the store but that's because it's what you want where you're going. Scope, and accurate a long way off. Wolves, hnn.

He just said, "Whew!" and that set her off.

"My land it is huge. It is silent even with the truck so noisy. You can just feel the silence. I don't know, Clarence. I don't know."

Washouts more worrisome to him. They were silent he supposed. His appeared to be the first vehicle to go up the Taylor Highway in 1972 if that was the year. Beat the repair crews anyway. When the snow melted fast, which it was still doing, gray mountains looked like lace, with snow in every pocket, these culverts were not always big enough, the water cut a half-circle out of the road and barely enough left to pass, the trailer wider than the truck. If you slipped, down the mountainside, hell for leather, you could imagine it, so steep. Down in the bottom there, the bigger river still full of ice. They were following a fairly big river basically but had to follow way up every tributary and then back down the other side to the bigger river again in order to keep to a reasonable gradient. Many miles between points not very far apart. Burning gas all the way but Duke II thought of everything, jerry cans in the bed of the truck which was awful full and very heavy all by itself say nothing about the horses and the trailer.

A long way down, sometimes not so long, the road following the best it could. Huge eroded country not very green because so far north. You get to a kind of country where the frost stays in the ground all year and that changes the vegetation. It is hard for the trees. They are like dwarfs and down in the valleys you can see, they do better, some of the islands in the streams are dark green with spruce and pale green leaves were coming out in the poplars. Or, looked like poplars to him, or some relation of theirs.

They stopped where water was running in a culvert and waited for Pippa to come up. Just past a derelict vehicle that stopped here long ago and never left. Somebody shot at it from long range, hit it all over, now covered in brown dust. A pickup truck, red like his under that coat of mud. Down in the bottom the ice was solid white in the middle of the river and it looked as if it was arched across the valley from side to side, because blue water ran in a stream down each side on top of the white ice, between the river ice and the shore ice. In the sunlight up here it was hot, the middle of the day.

Pippa brought out binoculars and Clarence thought good for you young lady. What else do you have in that vehicle that will come in handy? Fears of this wilderness went away when you could see along up the valley a long way and see traces of a place where somebody dug a ditch, built some sort of contraption, for mining gold he supposed. Long ago but it gave you an idea you could survive in this territory. Of course. Nothing to fear. They had everything necessary for a long long time and it was early spring here, perfect timing.

Duke Arquit the Second had said there was a gold boom going on right now. Government did something, let gold float on the market. Gold floating, well. And it went up to $200 an ounce for a while, then back down a little but still high, $150 an ounce and going back up. The old timers had not found all the gold, not by a long shot, how could they?

Gold fever was like malaria, he said. An awful disease. Very few miners got rich but a lot of them got sick with the fever and never shook it. Found just enough to keep going. Lived a dream. "That ain't all bad," he said. "The people that got rich is people like me, that supply the miners, ha ha." Ha ha, Clarence thought. But he left him most of what was left in the envelope, an awful lot of U.S. dollars cash. Never mind, not counting. Clarence hefted that envelope once in a while, felt its thickness. He did not begrudge the thinning. Was proud of that money. What went out went for a good cause. The new money, hidden elsewhere, didn't like the way he acquired it, might not ever use it. Would have bought Hesther back with it if he had to but that was different.

Wheat berries, canned bacon, sugar, coffee for two years! Everything but meat. "You'll eat moose three meals a day!" Duke the Second inspected his tools, insisted on selling him a Swede saw, of the bigger size. What is a Swede saw? Well it is nothing but a bow saw. Sold him fishing tackle stronger than Clarence was used to, why, bigger fish. He admired their mukluks for most of the year including the winter if you put in these felts. But no good in water. For that he was satisfied with Clarence's and Pippa's Bean boots, sold Hesther a pair and another for Lucas. He said the temperatures would get down to 70 degrees below zero but it wasn't as bad as you think. The winter air was so dry, he said. Snow light, never very deep. Just cold, ha ha. Get used to it, you won't mind it. Clothes will be rags, you'll be half naked, still won't mind the cold.

Clarence thought, Ha-ha-how about a cabin with a nice warm stove? But winter was far from his mind because Luke had been drawing a picture, over by the stove, with his crayons, entertaining his little sister. He could make a thing look better than real, that boy. And there on the paper was Merlin, black-maned, red-hide Merlin, with Clarence up on his back, unmistakable in the tall black hat! Am I going to learn to ride? And Buck with his panniers. The new Winchester in a scabbard. There we are, high on a mountain trail with a view of white-capped mountains far in the distance. What's this, brochure for my new business?

224

"Mountain man!" Luke cried. "Guide! Scout!"

Duke looked the picture over and went looking for a scabbard. "Might have one here somewhere left over from the Pony Express."

After a day of slow progress up the Taylor Highway Clarence was feeling more at home. Hesther had gathered folders and brochures about the interior, about Eagle, a little town on the Yukon, at the store in Tok and was now quoting, "'Sportsman's Paradise,' 'abundance of fish and game,'" while Clarence had been noting the stunted sorry trees and what looked like, certainly must have been, a burn, and was imagining the fire, the holocaust it must have been which swept over the road. In this territory you wouldn't talk of tens of thousands of acres, like Rockefellers to-home. Here it would be millions except nobody owned it, it was free, empty. "'Famous Fortymile Caribou Herd!' Right where we're going! A hundred fifty thousand caribou! They's like reindeer, en't they? But it says they've disappeared, haven't been seen lately. Well, so what? I's getting' gold fever!" she exclaimed. "Little care I for the birdsong of spring. Let's go! Let's stake our claim ere the best be gone! We needs a dog."

He didn't know if she was pretending to be fearless or forgetting. She showed him a photo of a fellow in a floppy hat tilting a wide-rimmed pan, water sparkling, big shepherd lying on a pile of gravel.

After a night camped in a gravel-pit turnout, near a running culvert where they could fill their water-jugs, a restful evening in which Lucas fed him his stew, mouthful by mouthful, and Clarence took to telling him stories from his past, between bites, the same old tales he used to tell back home, to the point where people made fun of him and Leo Weller could finish his sentences for him, as in saying, "Yes, that was the longest ride anybody ever had on a railroad, without no locomotive", and yes, little jars of kerosene with a wick in them, set on poles stuck in the snow alongside the ice-road, which he had to drive a team of horses and a wagon over every day before dawn, going twelve miles into Santa Clara and back every day for hay and grain and supplies, yes, "there's your 'lectric lights"—Lucas fascinated, Lucas wished he'd been a boy when Clarence was a boy, in the lumber woods or anywhere. "No good with machinery and never was," Clarence said, and Lucas said, "Me neither!"

Next day they switched shotguns, Lucas rode with Clarence, in the pickup ahead, and the Microbus well behind out of the dust cloud and the two women getting their heads together probably with no good result although you never knew, might be discussing sleeping arrangements. He wouldn't put anything past Hesther, not since Whitehorse, ha ha. Telling stories to Lucas Clarence was hardly paying attention to the country and the sky, hardly noticing the darkest blue he had ever seen and more small clouds like puffs from a steam engine or the occasional glimpses of white ranges that must be in Canada, to the east or up in the Brooks range north of the Yukon. Then the country would suddenly come back to him, the deep gullying of the terrain down to the frozen streams and he'd say, "If I'd been paying any attention I'd been afraid. Don't look, you're in danger."

What was that? Not up ahead but across a gulf beside them. Couldn't tell, but something the color of a dead fish, shaped like a trailer. Couldn't turn his head far enough but then they skirted another washout in the crotch of a hairpin turn and then it was right up ahead of them, alongside the road, clad in dust, leaning as if it would roll over, and when it did that, never stop.

They went by. Bullet holes. That was just a ordinary panel delivery. Lucas craned around as they passed it. "Any dead people in there?" Clarence asked.

"Nope! Who shot it?"

"Hunters."

"I don't get it."

"If you haven't got anything else to shoot at a old abandoned car is hard to resist."

"Shall we shoot the next one?"

"I have never been one to do that."

"What happened to the people?"

"People got a lift."

"How do you know?"

"Because I am older than you."

"You're a guru!"

"What is a guru?"

"I don't know!" he sang, laughing at the same time.

Clarence liked this running in a caravan, with two sets of wheels and two sets of people. Too good to be true. Only a hundred more miles to the end of the road. He asked himself if she'd run away, this Pippa, quick as she joined them. No, I have a hostage, this boy that feeds me my lunches by hand, laughs at anything I say.

Good except I never ate potato chips before. Now, I have no choice until they run out. "Open!" he says, laughing with delight and dipping another in the onion sauce. "Now, Coke!" which will run out quick too, today. Wants me to suck from the same straw he sucked from. Same as kissing him, am I blushing?

There was nobody else on the road, nobody at all. Where the gravel or sand was soft enough to hold an impression, no tire-track. The horses found some sort of lichens and ate for all they were worth when they stopped to stretch their legs. Put their noses in the culverts and pumped their ears full. Took a good look around and decided not to run away.

One more derelict small pickup truck full of window-glass you couldn't tell the color of for the mud all over it top to bottom.

Clarence saw black oil underneath, dinged the oil-pan did they? That made him steer cautiously around the grapefruit. Then they passed a huge tan metal covered building big as an airplane hangar or a hotel but almost without windows and looked to be made by giant children, a house of cards made with sheets of corrugated steel. They said it was a dredge, it was on Hesther's maps, fifty years since it worked but Clarence could not imagine how it ever worked or what work it ever did. Not a machine. Just the ugliest thing ever built, glad it was shut down if that long pile of gravel down the middle of the creek is what it left behind. Did it move? Dredge. I would call it a Destroyer. Next, General Merchandise, Café, Saloon, more to the signs than the buildings but this was Chicken, last place to get gas, gas the price of blackberry brandy. Not open. Didn't think there was anybody there awake until this person that seemed to be very sick came around the corner, sick or stupid, too stupid to talk or count the money. Hesther had to close the person's hand over the bills, turn it around and give it a little shove to go back where it come from. Boy or girl, young or old, I don't know and neither did she.

Café was closed but they looked into the Saloon next door, "Just for the fun of it," Hesther said, and came right back out because, three o'clock in the afternoon, three people in there all too drunk to stand or say hello.

Soon, turned north again after the fake toward Canada and a fork in the road that did go there, now headed for the end of the road and won't need to go nowhere evermore. Hesther saw a cairn beside the road. No place to turn out but so what? Stop and stretch. Look at that cairn if you want to. See if the owners left us a note. Clarence let the horses out to see what that water in the ditch tasted like. Hesther looked, found nothing, filled a canteen and said, "Lordy, taste that!"

Clarence sniffed, said, "Smelling it is enough."

Pippa yelled, "The truck! The truck! Where is Lucas?" the last word a scream, the truck and trailer going, slowly at first, faster and faster, ahead down the road. Clarence stood with his hands forgotten at his sides, what could anyone do? No problem if anybody was driving but there at the bottom of the dip was your typical half-road crater, washout, only a narrow bridge of packed gravel across, for once no hair-pin turn. They had been negotiating these one after another, the horse-trailer always threatening to cut off the turn and drop a wheel into the crater. That would be the end.

He almost didn't watch, thought he'd closed his eyes but clearly saw the front end swerve, the right wheels just barely skirt the washout, the left barely stay on the road, and the trailer follow, wider than the truck, wheels partly over both edges, digging in a little and slowing the truck already slowing on the upgrade beyond until it almost-stopped, and the door swung open, the boy out on the road with both fists in the air and his head thrown back, his shout coming a split-second later, "Yahoo!"

Clarence felt shame drain off his face like mud. Come too far. Took one chance too many. Not cut out for pioneering. No business in love with a eight year old boy. Pippa sank to her heels, head down, shaking, one kid in her sling in front of her and the other on her feet, hiding her face on her back.

All the rest was foreordained. The truck and trailer backed down, picking up speed but not much before the trailer wheels hit the washout. The rig jack-knifed down the low side, the trailer not rolling but pulling the back end of the truck off after it and then the truck turning its front end toward the onlookers as it dropped and heaved over, going down on its side on a slope far too steep for the side to check the rotation, making the trailer roll with it, the trailer's taller side too fragile to stop it, smashed sideways and anyway separating at the hitch with a sound like a maul hitting a steel wedge. And now the two heaps of metal in a single cloud of dust rolled and bounded in separate rhythms down and down and down ever faster, out of sight behind the slope, and then into view again out onto the shore ice, very small, very dark against it, splashed through the nearer stream of running blue water on top of the ice and rolled right out onto the middle of the arched frozen river, where they stopped still, close together. Silence came back up from them, battered shapeless things. Six good tires upwards, spinning.

Of the tent and poles and many other things that were in the bed of the pickup, axe, adze, cooker, not much in sight. Scattered down the hill presumably. Many supplies piled in the forward compartment of the horse-trailer. First bend in the stream two rifle-shots away. What did the cairn mean?

Lucas first to speak, said, "Oops." His mother hugged him close, swaying.

There was a click, so Clarence said afterwards. Sometime in the next few minutes as this group of people looked at the country they were in and at each other. They were not going to Alaska anymore. They were not travelers. They were here. Had no need of that pickup truck and that trailer, good for nothing but going down the road. At the end of the road another little place like Chicken, Alaska, only a little bigger bird, Eagle. Another Mercantile Emporium, Saloon, and Café, closed or full of drunks. If you ever got there you would have to get away from it or else you might as well have stayed home. A click in himself as he realized this and he thought a click in Hesther, maybe a different click. They were where they had wanted to get to and what was more they still had everything they needed. Sure it was scattered up and down that mountainside and maybe sealed up inside folded metal down there on the ice, hard to pry open, but, everything they needed and here was the country that they had been coming to. Nobody in it but them. He could not have imagined it. This was a dream come true, more than any dream he could have dreamed. No engine sound. True wind on their faces. Nothing ahead that they couldn't do, one step at a time. No motors no clutches no electric wires, no Duke Arquit no sisters.

Couldn't tell about Hesther. He looked in her eyes and thought she was maybe a different person, never known. Before he could transfer to her his confidence she was seeing unseen things, up over his head, her eyes rolled back. A horrible presence, the only thing in the deal that scared him. He figured she would come back the way she was once they were snug in the tent again if it wasn't torn to bits and the poles all broken. But that wouldn't be no problem, look at the tent-poles all over the islands in the stream. She had needle and thread somewhere, a white-on-white quilt in her chest with fine-work to beat anything.

How was Pippa? Pippa gave him a wicked smile with her tongue sticking out the corner of her mouth. The devil was always around somewhere. Afraid of nothing, that one, and the little man too, on the jump to get down there in the bottom and make camp. Didn't say sorry because, wouldn't mean it.

Down the valley, to the north, cut into the near side of the tongue of all-but-barren mountainside that closed off a farther view of the descending river, was a road, or something like a road, a ditch maybe, an edge of gravel following a level line around the tongue and into a draw, out of sight again. Pippa brought binoculars. It looked more like a ditch than a road but they couldn't tell and Hesther would not look, her eyes still rolled up in her head, a face on a totem pole part human part bird or animal. And across the valley, another sign of human history, a field of wildflowers and low brush that might once have been a clearing, and almost lost in the brush, two rusted things, oil-drums his guess.

They walked and drove along slowly, Clarence and Lucas ahead, the horses snorting and catching up and then plodding along close behind the creeping Microbus. Clarence directed Pippa carefully over the washout where the truck had gouged out the gravel edges and narrowed the way. There would be no going back if that eroded any more.

What they were looking for, some way to get down to paradise, also to get the Microbus off the highway where nobody would shoot out the headlights and windshield. The bus would be no use to them for a long time but some-day, might need to borrow a cup of sugar from a neighbor, ha ha. For which, already planning to come back and start it now and then, keep the battery up.

Every little way as their progress exposed new walls of the valley Clarence stopped and scanned the far sides. Now rounding that tongue, he could see farther down, closer to the river of ice and closer to that road or ditch that paralleled it along a contour twenty feet or so above it. More and more it looked like a ditch though he wished it was a road because it headed back toward the treasure.

No way for Clarence Shampine to have any idea that in almost every one of these dendritic tributaries of the Fortymile River, itself one of many tributaries of the Yukon, any travelers such as themselves might have found signs of gold mining from as long ago as 1878 or as recently as 1971, major activities in the earliest time, more recently the work of loners with gold-malaria, or just as likely, not miners but lone trappers including the Athabascan Indians on their long lines from a village on the big river near the border, but few of them and far between. No idea how far from a miracle it was that after they found a flat turn-out that led them to that ditch, and straddled and followed that level ditch until it too washed out, and left the bus uphill from the ditch on a knoll from which they might be able to coast it down and bump-start it in an emergency, and followed it around another bend, they saw something more, that brought Hesther partway back to herself.

"Land sakes alive," she said, perfectly human.

They would have had a fair chance, if they followed this tributary or another down to its mouth on the Fortymile, of finding at least the remains of a low, ten by twelve log cabin and the small diggings of one or a pair of miners who perhaps followed a bit of color down into an old dry stream-bed all winter, hauling out the gravel by the bucket and piling it in that waterless season, to rinse it through their wooden sluice-box with the plentiful water of the next May and June. Gone now, driven out of the country finally by age or illness or the cold or the same fever that brought them there redirecting them to some other glory hole; their cabin and even their cache of supplies still there, undestroyed if they left the doors and windows open so the bears could get in and out without wrecking everything.

But of course they did not follow this nameless tributary down toward the Fortymile. They necessarily followed their chiseled contour up to the right, westward, toward their wrecked vehicles and scattered supplies, their tent, their tools. It was looking up and across this valley, now from down deep in its vastness, that they beheld, close under the spruce and aspen forest of the slope behind it, a two-story log house not yet a ruin, very old no doubt but enduring as no such building would have endured back home, with a porch along the front and a shed to one side, a two-story cabin if those two windows over the porch lighted a low-roofed room above the above-ground floor and not a loft reached by ladder, but either way inviting, adequate, astonishing. No cellars to these places, not to disturb the permanent frost beneath, any storage space in separate buildings of a cache, another smaller cabin high up on poles.

Inside such a building there would surely be some sort of a stove, probably made from oil drums but once in a while a proper-made one, possibly even cast iron, brought up the Yukon any time in the last eighty years by a river steamer, a paddle-wheeler just like those on the Mississippi, that nosed in to the shore every so many miles and sent its crews out to denude the valley at the rate of ten cords of firewood a mile, against the current, or bought the cordwood from an Indian village. There might be anything. Pots, an old calendar, books. Clarence hoped for a bar of steel to pry the folded trailer open with. The ice was a road up to the truck and trailer, until the thaw, and their waterproof boots would get them back and forth dry-foot. The horses would be skittish on the ice, and in the event the ice, hollowed out by currents flowing underneath, would give way under them and give everyone but especially the horses a fright. But they would get out in panic and never be asked to cross again until low water, August, at their ford, and then only while Hesther, deadly marksman, watched from the porch with the Model 70, for predators.

Eighteen

NOTHING AMAZING ABOUT THIS SURVIVAL ITSELF, the following May, to the people of the little village of Eagle, on the Yukon, alerted by the howling of its dozens of sled-dogs, staked out in the yards of its few streets of small log houses no more elegant than this one, on one-eighth-acre lots, none with running water either, though a few with electric washing machines served by a portable generator shared and borrowed around. Those whose houses were on the southern side of the settlement on the Yukon, hearing the hullabaloo, looked out where the Taylor Highway sloped down into town, past the old parade ground of the army fort, now the air-strip, idly curious to see what so agitated the dogs.

This is after all the place where Roald Amundsen once arrived alone on skis in December, having crossed seven hundred miles of ice and snow from the Arctic Ocean, on foot or Nordic skis, to report his discovery of the Northwest Passage, via the wireless the Army then maintained. Couldn't wait to tell the world! Doubtless the town's dogs made a lesser outcry on that day, since Amundsen skied straight up the Yukon into town. Like this party coming in now, Amundsen made himself a well-liked guest in Eagle. He wintered there and then skied seven hundred miles back to the Arctic Ocean and his ship and crew in time to meet the spring and sail home.

Still this was notable: the two mismatched horses, neither obviously a draft animal, drawing a powerless dust-encased Volkswagen Microbus, the head and cape of a large grizzly bear draped over the VW logo on the front, the roof piled high with moose and caribou antlers, a pole travois attached to the back bumper scraping along behind, loaded with bulky cargo wrapped in some kind of whitish tarp.

A large shaman-looking Indian woman rode the taller of the horses, a lean man in a tall-crowned, wide-brimmed black hat and otherwise in rags including a holey buffalo-plaid jacket led the same horse by a mere halter-rope. A slim young woman with a big tummy and a papoose on her back walked beside the other horse, two more children of different heights behind her, the taller a very long-haired boy, dancing in circles of celebration.

The harnesses attaching the unusual draft animals to the silent Microbus appeared to be made out of babiche and rope, the breastplates and collars of bearskin with the fur still on, turned inward. As would be seen, no one in this party had any notion of tanning hides.

The horses were gaunt enough but they did not show any sign of complaint. They appeared docile and willing. The Taylor Highway was ending before them in a long gentle downhill grade, with water, the very full, ice-choked Yukon River, sparkling at the visible end of it. Their ears were up. The travelers spoke to them and they spoke back. As if they knew Hesther would shoot any attackers, they paid no mind to the wailing whirling huskies crashing against their chains all down one side of the road. She did have the Model 70 in its scabbard at her knee.

The first to join them were the children who saw them first, soon joined by others, some of them in wheeled sleds or carts drawn by their particular dogs, now coming alongside the other children and asking Where from? How long? What's your name? Who shot the bear?

By which it quickly learned that nobody shot the bear, Mama killed it with a spear, the boy said. The pregnant lithe young girlish woman killed the bear in the mythical fashion of the early indigenous people according to hearsay or legend, believable only with the proviso that for every successful such kill, a lot of Indians died trying. That is, his mother killed the bear with a long sharpened stick or spear, planted butt-down on the ground in front of the huge standing squinting nearsighted animal, so that when he dropped to his forefeet to charge her, he drove his rib-cage down over the spearpoint, impaling his heart on axe-sharpened wood. Dead, Clarence told them with great pride, at the Post Office a little later in the afternoon (the long, long sub-arctic afternoon), "before he hit the ground." "He" in the honorary form. He was a she, as is often the case.

Much was learned of this arriving party in the course of their progress to the riverbank, a progress that over three quarters of a mile became a parade, the children circling off to report, adults walking along behind to get the picture when the procession came to a halt at the village well. The van was not out of gas, they don't know what's the matter with it, he's not a mechanic. They've been in the Fortymile country on a stream of no name. What's under that white tarp?

Well, hnnh, what's under that tarp is furs, young feller. Lynx, fox, wolf, muskrat, ermine. Just by the size of that heap the parents calculated the value of the pelts in the range of three to five thousand dollars. This man could buy himself a new set of long-johns at the general store. Plus, they've got a bag of gold!

The gold could be seen dragging down the breast pocket of Clarence's lumberjack jacket, wool, red and black, holes in the elbows patched with moose hide and holes in all the rest of his garments un-patched, nothing to patch to, so that you wondered what held them on him, except that this apparition was no worse than the people of Eagle were used to, no worse than some of the river people who lived in the country down-river and used Eagle as a place to leave their junk and prided themselves on lacking respect for anybody in a cluster of more than one house and doing without money and not noticing the cold that came through those holes, men of maximum practical application according to themselves whose women knew when to keep their mouths shut.

The shrewder question was where did these horses come from? Horses had not been seen in Eagle since the last bit of the Army left in 1921 - if there was any then. Anyway the Army used mules, mostly. There still was a mule barn back there across the parade ground or airport with room for 57 mules, empty. "Is that so," Clarence said. "Well, I'll be."

Well but the horses, how did the horses get here? Horses came in a horse trailer! Pulled by a pickup truck! Where were the truck and trailer? "Both of them went down the river on the ice last year," Clarence said. "Didn't anybody see them float by?" So they knew before the procession reached the well that he was a wit, too.

What was this about gold? Indeed that was one of the more interesting lines of questioning in the Post Office, everybody in there with the postmaster that would fit and the doors and windows open for the rest to hear and the new guests seated in the armchairs of the town fathers. The big lady said nothing (Hesther had lost or broken her pretty pointy glasses, and her contacts without the necessary rinses threatened to damage her eyes; she told Clarence that her deadly shooting was "purely psychological.") The apparent blindness gave her an aura of great power. The one who was apparently given to motherhood under any conditions whatever looked frankly around, smiling, as if searching another mate, and there were already volunteers. Pippa pregnant looked very appealing in Eagle, Alaska. But what was this about gold?

"Well-l-l," Clarence said, "ought I to tell you?"

"The kid said you found gold."

"Well-l-l, maybe we did. We come upon a gold mine, you see."

"He says you had a hose like a water-cannon to wash the gravel."

"Who told you that?"

"The boy, Lucas, the boy!"

"Well-l-l, we found a aqueduct, led right from a old reservoir to a pond, and there was a pipe, made of old oil drums. Some'n was a good welder. Inventor too, rigged a nozzle counter-weighted with a box of stones that let you aim the blast with one hand. Don't you think we'd go to mining? Somebody took away the bulldozer, but that was all right with me, I wouldn't want to listen to it or smell the smoke, nor know how to drive it. We made a drag-plow. I will tell you what: how we done everything we did, including get here. Horses. And everything the horses done, depended on her. That one."

This referred to Hesther, the large Indian woman, so assumed to be because of the cheeks puffed right up almost to close her eyes, who didn't appear to have heard her praises.

"Because she taught them. I am a team-es-ter but I wouldn't no more been able to do that. But she did it. Them two light horses drawed us half the way here, uphill and down. Hard work for a team twice or three times the weight. And she made the harness, such of it as wasn't rope, out of hides. For the rope we thank the man in Tok that made me buy it. Now, is there a house for rent in this burg?"

"And is they any postcards?" Hesther suddenly croaked.

Suspicion in a few old Eagles, over the next days. A garrulous, suspicious, back-biting town, ask anybody there if they have a single neighbor not badly flawed. "How did they keep those children alive, without any dogs to alert them to the wolves? There would have been a pack of wolves got on to them for certain. How did they keep the horses alive for that matter? Listen, I don't think anybody could. No, something wrong with this story. It is not possible. Who's the father of the unborn one? Not that old scarecrow. Been in the Fortymile since last spring this time? I don't think so. Whose old claim did they hit, anyway? Never heard of anybody up that way hydraulic mining with a bulldozer. The clothes, though. Holey clothes like that were earned, somehow. I don't know. Let's see this gold. If he's really got a bag of gold in that pocket I'll have to doubt my words. And if there's really any link in that pile of furs he's hit it just as lucky, prices what they are now."

Next morning Clarence took his little caribou-hide bag to the assessor's, that is, the General Store, and got some kids with their dog-wagons to bring along his pelts from the Roadhouse since that is where you traded your furs, too. Somebody in there heard the little bag hit the counter. Just the sound made you look. The gold would have half-filled a peanut-butter jar and weighed more than two bags of sugar. At a rough guess, $170 the ounce, twelve-thousand five hundred dollars. And there were indeed several lynxes among the furs, lynx at a premium, and beautiful wolf-hides, they must have taken the whole pack, one bullet hole each hide. Five thousand dollars there if a dime. No, it didn't figure. Fur was high but this was in fact poor trapping country, hard living for the game as well as the humans, you needed twenty-five miles of line. Just like placer mining in a worn-out country, the barest subsistence living. Though you never know. You'd be jealous if this old coot wasn't such a modest soul. Let's see about this truck and trailer floating down the river.

As usual he started with his "Wel-l-ll," apparently thinking both about how he could keep his cards close to his vest and how he could draw a chuckle from the natives. "Riding high and handsome on the ice when last seen, the tributary high and wide and nothing to stop them or destroy the ice they were on for as far as the eye could see." He and his party had pried them open and picked them clean of anything he could use (Clarence didn't mention the Manila envelope, by no means empty even after the spree in Tok—don't forget that flybox full of white powder! The envelope was found intact in the crushed pickup and was stowed somewhere about Hesther's person at this moment) and watched them go without regret, "except I was sorry for making a eyesore wherever they landed." Said he knew of a good snowmobile at the bottom of a pond back home, no one to see it there but still a shame. Said when asked, No, the ice never did back up and flood their camp, bottlenecked somewhere below. That could happen as these old-timers well knew, but it did not. So who knows how far down the Fortymile those three tons of steel floated? Or how far down the Yukon after that, to Eagle and beyond, passing in the night. Although: four heavy-duty tires, brand new back in Whitehorse, on the pickup, good rubber on the trailer too. Somebody would want to scavenge that. If anybody saw those items approaching the junction town of Fortymile in Canada, somebody surely would have found a way to drag them off into some shallows and get at least those tires but probably the trailer too, make something out of it. That engine might be good, rebuilt. Wheels, brakes, whatever parts. That trailer beat back into shape and sawed in half horizontally would make somebody a barge, capable of sailing two thousand miles to the Bering Sea. Nobody let anything go to waste in Fortymile, in Eagle either for that matter, Alaska generally.

Talented people here, could make something out of anything. That's why everybody's yard piled with you name it. No such thing as junk.

That was Clarence's typical place for days, in the armchair in the Post Office, surrounded by the jury, unaware what a judging, divided little place it was, the Christians hoping he would prove to be one of them but increasingly doubtful, that adorable tummy one big question mark. While the girls were establishing the family in the old Roadhouse, a sort of a community institution which had not been in operation for the last few years but quickly put up to them, would they like to take it on? First take shelter in it and muck it out and then stock it and run it?—Clarence having breathed that she was a cook as well as a horse-whisperer. Clarence had been bound to pitch his tent anywhere and make do until he could build a cabin. The Roadhouse? "That would be a change of plan but all right," he had said.

So the girls were not beside him now and by the second day someone felt familiar enough to ask or hint toward asking was he the father? And Clarence looked down saying, "Wel-l-ll," drawing it out to a near-chuckle, "I-I-I didn't keep an eye on her every minute, she went down to Tok once for contact-lens solution," letting them hide their smiles a few beats before adding, "but I will take the blame if nobody else shows up."

And he went right on, "Next you will ask if the other one is my wife, other way of saying Do I have two? Which is the kind of questions I come on this expedition to get away from. Want me to ask you who is that you're living with and what do you do in the dark? I am not fit for marriage and thought I looked it." Up until then he had not showed any bite, but a man that had just got this party through four seasons in the Fortymile had to have some, it stood to reason.

"Now now now don't be touchy," said a tall man leaning on crutches, his leg in a cast. "But you better be told that this town is run by the Christians. They give each other all the government jobs, starting with the Postmaster Customs Agent Historian Climate Reporter and River Measurer et cetera here," indicating the kind blushing man in the window, whom Clarence had found most courteous. "Maybe if they think you are a bigamist they'll take back the Roadhouse."

"Wel-l-ll, what do I care?"

"Even if you don't care about having the Roadhouse to live in, you might want to put your horses in the Mule Barn."

"Yes I might." He already had, the first night, on the advice of others who told him that was none of the town's business. "That's Federal," they had said. "You might even find a real harness or two in there." Already had, dried out to the point they would fall apart if you looked at them.

Had to put the horses in somewhere, they weren't used to so much green grass. And these here dogs were no better than wolves. They were wolves; would tear the horses to bits but fortunately chained to their hovels next their owners' cabins.

"I warn you about this town," Crutches had said. "It ain't that much better than the lower forty-eight even if there's only thirty-six people in it. You will wonder why you left paradise to come here."

"No I won't," Clarence said. "Other than to cash in my furs, get more coffee and sugar and ammunition. I wouldn't need a airdrop of hay and grain until fall. No. And for that I would gone to Tok, cheaper."

"Why did you, then? We thought maybe it's for school. The boy's school age. You can't legally keep him out there without mail-order school at least. And health-care...? We thought maybe . . ."

"Wel-l-ll, ye-e-e-s, when the time come. Why did we come in? Would have stayed forever but we was run off, by helicopter. The federal government boys dropped out of the sky, said if we spent another night in that cabin, we were trespassing on the People of the United States of America."

"Oh the bastards!" said Crutches. "Don't tell me!" said Crutches. "I know all about it. Kill the bastards! Kill them all. Kill! Kill! Secede!"

Crutches went nearly crazy at the mention of the BLM's new rules, running the river people off their places, ruining everything. Clarence more calmly told how it was, "That's right. Trespassing on the people of the United States. I said 'Never mind, I am one of them and here's five more.' He said you are six of them trespassing on all of them. They want this to be a wilderness. I said, 'This is a wilderness and nobody knows that better than we do.' He said 'No it's not you are moving the gravel, you spoilt it forever. You have to leave.'"

"Kill! Kill the bastards every one! Secede!"

"I said, 'Where's the next place further north that is a wilderness that is not trespassing on the people of the United States to live there.' He said 'Are you a Indian?' Said Indians are the only people free to live in the wilderness. I said, 'I am close'ter to a Indian than you think. I have been getting close-ter to being a Indian all my life and now I am ready to make the last jump.'

The boys in the Post Office were chuckling by now. Clarence said," He was a nice young fellow. He said, 'Looking at your wife you're almost there.'"

"But she ain't your wife," the man on crutches said.

"She isn't Indian either."

"So much the worse for you."

"Hoot, get another one!" said another grizzled old character, going out the door. Quite a few of the people of Eagle already had their curiosity satisfied, didn't stay to listen any more. Clarence and family soon fixtures of the town, information accreting more and more slowly, some of it going the other way. Pretty soon Clarence was stupid, old-fashioned, pigeon-toed, stubborn, dull, a mere boy of seventy; Hesther the one with respect, good cook, good-natured but took no sass, open your mouth she'll give you some work to do; Pippa the one kept in awe, for planting that spear in front of the bear to defend her brood.

She said she'd felt somewhat naked, carrying her baby everywhere she walked, without a weapon. In fact that time of the year she generally was naked. Asked Clarence to make it for her, because the bears were there. They knew the bears could be anywhere. You'd see them stand up out of nowhere, never see them until they did, and someday it might be right beside you, when they were berrying by chance along your path. They were berrying themselves in this case, and could not see for the bushes. Clarence had just drawn a bead on this big boy with his Colt's revolver, fired just when it dropped to charge. She left the spear standing there by itself and skedaddled. Things could have been very different but this is the way they turned out, fortunately.

Nineteen

NOW THEY WERE ON A CAMPAIGN to get house-logs for Henry Begay, the young chief of the Han tribe whose village, Eagle Village, just called the Village, in distinction from the town just called Eagle, lay three miles up the river. Henry was an unusually young man for the position of chief and college educated, but people in Eagle gave him no chance of accomplishing anything for his people because, first, nobody could accomplish anything for people who were paid for doing nothing, given free educations and health care and millions of acres of land nobody else could use and fishing and trapping rights on even more, and besides that given almost two thousand dollars a year per person from the state's oil revenues just for being Indians. And who were supplied with alcohol illegally by Eagle bootleggers while Eagle was a dry town and who fought and shot and died under the influence of alcohol at a terrible rate. Beyond all that, Henry was a moody and unhappy man, active only in fits, mostly sitting there in the bachelors' house in the Village meditating what to do to change matters while the other young men drank wine and shot off pistols and threw bottles over the bank toward the river below.

This young chief had been planning to build a cabin a year ago but a tragedy stopped him. He was going to build the house and marry his beautiful sweetheart, but first he went off to make some money on the pipeline. He could make a thousand dollars a month, driving a truck on the service road to the North. While he was gone, somehow or other his sweetheart died. This made him a more sympathetic figure in Eagle but it was just confirmation that the Indians would do nothing to change their ways as long as he was chief. His father had been chief and nothing happened. The Indians did nothing but what they had always done. They sat around all day and walked into each other's houses not even saying hello and sat down and waited to see if anything was thought or said by anybody else, going away just as purposelessly leaving a pair of ptarmigans for the woman to pluck and cook if she wanted to.

(Because, as Crutches said, what can you expect? That was the deal with Statehood. Give the Indians everything they could dream of, mineral and gas rights and all, and give the rest to the Texans filling up Fairbanks with trailers and pointy-toed boots. Secede!)

But now a fit was on Henry and he was going to build that cabin. Maybe he had another girl in mind. Certainly he had learned of this man recently come to Eagle with horses trained to haul, horses that were capable of skidding the logs out of the burn upriver where he had given himself permission to get them. There the logs could be formed into a raft and floated down to the Village, and then a horse could skid them out of the river and up to the site of the new cabin.

So Clarence and some of his family were on an outing to the Village and on upriver with the chief. He and Lucas and Pippa left the other children with Hesther at the Roadhouse. Clarence was no river person and walked the shore with Buck towing a square-sterned aluminum canoe on a long line, Pippa in the middle with a pole for fending-off and Luke in the stern with a paddle for steering, and light camping gear and food for two or three nights, everything casual and indefinite with Henry.

They stopped at the steep bank under the village and Pippa ran up the bank despite Clarence's move toward the natural gallantry. It was not just gallantry, which he knew she had no use for, but the feeling that this young woman running up there into the Indian village where occasional shouts were heard and shots fired and bottles rolling down the bank, was improper. She had no use for what was proper either. Was still more pregnant with the baby she had been pregnant with when they came into Eagle, though in good condition, light weight but active. She wanted to do this rather than hold the horse, and she did it.

In ten minutes she came skidding down the bank on the seat of her pants and in a few more the chief stepped down it with his chainsaw, and they got into the boat and set out up the river. When Henry Begay went up to the burn usually he used a canoe with an outboard motor but this would not bring the horse. Clarence was going to help him build the cabin and he had told Henry that he ought to let him try something never done before in this country, build a double-log cabin, an inner and an outer log all the way around every course, the spaces between all chinked with moss. That way you would have a warm cabin, use less wood to heat. Clarence said he would not know how to build such a delicate structure as the typical Eagle house, how to notch such spindles, would break them trying. It might fall over. Had lived one winter in such a place up in the Fortymile and wouldn't wish that on anybody, though he didn't mean to complain. He liked to be warm when he was indoors.

They arrived at the burn, six or seven miles up the river, with all they needed to spend a number of days, two of Henry's cousins, come up by the trail, making their own tarpaulin shelter, bringing their own food, and the only problem was that Henry forgot to bring the gas and oil for his chainsaw. So it turned into a sort of recreational outing, Henry letting the cousins go back to the village, the three new friends marking the trees they were going to cut but otherwise fishing and resting and, since the cousins did not go back and had wine as well as freshly-snared rabbits, eating and drinking. The fishing saved a dead loss for Clarence because cutthroat trout up to four pounds kept him laughing to himself and he thought Pippa's presence was cheering up the chief.

This was where he learned more about Pippa than he had ever asked to know, not an inquisitive person but a respecter of people's privacy. Not that Henry Begay pestered her with questions, either. He was soft-spoken and polite too, but a story emerged, of two young people going to college in Denver, Colorado to study art, and the boy's birthday being unlucky somehow, something to do with the Viet Nam, so they quit college and went to Canada. They lived on an island off the end of the Gaspé Peninsula in Quebec. The boy loved boats and used to row the bird-watchers around the island which was rich in migratory waterfowl. Then the Canadian government turned the island into a bird sanctuary and boarded up all the houses on the island. That was when, Pippa said, the man's parents "reeled him in." But they didn't reel her in, or her children, she said.

Good enough, Clarence thought. That was the Pippa he knew, at the end. He had just been reeling in the cutthroat and he thought he probably ought to give that up as a thing to do for fun. Either kill them and eat them or don't reel them in in the first place.

Eventually the logs got cut and floated down to the Village and Clarence and Henry began to spend a relaxed portion of their days laboring on that double-log cabin, drawing curious onlookers who would ask how they were going to do the windows and doors, the roof and eaves, which Clarence did not know, except that they would do them when the time come. Clarence came to understand the Indian sense of time a little better and to revise his notions of work.

There was no hurry. Life was all around you. Nature was offering to converse.

Hesther would not have let him form any notion of rivalry with Henry if he had suspected, and anyhow he had enough rivals, if that was what they were, with these other bozos of Eagle flocking to the Roadhouse for a look at Pippa. And as summer wore on new ones, incomers, crazy-eyed young men from anywhere in the lower forty-eight who heard that this is the ultimate Interior, ultimate test of self-reliance, which it was, come to prove themselves against it. They all came to see Pippa across the counter of the Roadhouse and later in the day across the mahogany bar of the speakeasy around the block, competing for the glance out the corner of her eye, that little smile-dimple at the corner of her mouth, a look at that dear little tummy. Well, Clarence said, he was not nobody's keeper. And as if he hadn't said it his own self, Hesther added, "No, that's right, you isn't."

One particular bozo looked like he had a chance with her, too, a fair-haired healthy poetical fellow who had already toughed out one winter alone learning to trap and try to keep a dog alive in wolf country. Now he had renamed himself River Breeze and was ready to challenge the Yukon itself. The ice had passed through, the river was a thousand feet wide and thirty deep, moving at seven miles an hour, saying "Come on!" to him, and he could not resist it but he wished her to come with him (all the kids as well, if Hesther and Clarence wouldn't keep them), two thousand miles down to the sea. He had sawed the top off a school bus, tipped it over and made a boat of it, had no end of room. "Just to do it, Pippa! I want to do this! Come with me! Come!"

Hesther was just then preparing to fly to Fairbanks to be fitted for new glasses, and she was afraid the girl would do something "drastic" while she was gone. The devil was in Pippa. She seemed to be looking over the whole crew of bozos, getting ready to make her choice. Every night the young men beat down the door of the speakeasy next door, joined by many not so young, and the mayor decided to appoint himself the law enforcement and shut it down at last.

But the mayor arrived too late. Henry Begay came down by canoe from the Village with several black-haired cousins and for two thousand four hundred fifty dollars he bought every bottle in the place, cases and cartons in storage and all. Pippa stuffed the money right in her apron. The young chief stared around at the other men young and old, should any dispute the purchase, while his cousins smashed every bottle, almost, and then they marched down to the beach and shoved off home, in the dark, their boat moving very slowly against that powerful river, black silhouette inching northeast. Easy for Pippa to catch up. Above the village, out of sight around the first bend, in a place where they could eddy out, Pippa was wading barelegged and barefooted.

"Well, you said you wasn't nobody's keeper," Hesther said. The children were all to bed, Lucas wide awake and dreaming of beads and feathers. "So don't pout."

"House isn't ready," Clarence said. "She can't live in the bachelors' cabin."

"Well, get the new one done."

"You sound just like a white person," Clarence said.

"I's going to Fairbanks."

"Nineteen cents a pound, both ways. Cheaper to fly the doctor here."

"That's the first mean thing you said to me since I don't know, Whitehorse."

"And I take it back. I'll get along, or maybe go with you."

"That wouldn't butter no parsnips."

251

"There you go again. White person."

"I don't mind you calling me Indian."

"You have to earn it."

"I think you have got some mischief in mind."

"So I do."

"Move into the Village with her."

"I like the pace there. Also, friendlier. And the Village isn't dry."

"Clarence be serious. We can't go there. No way we can become Indian."

"There's one or two white people in that village. They call them land-grant bridegrooms."

"You think they's a Indian woman would marry you?"

"Wel-l-ll, maybe. Or a Indian man that would marry you?"

"What's all this talk of marryin'?"

"Well, if you're married to a Indian, you get the privileges of a Indian. That's why they call you a land-grant bridegroom. You're the one always wanted to marry."

"Did not!"

"Did so, or so I thought."

"Well, I did. But that was then. I was a mere girl."

"I think the goverment would let us alone if we was living there. Go up the country anywhere, and build a cabin for ourselves, dig for gold and trap some more. Wouldn't be no helicopters. Why, because Indian territory. Always said that was where I was headed. Have another little house here near Pippa's for the darkest months, help them look after the children."

"I likes Indians but I don't want to live there, amongst those drunks, Clarence. They's too many of them. Even the women, I hears. In the winter, when the sun don't even come up for ten minutes? I might get to drinkin' myself, you know me! I want to see those children brought up right, educated, ambitious! Yes I am

252

white, without prejudice. You and me are all right together, live and
let live, one thing and another, been through enough and wiser now.
You know where I's been, off where the moon don't shine awhile.
I's only partway back, still seeing things behind things. After I see
that bear about to land on Pippa! Sees things so sharp it hurts, and
that without my glasses. Don't ask the world of me. Eagle is all right.
I don't mind the Christians, foo! It's restful, compared. You can't
live in paradise forever and once you lived there I don't think you
can go back. I see a future. The Roadhouse is good. It's just right
for us. You know who I'd like to have come help cook? Your sister
Bessie! And look at all these people asking you to take them up in
the country, just like Lucas's picture. Learn to ride! I'll teach ye!
Shampine's Guide Service, mountain sheep and grizzly bears or your
money back! There'll be more tourists and hunters every year now,
so they says. And lately they say the Army Fort is going to be a National Historic District. You'd think Alaska was a thing of the past,
folks here says it's ruint, but shoot, the country is still here, we'll
make ourselves useful. Pippa'll be practically next door."

Pretty long speech. You certainly are not a Indian. Time was
you knew when to put your hand over your mouth. But there is truth
in every word you say, so I will keep mine shut.

In bed together now (second floor room, Roadhouse), just as
they were the first night, the real beginning of this trip. He was sunk
over against her the same, no use to struggle against it, the mattress
sinking deep on her side. Why was he unafraid to venture still further north? Why, because he did not mind the long winter nights.
Longer the better, with his partner beside him, soft and plenty of
her, radiating heat. No need to feed the woodstove and crawl in, no
matter how the wind may sing.

253

AUTHOR'S NOTE

The author is in somewhat the position of Patrick O'Brian when, preparing to write *The Nutmeg of Consolation* and so needing to research the penal colony at Botany Bay, he discovered Robert Hughes's newly published *The Fatal Shore*, an abounding source for everything he needed. In my case, I already knew the perfect resource for farthest Alaska: John McPhee's *Coming Into the Country*. But I didn't realize until I re-read that book that McPhee had been visiting Eagle, in the deep interior, at practically the same time my characters would arrive there. In fact I didn't know where they would arrive until I found McPhee's Eagle.

I have mined his pages for the ending chapters of this book, freely upending reportorial facts into fiction. And once, in grateful homage, I come close to quoting. Where Clarence is overwhelmed by the country and feels unprepared to cope with it, he's talking to himself almost in John McPhee's own words.

One other borrowing: I could not resist giving Clarence a line I once heard Wendell Berry utter: Computers are expensive, heads are cheap.

CPSIA information can be obtained at www.ICGtesting.com
Printed in the USA
LVOW120044201212

312531LV00005B/186/P